By the same author

Land~

the World

A book for all who delight in   ...as to offer

From readers ...

'What a fascinating, generous tre   ¬-trove of history and stories
... all connecting back to the Clumps. Brimming with intriguing
revelations linking famous names (and infamous antics) and
historically pivotal events and decisions to the very ground here
under our feet.'

David Gentleman, Dorchester

'Not only are the stories fascinating, the manner in which they
are told is wonderfully light, witty and conversational.'

Oscar O'Connor, Dorchester

'To say that I have enjoyed *Landmark in Time* would be an under-
statement; I believe it's a little masterpiece ... a delightful but
serious picture of our history and our society.'

Dr Lucio Fumi, Henley

'An inspirational journey of keen observation and research and
one I don't want to end.'   *Sally Worsley, Wallingford*

'The only book that has held my full attention in years.'

Chris Charlesworth, Cholsey

The Tuscan Master
(Sceptre, 2000)

'A tender and joyous celebration, a book that shows that ordinary
lives, half-successful lives, even failed lives, can be lit with glory.
At the end I was weeping with happiness. A beautiful, subtle,
and very loving book.'

William Nicholson

The Kennedy Moment
(Myriad Editions, 2018)

'The Kennedy Moment is that rare and clever thing – a gentle and moving thriller.'

Staunch Book Prize, 2019

'In lucid, persuasive prose Peter Adamson tells a truly gripping story about something profoundly important.'

Literary Review

'Reads like an Elmore Leonard novel, only with more emotion and more depth. I was spellbound, in genuine suspense.'

Adam Fifield, author A Mighty Purpose

'I was captivated from the start and found it hard to put it down until I'd reached the last page. It is a book that will stay with you long after you've finished it.'   *NB Literary Quarterly*

'It was that rare book which makes you feel sad when you finish it because the process of reading it has been so enjoyable.'

Fionnuala McCredie

Facing out to sea
(Sceptre, 1997)

'I was captivated by the atmosphere but it was the sheer thoughtfulness of this novel that interested me…one of the most consistently intelligent and fascinating novels about what goes on in people's minds that I've read for a long time. Quite mesmeric in its hold.'

Margaret Forster

'It took me into a world I knew very little about and opened my eyes to its beauty and interest. What I especially admired was the way the characters were both representative of large ideas and yet also fully human … it's a huge achievement.'

Alain de Botton

Peter Adamson

I need you to be Harold

and other stories

P&LA

First published 2023 by P&LA
© Peter Adamson (b. 1946), 2023
The moral right of the author has been asserted
https://peteradamsonwriting.com

ISBN 978-1-3999-4874-6

A catalogue record for this book is available
from the British Library

Every attempt has been made to obtain the necessary
permissions for use of copyright material. Apologies
are offered for any omissions; future editions will
include appropriate acknowledgement.

Designed and typeset in Palatino and Trocchi by
Charlie Webster, Production Line, Minster Lovell, Oxford

Cover and chapter illustrations by Rod Craig (www.rodcraig.com).

Printed and bound by Short Run Press, Exeter, England

For

John Williams
and
Mehr Khan Williams

The Stories

I need you to be Harold   1
> A weekend in New England begins in all innocence –
> until Paul agrees to stand in for a boyfriend who has
> failed to show.

The Hand of Nicias   19
> Art restorer Hana Kerosi is on the verge of abandoning
> her chosen career when she is offered an unusual
> commission.

Up on the Downs   37
> The year is 1917 and a chance encounter on the
> Berkshire downs brings together poet and painter,
> both with memories of a less peaceful place.

Sahel   53
> In a village on the edge of the Sahara, all the whispers
> are of whether Kadré will be one of the ten boys,
> chosen from thousands, whose names will be on the
> list pinned outside the office of the Préfet.

The Chosen One   67
> An incomer to the village is flattered to be invited to
> dinner at the Manor, home of a well-known recluse.

Incident in Assisi   83
> His wife is a high priestess of the contemporary art
> scene, but Tom is finding it hard to keep the faith.

The Greatest Journey   99
> Passionate Socialist George Bernard Shaw is persuaded
> to co-author a book with his ill-tempered Tory neighbour.

To Helsinki and back   126
> Celebrating their silver wedding by recreating their
> first date seemed like a romantic idea at the time.

The Wine of Forgiveness   140
> On the evening of her retirement, Kat Sokalska dines
> alone at a bistro on Manhattan's Lexington Avenue.
> But from downtown, the chanting is growing nearer.

Comfort   154
> She had agreed to meet him for a drink, but will she
> turn up? And why hadn't he chosen a place where he
> could be comfortable?

The Institute   161
> Billiards practice night at the Men's Institute and top
> board man Arthur Tingle is sizing up a new member
> who looks like he can handle a cue.

The Unposted Letter   172
> A few days after Dora's funeral, an unexplained letter
> is found among her effects.

Boiled Egg with Rosie   187
> When Martin volunteers to take over the cooking,
> Rosie couldn't be more pleased …

Desiderata   196
> Iris sits in the church each week hoping she will not
> be seen as she reads The Gospel according to Sharon.

The Wall   211
> Class walls are usually metaphorical, but in this case
> the wall between slum and shanty is built of bricks …
> until one night the wall is breached.

Acknowledgements   231

I need you to be Harold

I T WAS A DAY THAT BEGAN IN INNOCENCE. A hard, cold, blue New England sky, a weekend without commitments, a straight-from-the-oven bagel and the leaf colour at its scarce-believable best as I crossed the river and picked up Mass Pike heading east out of Boston.

Ever since I had first seen the photos, I had been drawn to small-town New England. Don't ask me how you can be nostalgic about somewhere you've never been, but there was no denying my soul-tug towards those white clapboard houses glimpsed through sycamore trees or arranged around village greens and watched over by modest Congregational spires. And so after settling into my year's teaching appointment, I had taken the first opportunity – a Thanksgiving weekend – to rent a car and head for the Berkshires.

That first day was all I had expected of it. But rather than following my itinerary, I will check my story straight into the Red Lion Inn, Stockbridge, where I had reserved a single room for three nights. These New England coaching inns – open fires and polished floorboards, rocking-chair porches and herb-scented gift shops – are all part of my iconography and the Red Lion, which first opened its doors at the close of the French and Indian Wars, did not disappoint. My room was on the third floor and its parchment lampshades and hand-quilted bedspreads were all I had imagined. I stowed my overnight bag in the wardrobe and sat on the edge of the bed, savouring that moment of anonymity that all hotel rooms offer; that moment of reluctance to claim bare surfaces and take possession of empty drawers, that moment that whispers seductively – 'you could be anyone'.

I had not eaten since Bagels-R-Us but didn't fancy a table for one in the main dining room where families and friends were already arriving for Thanksgiving dinner. Instead, I took a stool in The Widow Bingham's Tavern, picked up the bar menu and ordered the 'Famous Red Lion Bloody Mary'. My surroundings – low-ceilinged, oak-panelled, lamp-lit, with ketchup bottles on check tablecloths and antique kitchen paraphernalia strung from the rafters – fitted perfectly into my idea of the weekend.

Perhaps it would be better to preface what happened next by acknowledging something about my state of mind at the time. I had spent the day, as intended, pootling around quiet villages and stepping inside achingly simple white churches with box pews and clear-glass windows. Unlike de Tocqueville (the subject of my first teaching semester), my attraction to such places was almost entirely unexamined, a vague yearning without much thought as to what I might be yearning for. Perhaps on that account, as well as the Bloody Mary on an empty stomach, I soon began to sense an undertow of dissatisfaction. Was it perhaps the sense of having been only a spectator, my face pressed up against the window of a world in which I seemed to have invested some unarticulated hope? Or was it to do with what I imagined those New England villages to represent: a world of more stable norms and values, of community and belonging, a world that could still be understood? I should perhaps also mention that, even at the best of times, I am given to this kind of half-think.

A long pull at the icy furnace of the Famous Red Lion Bloody Mary jolted me back to The Widow Bingham's Tavern, now rapidly emptying itself into the dining room. It was just after half past seven and soon the only ones left at the bar were myself and a woman of about my own age who, when not looking at her watch, was twisting round to check the lobby for arrivals. Embarrassed as I am to confess to it, the words that came to mind were 'Bergdorf-Goodman'. The one friend I had made on the faculty, though progressive in all the usual campus ways, had a habit of classifying the women of his acquaintance by a department-store metric. If I have it right, this entirely subjective scale ranged from Walmart and Macys through Bloomingdales and Saks and finally to that rarity among women, a Bergdorf-Goodman. In case it comes up again, I had better also mention that such problematic ways of thinking have a tendency to surface in unguarded moments and have to be quickly slapped down in a kind of woke whack-a-mole. On this occasion, I paid penance by ordering a second Bloody Mary and devoting my attention to the bar menu.

I had decided on the Red Lion's Famous Hand-Carved Turkey Sandwich with sage stuffing and cranberry mayo and was hesitating over whether to start with a cup of New England clam chowder when my weekend took its bizarre turn.

'English, right?'

I had only spoken two words in her hearing, but it had obviously been enough.

We talked about the Berkshires for a while, and I think I might have gone on a bit too much about my feeling for New England domestic architecture because her attention kept straying towards the reception desk out in the lobby. Eventually, with another glance at her watch, she asked for her tab. I stood to help her with her coat, a camel-coloured cashmere that I imagined might have cost more than my entire wardrobe. Smiling a speechless thank you, she picked up her purse from the bar and walked out through the lobby into the night.

Alone now, apart from the barman who was checking optics, I drifted off again on that same current of something unfulfilled. Could it perhaps be a sense of not really belonging, of lacking an authentic identity of my own, some place to stand? Through the bay window of the Widow Bingham's Tavern, I saw the indicator lights of a car flash once as the doors were unlocked.

'Get you something to eat, sir?'

I was on the point of ordering the turkey sandwich with a side order of fries when there was a swirl of the camel coat and Bergdorf-Goodman reappeared on the barstool next to me.

'Sorry, but could I just ask you something?'

'Sure,' I said, wondering why I suddenly seemed to be performing a bad impression of Brad Pitt.

She took the menu from my hand and placed it back in its stand, dismissing the barman with a smile. 'I was thinking, if you're about to dine on your own this evening, how does a traditional Thanksgiving dinner in one of those lovely old New England homes sound?'

Faced with nothing more than a dumb look, she proceeded to unburden herself of a narrative about a new boyfriend who was supposed to be driving up from New

York to be taken to meet her family for Thanksgiving and who ought to have been here an hour and a half ago. 'Rather obviously,' she concluded, 'he's a no-show.'

'So… you're asking me instead?'

Floored by this scintillating repartee, she placed both hands on the bar rail.

'Look, this is the thing right here. There is no way I can go back and say I've been stood up. No-oo way. It's too long a story but… way back… I guess I made up a serious boyfriend.' She paused to let this sink in. 'Like lots of girls do that?' she said, as if she had been accused of something. 'Anyway, thing is, I over-elaborated and got found out. Ever since, my Mom and sisters and all, well… you get the picture?'

The barman, perhaps aware of a small drama being played out, was polishing glasses and pretending not to listen.

'You mean you'd like me to… stand in for …

'Harold, yes'. She tossed a fall of soft, shining hair back from her face. 'It's just that when I heard you speak it just seemed like serendipity… you know? Harold's a Brit, too.'

I also took a glance at the reception desk in the lobby. 'Well, it's very nice of you to ask me.'

'Does that mean you'll come?'

'Would I… I mean… would I have to impersonate him?'

'No. Well, yes, I guess. In a way. But it's okay. No one knows a damn thing about him. Expecting me to show up with a Brit in tow is all.'

'You mean I could just… be myself?

Outside in the street, she took my arm. 'This is so-ooo good of you.'

My rental car was the first in the lot and I already had the keys in hand.

'So, I just follow you?'

'Why don't we take mine?'

'Then you'd have to drive me back.'

'No problem. The thing is' – she glanced at my compact Chevvy Malibu with the bent Massachusetts license plate – 'I think I might have mentioned that Harold drives a Porsche coupé.'

Her perfume hung between us in the cabin of the SUV as she drove us out of town, heading west on Old Main. 'I'm Candice by the way, Candice Eliot. Don't tell me your name. I need you to be Harold. You cool with that?'

I had the sensation of wading out to sea and being about to lose the sand between my toes, but we were already turning onto a broad avenue lined with Colonial and Greek Revival homes discreetly hidden among the trees.

I struggled to engage my brain. 'Isn't there anything I should probably know?'

'You're divorced and you work on Wall Street is all.'

We were turning again now onto a gravel drive winding through tree-shadowed lawns.

'Great,' I said, 'I don't know anything about finance.'

'Just stay wa-aaay off the subject. Pop loathes bankers anyway.'

Between the rhododendrons, I saw that we were approaching a well-lit Federal Era mansion.

'Maybe I should know how we're supposed to have met?'

'Motivational training course in the city. Don't elaborate.'

'You work on Wall Street too?'

'No, I was running the course. I'm a psychologist.'

The entrance hall was all sconces and chandeliers as the stranger I had become shook hands and smiled through a blur of Thanksgiving wishes and half-heard introductions.

Supper had obviously been delayed and I had the inspired notion of apologising to Candice's mother for my late arrival. 'Oh, we expected it,' she said graciously, 'I95 is a pig anywhere near Thanksgiving.' And then we were ushered into a candle-lit dining room reeking of furniture polish and old money. To my relief, I was seated between Candice and her nephew, who must have been about ten and who solemnly shook hands and introduced himself as Aldus Franklyn. The scene was splendid: leaf and flower arrangements in fall colours glowed on the oak of the refectory table; pewter chargers gleamed dully amid the sparkle of cut-glass goblets; fat beeswax candles made bright halos making it difficult to see the faces opposite, half-hidden in any case by the vegetation and a line of swing-lidded tureens.

Unwrapping a warm roll from a cotton napkin, it occurred to me that gastronomic curiosity might see me through the first few minutes and was soon being informed that the sprouts were dressed with maple and walnut, the stuffing studded with chorizo sausage, the parsnips glazed with cider and honey, with a choice of caramelised sweet potato or mash with buttermilk. Once or twice I failed to respond to people who began with 'So, Harold, tell me…' but the general noise level, amid all the carving and the passing of plates and pourings of wine, offered blessed cover.

When dessert was eventually brought out – marshmallow pumpkin pie with walnut crust – I struck up a conversation with the nephew, who was making no effort to conceal his boredom. When I asked if he found adult conversation a little dull, he suspended his spoon and delivered himself of the opinion that it wasn't really conversation at all because everyone kept interrupting and so no one got to finish what they were saying and so none of it made any sense and it always ended with everybody laughing at something that wasn't even funny.

Coffee was taken in the drawing-room – log fire, plaid armchairs, Hepplewhite-Sheraton style antiques, Audubon prints on the walls – where the conversation continued to be much as young Aldus had characterised it and was too disjointed to pose much of a threat to an impostor.

Towards the end of the evening, Candice's mother stopped by the two wing-back chairs in which Candice and I had been facing each other, half-hidden. 'And where might you two be planning on going tomorrow?'

The idea of tomorrow seemed oddly alien in the situation but at least the question offered me safe ground and I stuck to my actual itinerary: 'I'd been rather hoping to see Hancock Shaker Village, Mrs Eliot.'

'Isabel, please. Oh yes, you must see Hancock. Don't miss the Great Barn. And there's Edith Wharton's place of course, just up the road. But you must be dreadfully tired after that beastly drive. Your room's all ready, so you two just go on up whenever you want. There'll be plenty of time to talk tomorrow.'

Candice grimaced an appeal for me to play along and reached for my hand. 'Yes, I'm quite tired too. I think we'll go on up.'

Still holding my hand, Candice closed the bedroom door behind her.

'Oh my god, was that just amazingly awful?'

'No, but...' I gave a trapped look around the room and its centrepiece – the enormous mahogany, paisley-quilted sleigh-bed on which a dozen cushions had been scattered with careful abandon. She grinned and was about to say something when her cellphone rang: like the world inter-rupting, or an alarm clock breaking into a dream.

'Darling, what happened? Where are you?'

She gave one of her apologetic grimaces and disap-peared into the bathroom, closing the door behind her.

The bedroom décor should have been calming: beige wallpaper with a faint silver stripe, rag-work rugs on mellow old floorboards. I crossed to the window seat. Outside, what I had at first taken to be a small balcony turned out to be the platform of a fire escape from which white-painted ironwork zig-zagged down into the darkness.

I tried the sash and felt an initial give. Directly below, another gravel drive headed out across unlit lawns. As far as I could tell, Candice seemed to be doing most of the talking.

It was almost a quarter of an hour before she emerged.

'That was Harold. He's been stuck on I95 for two and a half hours with no signal.'

'You told him what happened?'

'Laid the whole thing right on him. He's cool with you. He'll be here in twenty minutes.'

'He's coming here?'

She raised both hands and made a calming gesture.

'Okay, we have ourselves a situation. Now, here's what happens.'

She tossed the fall of hair back from her face in the manner that was becoming familiar.

'He takes the long-cut and comes in off Glendale. Brings him in right here under the window. I told him not to slam doors. He comes up the fire escape' – she took a step towards the window – 'says how-d'ya do and all, and tosses you his keys. You shoot down the fire escape and take off. Hang a right on Glendale and a left when you hit

20. Five minutes and you're tucked up at the Lion. In the morning, it was all a dream.'

'But... what about you – tomorrow, I mean? You just... tell everyone the truth?'

'Exactly what Harold said. But that's not what's going to happen. No way can I go down and 'fess up. I told you before, I have form.'

'But you can't just go down to breakfast...'

'With a different guy? That's exactly what I can do. Ever hear of change blindness?'

Dumb had become my default expression.

'Dan Levin? Kent State? Come on, it's about as famous as the one where the guy in the gorilla suit walks across the court in the middle of the game and no one notices.'

At this point, I found something in me starting to push back. 'Candice, I haven't the faintest idea what you're talking about.'

She sat down on the end of the bed. 'OK, get this, right? Unsuspecting sophomore gets stopped on campus by some guy asking the way to the library. While they're talking, two other guys carrying a door come between them. When they've gotten by, the guy asking directions has changed places with one of the guys carrying the door. The subject doesn't even notice, just carries on explaining the way to the library. Change blindness. Got it?'

'You mean you're just going to go downstairs tomorrow morning with a different guy and no one's supposed to notice?'

'God, you sound exactly like Harold. I know it sounds weird. Everyone thinks they wouldn't be fooled. But trust me, it'll work. Some other campus someplace, they offered a bunch of students five bucks to be in some dumb psychology experiment. When they trot off to sign up, the clerk at the desk disappears to get the consent forms. Comes back, he's someone else. Do they notice? They do not. 'Real-world change detection paradigm', Daniel T Levin and somebody, 2002 or thereabouts. I know Dan. Smart guy.'

'But, I mean, I was down there for a couple of hours tonight…'

'Doesn't signify. Look, I don't have time right now to teach the whole semester, but here's the four-one-one: retaining visual data so as to be able to reproduce it later is not a strong point of the species. There's a bunch of names for it – inattention blindness, encoding failure, representation failure – but the take-home is you have to be paying a whole lot of conscious attention if you're planning on retaining any specifics over time.'

I started to shake my head but she tossed her hair back again and waved the doubts away.

'Fact is, Harold – what's your real name by the way?'

'It's Paul.'

'Well, fact is, Paul, you need to encode data if you're going to retrieve it. And all those folks tonight, in the middle of all that "have some more pumpkin pie and no I shouldn't really and okay maybe just a small piece", let me tell you, no one was doing a whole lot of encoding. Data you take in like that just isn't retained because it's not organised. Retrieve and compare? Forget it. Makes you think about the justice system, doesn't it?'

But I wasn't thinking about the justice system. I was listening to a voice telling me I'd been given an out and should take it.

Candice looked at her watch. 'Harold was the same, circling the airport for an age before touch-down. But, believe me, it'll be fine. We'll go down in the morning – beautiful day, did you sleep well, yes thanks very well, try the blueberry muffins – and no one will say a damn thing. Even if they think something's not quite kosher, they'll think it's them – their confusion, their hangover, their poor memory for faces. And everybody else will just be carrying on like nothing's different, so we get the bandwagon effect going for us as well.'

'But, I mean, does this Harold even look like me?'

'Doesn't signify. God, the guys who swapped places at Kent State were a whole lot different. You and Harold, not so much. But I'm telling you, it's not what people saw tonight that matters. It's what they can pull back in tomorrow morning. What they encoded. And given that you haven't got two heads I can tell you right now the encoding number they did on you – male, white, British, college-educated, acceptably middle class, period.

I looked down from the window to the disbelieving lawns.

'Well, if you think it could work...'

Harold performed an exaggerated impression of a burglar climbing in from the fire escape. He grinned, shook my hand, said 'Hi, how was my dinner? and then hugged Candice, swaying her from side to side while rolling his eyes at me over her shoulder.

'So, I just need to get this straight,' he said, releasing her and brushing a few flakes of fire-escape paint from his jeans. 'The master plan is, I go downstairs in the morning and pretend to be someone who was pretending to be me tonight?'

I smiled back nervously. 'You think it might work?'

'Can't see it myself,' he said cheerfully, 'but Candy "trust-me-I'm-a- psychologist" seems to think it'll be okay.'

'Of course it will,' she said, 'and don't call me Candy.'

She came over to take my hand. 'Tell me your name again?'

'Paul. Paul Morley… I think.'

She smiled and placed both hands lightly on the tops of my shoulders. 'Well, thank you, Paul Morley, for being my knight in shining armour. You were so-ooo great tonight.'

'No problem. But, look, do you think you could, you know, ring me or something to let me know what happens? It's just that I'd be curious to know…'

'If we get away with it,' said Harold, still grinning.

'Sure,' said Candice, 'I'll call you.' She punched my number into her phone while Harold forced the window up another couple of inches.

'I'll go then,' I said, hoping I could manage Harold's way of stepping elegantly over the sill.

'You'll need this – careful not to spit gravel.' He was handing me the key fob, emblazoned with the famous Porsche red, black and gold crest. 'It'll be okay in the lot for a couple of days. Just leave the key at the front desk. I'll pick her up Sunday.'

From the foot of the fire escape, I gave a wave to Candice and Harold, silhouetted against the light of the bedroom window, their arms around each other's waists. And then I was driving tentatively through the night, listening to the slow crunch of gravel and wondering how the perfect innocence of my New England day was ending in the bucket seat of a $300,000 Porsche 911S having just left the bedroom of a Bergdorf-Goodman by the fire escape.

She did not call until the evening.

I had slept long, breakfasted well and, despite the cold, taken coffee in a steamer chair out on the porch where a notice offered guests packed lunches and 'curated New England experiences'.

Hancock Shaker Village may be a museum, the ghost of a community strangled by its own strictness, but it did the job of bringing me closer to whatever grail it was that I was searching for. Those quiet, whitewashed rooms, the timelessly crafted furniture, the patient spinning wheels and looms, the worn and sculpted shovels, the delicacy of copper-riveted boxes – all of it pierced me as nothing else had done. It spoke of an aesthetic liberated by restraint and was as moving to me as whole galleries of fine art.

Glad to have my mind differently stocked, I skipped lunch and headed east toward Historic Deerfield. A long drive in the country, I have found, works like a gimbal, allowing the mind's quivering compass to align itself with the field of underlying concern. And so it proved as I was passing Bryant State Forest on that Friday afternoon. The Shakers of Hancock Village were more than a tourist curiosity: they had known community and belonging and purpose in full measure, and it was a knowledge reflected in all that they did and made and owned and used. Not even for one evening would it have been easy for them to assume any other identity. Nor, I speculated, would they have failed to devote their full attention to what was before them.

By early afternoon, I was visiting the first of the homes on Historic Deerfield's Old Main Street. It was as rich an afternoon as I have ever passed, and as close to time travel as it gets. But more important than the signs marking the years outside each of the houses along that tree-lined village street was the journey along that poignant continuum from brutish survival to a gentler, more refined existence: lap-jointed log homes became mud-caulked, then shingled, then weatherboarded, then finished in a lime of crushed-clam shells or built in stone or ballast brick; batten-and-plank doors with strap-and-pintle hinges acquired panels, transoms, sidelights, porticos, while interiors that had been plastered with mud and dung became limed, whitewashed, and eventually lined with duck-egg blue wainscoting and floral wallpaper; open three-stone fires gained hearths and chimney breasts, oak lintels, carved wooden mantels and, later still, marble surrounds. To walk the length of that street was to walk through a history that was not about the strut of politicians and monarchs but the struggle of families and communities to leave behind the primitive, to win for themselves a measure of comfort and refinement. I felt their struggle in everything I saw and was moved by their silent presence.

The traffic was light for a Friday evening and I was free to settle down with my thoughts on the hour-and-a-half drive back to Stockbridge. I still had not heard from Candice. And when she came to mind now, as I took the road running parallel to the river, even her name seemed to have come from a world and time more distant than Historic Deerfield.

Somewhere near Conway Hills, I stopped to take on coffee in a roadside general store and found myself in a wooden labyrinth of aisles that wandered between grocery mart, barbershop, hardware store, haberdashery, apothecary, stationer, dairy and ice-cream parlour. When I found the counter, I helped myself to coffee from a jug and carried it out to the stoop where half a dozen chairs were arranged around barrels.

As a pair of motorhomes passed in a sedate convoy, I checked my phone and reflected on the past twenty-four hours. It was easy enough to see Candice's home – with its chandeliers and gilded mirrors, its excess of foods and wines, its streams of information and entertainment accessed from leather recliner chairs – as just a continuation of the centuries-long journey I had followed at Deerfield. Easy, too, to lament what had been lost along the way – something that was perhaps too far gone to see clearly but which might still inspire a longing. Maybe it was the loss of an intelligible connection with the workings of things, or perhaps it was the thread of belonging spun too fine, the identity attenuated, the seeing and the experiencing gradually becoming less conscious, life less encoded, as the pace of the undreamt-of had quickened to a blur.

I looked out across the highway. Set back from the road behind deep lawns was a Greek Revival home whose columns would have been more to scale on the Parthenon. Only when concluding that what had been lost was the nobility of the struggle did I remind myself of what had also been left behind: lives cut short by illness or blighted by boredom and bigotry and the cruel censoriousness of closed minds. I stood to go back into the store to help myself to a refill. Over the door, a hand-painted sign announced 'If we ain't got it, you don't need it'.

I had just returned the thermos to the counter when my phone sounded out the opening bars of 'Sweet Baby James'.

'Hi, how's it goin'?'

'Candice, what happened?' I walked back out onto the stoop.

'Nothing is what happened, like I said. Harold was cool, just hung in there and assumed they all knew who he was.'

'I can't believe it.'

'Yeah, only one who wasn't blindsided was the nerdy nephew. The one you were talking to?'

'Aldus? He knew?'

'Shuffled right up alongside after breakfast. Asked me out of the corner of his mouth – "what happened to the guy you were with last night?"'

'What did you say?'

'I told him there was a ten-spot in it if he kept schtum. He's saving for an astronomical telescope.'

'But, I mean, with your folks, it was okay?'

'Fine, like I said. We took off first thing to see that Norman Rockwell picture. You know the one? "Freedom from Want"? We're just having leftovers tonight, by the way. Harold was great. Pop offered him a cigar. Anyway, thanks again for saving my ass. I'll call you if I get to Cambridge, right?'

'Sure,' I said, 'that'd be great.'

I wrapped my hands around the K-Cups coffee. So it was true. Harold had taken my place, as I had taken his, and the switch had not been noticed. Except by Aldus, who thought all adults absurd. Or at least no one had noticed enough to break ranks. Candice had been right about the encoding, and about what it amounted to. Probably any reasonably well-spoken, white, college-educated Brit with some loose change in cultural capital would have done.

It was getting dark and I had miles to go. I took a sip of the still-scalding coffee. Did I feel used, anonymised? Or had it been a relief to be cut loose, freed by not being known? Without a community of expectation, it had been quite easy to imagine a different self, a self based not on anything that might be within but only on the expectations of others. Anything resembling a real me had shrivelled within the chrysalis of my pretence. Later, when I had time to reflect, I realised to my shame that the most disturbing thing about the experience was not its strangeness but its familiarity. I slipped the phone into my jeans pocket. One more whole day of unmoored anonymity still lay before me; one more day when I could be anyone.

I left the last of the coffee and reached to pick up the key fob with the famous red, black and gold crest.

❖

The Hand of Nicias

T HE EMPTY NICHE was a daily irritant to George Palmer, retired financier, philanthropist, and proprietor of Flint Park in the county of Berkshire. Whenever he ascended his staircase to the halfway landing, he was brought face to face with that unoccupied recess and went to his bed dissatisfied.

The niche itself did what niches are meant to do, its concave surface concentrating the light from the fine Venetian window above the entrance. But this was merely to advertise the vacancy. And as the sweep of the staircase was designed to lead the eye to this very spot, its emptiness seemed to proclaim unfinishedness. Almost as if he had run out of funds.

It was obvious what was needed to fill the space: a marble figure, an Aphrodite or a Venus, or a senator or a philosopher; a genuine antiquity, although of course a Roman copy of a Greek original would do. The important thing was that it should look as if it had always been there between the Doric pilasters and trailing acanthus leaves

Measuring the height of the niche at two metres twenty, George instructed his agent to seek out a Greek or Roman antiquity standing one metre eighty-three, plus or minus three centimetres. A month later, on receiving the intelligence that a first-century Roman Venus, originally unearthed near Grenoble and measuring exactly one hundred and eighty centimetres, was being offered for sale by Sotheby's, George had the catalogue couriered to Flint Park. After examining the colour plate, he authorised the agent to make the purchase. The suggestion of an independent provenance check was waived away on the grounds that the reputation of Sotheby's would suffice. The hammer price was expected to be in excess of four million pounds.

When the Venus of Grenoble was installed a month later, its new owner felt himself well pleased. She seemed instantly at home in the niche on the staircase. The nagging emptiness was gone.

Unusually, for a man of great wealth, George Palmer nursed progressive views and cultivated a diverse social circle. He sponsored the Black British Theatre Awards, donated to the Transform Drug Policy Foundation, and made Flint Park available for the Berkshire Literary Festival and an annual Gay Pride picnic. While not scratching the surface of his fortune, these involvements had the added advantage of furnishing interesting guests for his weekend house parties. Since his wife's death, he had felt the vast loneliness of the place and was rarely in residence without one or more of the guest suites being occupied.

Among those invited on this particular evening was Cinzia Fielding, art critic of a left-wing newspaper and an occasional panellist on Question Time. A regular guest, Cinzia could be relied upon to spice the dinner-time conversation with her iconoclastic views on almost anything.

'Allow me to congratulate you on your new guest, George,' was her opening gambit, addressed to her host as she slid her fork into the delicate sformata of asparagus and pancetta.

'I assume you refer to our Venus of Grenoble,' said George, already sensing that trouble might be heading his way. 'Just moved in last month. Settling in nicely, I feel.'

'But a fake, of course.'

George managed a smile that implied Cinzia was being tiresome. 'Really? Sotheby's seem to think it a first-century Roman copy of a Greek original.'

'Oh, I don't mean to imply it's not a genuine antiquity, George. What I mean is, it's fake in perpetuating the idea that classical civilisation and its statuary were white.'

In the silence that followed, Cinzia waited a moment before adding: 'Of course that's just a bizarre western notion that neither Roman nor Greek would have recognised.'

George smiled. Nothing delighted Cinzia Fielding more than giving a good shake to any foundations within reach. He listened as she pressed her point in that peculiar accent that contrived to combine Roedean and Brixton.

'The Romans had their unpleasant side, of course, but one thing they were not was racist. No way did they conceive or portray themselves as white. Italics, yes, but lots of them, including the great and the good, were Syrians, Arabs, Danubians, Transylvanians, Spanish.' She smiled around the table, implying that of course they all knew this. 'Emperors as well, of course, not just the plebs. Severus was a Berber from Africa. But naturally a racist mindset finds it impossible to conceive of them as anything other than white.'

'Are you sure they weren't just the tiniest bit racist themselves, Cinz?' said the television producer sitting opposite. 'I mean, weren't their slaves black?'

'Wrong again, Marcus. Any captives of war would do very nicely thank you – Germans, Britons, Gallics, and lots and lots of Greeks.'

'You do know, don't you, Cinz,' said a sarcastic voice from further down the table, 'you're becoming the go-to-girl for a hokey-wokey take on practically anything?'

'And your point is, James?'

'My point is that it's typical of you to ignore the obvious explanation for anything if it doesn't happen to grind your axe. Rome might have been fifty shades of brown but, like you might not have noticed, marble happens to be white?'

Cinzia affected an infinite patience. 'Marble might be white, James darling, but all those statues, including the recent arrival on George's staircase, most certainly were not. Every one of them was coloured, coloured, coloured. Good God, if an ancient Greek walked into the British Museum today she'd think she'd walked into a gallery of ghosts'

Are you absolutely sure about this, Cinz?' asked the actress seated on George's right. 'I mean, all of them?'

'Oh my Lord, where have you been Marcia? We've known all about this since Pompeii. Put your white marble under a UV microscope and little tadpoles of blues, purples, reds, pinks come swimming up like spermatozoa.'

'Well, statues maybe. But you're not talking about stuff like the Elgin Marbles?'

'What? After they'd been looted and stripped the poor things must have been scrubbed within an inch of their classical lives to get them looking like they do now.'

'It's hard to imagine, isn't it?' said a timid young man who had not so far spoken.

'Try,' said Cinzia. 'And don't just see togas and laurel leaves, Eric. Imagine the flesh as olive, bronze, ochre, mahogany, with copper lips and nipples, gilded earrings, grey beards and curls of black pubic hair, and maybe gemstones for eyes.'

George, who was thinking it would be typical of Cinzia to have made a private bet that she could work nipples and pubic hair into the evening's conversation, gave her a look of mock despair. 'So my Venus was … what colour, do you think?'

'Anything but white, George. I'll grant you that pale skin was a bit of a status thing for the women because of course it said you didn't work outdoors. But for the fellas being pale was plain unmanly. Brown was the colour of your soldiers, athletes, empire builders. It said moral and physical strength. Odysseus was black, by the way. And their statues weren't any more white than the people who posed for them. Sorry if this shocks you guys, I realise we've only known about it since the nineteenth century. Or rather we've known in theory. In practice, we still cling to the idea that all those busts and temples and columns were white.'

That night as George ascended the stairs he paused for a moment before the Venus of Grenoble, softly lit by a hidden spotlight. Bending, he peered closely at a polished thigh.

Next morning, strolling the grounds with Cinzia Fielding, he felt compelled to return to the subject. That classical sculptures were coloured he could accept. What disturbed him was her claim that putting white marble statues on pedestals was an expression – a promulgation even – of white superiority. Walking back to the house, he was not reassured to be informed that a marble statue from the age of Pericles had recently been adopted as a logo by a far-right group in Iowa. 'Not exactly subtle, George. But a neat way of saying that civilization is and has always been a white creation.'

Hana Kerosi was at a low point when the call came. In debt from six years of advanced education, she was now taking whatever work she could, mainly temping and waitressing. With a rent rise due at the end of the month and no savings, she was having to contemplate a return to Bzovík. Her parents would, of course, be welcoming. And too civilised to mention their opposition to her chosen career: worrying when she enrolled in the Academy of Fine Arts in Bratislava; exchanging meaningful looks when she failed to sell her paintings; despairing when she embarked on a masters in classics and archaeology in Munich; and saying nothing at all when she committed to a further year at the Courtauld in London. Since then, there had been a couple of studio commissions and a trickle of short-term and ill-paid restoration jobs, mostly the cleaning or invisible mending of old but gloomy family portraits.

She had never heard of George Palmer and had at first thought that the call might be a hoax. 'You've been very warmly recommended by a trustee of the Courtauld,' said the slow, confident voice. Did she have a moment to talk? Was she fully booked? Did she have any availability over the coming months? Would she like to discuss a somewhat unusual restoration project?

She was not foolish enough to go alone when he offered to send his car and didn't need to ask her brother to know that he would be happy to escape London for an afternoon in the Berkshire countryside. A week later, they were being chauffeured westwards in the back of George Palmer's limousine.

Eighteen months ago, when she and Cenek had both fetched up in London, they had become even closer, drawn together by exile and nostalgia for a childhood home that was falling into ruin. Their father had followed in the family tradition by neglecting his estates for weekends at the card tables in Vienna while their mother had devoted herself to poetry readings and private theatricals at which she floated about in dresses last seen at the court of Franz Joseph. The elder of their two children, a brilliant student, had been expected to restore the family's fortunes. But all Cenek had ever wanted to do was to work outdoors in harmony with nature. After a brief rebellion, he had bowed to the pressure of expectation and entered the world of finance, soon transferring to London where he had made a promising start in the City only to lose his job in the aftermath of the Lehman Brothers. Hana, the second string, had merely been expected to 'set out her stall' and marry well.

As they turned in between stone griffons and began to roll through the landscaped grounds of Flint Park, each knew what the other would be thinking. Although not on the same scale, Bzovík and its park had been a paradise for children to grow up in. Benignly neglected, they had had the run of the abandoned rooms, ghostly with damp and dust sheets, and of the tangled grounds where Cenek had known every plant and tree. They had swum and boated on the once-ornamental lake and sledged the carriage drive until dark on winter days. And what days they had been. No subsequent decay could erase the memories of those glittering December fêtes, necklaces of fairy lights in the pines, rag torches lining the carriageway, skaters in furs etching grisaille patterns on the pristine ice while brilliantly lit ice kiosks served hot Tokaj punch. Gone now, all gone, and the chateau itself contracted to a few habitable rooms furnished with fine ormolu tables and inlaid cabinets standing amid cheap, cane-seated chairs and metal fan-heaters with trailing wires.

The drive swept up through woods and lawns before making a final turn to confront them with the Palladian splendour of Flint Park. Half expecting to be met by liveried footmen, they found themselves being greeted instead by a large, comfortably built man of sixty or sixty-five strolling towards them across the gravel.

'Hana? Thank you for coming all this way. Glad it was such a fine day. Place always looks better.'

After introducing themselves, Hana and Cenek followed George Palmer up the wide semi-circle of steps. Halfway across the entrance hall, he stopped and gestured toward the great staircase.

'I thought we'd take tea in the garden, but it might be as well to just cast an eye over what I want to talk to you about.'

Later, after tea on the terrace, Cenek invited himself to explore the grounds, leaving the two of them to talk.

Hana remained silent as George Palmer explained the commission that was apparently being offered. When he finally rocked back in his chair to invite a response, she turned to look out over the maze of box hedges to the wooded hills beyond.

After a few moments, she stood. 'Would you excuse me, Mr Palmer, if I just take a few minutes to think about this?'

'Of course. And it's George, please.'

When she returned ten minutes later, her host stepped out from the conservatory and pulled back the chair for her to sit once more at the table.

'There are two things I should like us to be completely clear about.' Hana took a deep breath. 'First, about polychromy in general, there is of course no doubt. But you realise, I'm hoping, that not even the most extreme proponent of the 'white-isn't-right' school has ever suggested doing what you propose? It's been done with plaster casts and replicas, of course. But no one has ever suggested attempting it with the real thing.'

George Palmer nodded slowly. 'Which will make the statement all the more powerful, Hana. I may call you Hana?'

She smiled her assent and caught sight of Cenek disappearing into the arboretum. In the distance, the faint rumble of a train could be heard hurrying through the Thames Valley.

'And the second thing?'

'The second thing is that it would only be even thinkable if it were to be undertaken to the most exacting of standards. It would have to be state-of-the-science as well as state-of-the-art. Not just the painting – the research, the materials, the spectrometry, the lab work, analysis, testing. It would be painfully expensive.'

George Palmer smiled. He was beginning to like the serious young woman who listened attentively and spoke plainly. 'Fortunately, Hana, when it comes to expense my pain threshold is set rather high. I would expect to be kept informed, of course, but I would not expect you to work to either a budget or a deadline. I'm not flying blind, here. I've done a little research of my own. It's what led me to you. You have the background in classics, in archaeology, painting, conservation, restoration, and you have the contacts – a rare skill set, I'd have to say, and one for which I would not expect to pay less than, shall we say, eight thousand pounds per month?

It was not without misgivings that Hana began writing the protocol and assembling her materials. She knew that, whatever the other considerations might be, her decision had of course been influenced by the prospect of paying off her debts, especially as it had made sense for her to accept the offer of one of the guest apartments at Flint Park for the duration of the work.

It had also made sense to have the Venus of Grenoble moved from its niche on the staircase to the flagstoned square in the centre of the orangerie, empty now of citrus but filled with light.

A first look, using only a headband LED and hand-held magnifying glass, showed that the statue had been cleaned far more aggressively than would have been the case if its pigmentation had been lost only to time and the elements. There was clear evidence of a mild abrasive having been used on the more accessible surfaces but the interstices of the carving had also been denuded by centuries of damp and oxidisation. After hiring an Eschenbach, ultraviolet and infrared light revealed traces of pigment in all but the most harshly cleaned areas. In some places, it was true, the original pigmentation would remain unknown. Digital hue measurement of adjoining areas and comparisons with the known colouring of similar works would help, as would laboratory analysis of minute variations in the marble surface that would probably reveal the kind if not the colour of the paint that had been applied. All this was communicated to George Palmer as the work progressed, but his concern continued to be whether the problem could be satisfactorily overcome rather than how long it would take or how much it would cost.

Following standard protocol, she had opened an online file for logging each step, starting with research into the kind of primer that would seal the marble without rendering the painted surface too flat. This done, every square centimetre of the Venus of Grenoble was photographed and computer-mapped onto a grid cross-referenced to the daily log. Working with a six-micron tungsten needle under a stand magnifier, she removed obvious samples of pigment from the navel, nostrils, ears, and from the delicate 'Venus wrinkles' of neck and throat. One month in, the contract for spectrometry and x-ray fluorescent analysis was signed off by George to a company in Hounslow. With luck, this would reveal the exact chemical compositions of the ochres, madder, lead white, arsenic sulphide and a particular red that was probably mercury-rich cinnabar. Fluorescent analysis should also reveal the blacks of burned bones and the eggs and oils used to bind the paints. Less common organic dyes from two thousand years ago would be more difficult, but some had already been identified by the Brinkmanns at the Liebieghaus, including the deep purple known as Tyrian which had been traced to a compound found in the glands of the sea snail.

After two months, Hana had proceeded as far as research and scientific analysis could take her and she was face to face with the task of applying twenty-first-century brushstrokes to marble carved in the time of the Caesars. The oils and pigments for the day had been prepared according to the computer grid. Matching them up might seem a little like painting by numbers, but Hana knew that the weeks to come would call on all of her painterly skills. She loaded the first brush and said a silent prayer to Praxiteles who, when asked which of his marble figures he considered the finest, was said to have replied 'the ones that Nicias had applied his hand to'. But she knew that she was not Nicias: not of his time, not of his sensibility, and must make of it what she could.

As the work progressed, she strove for some of the subtlety that she felt must have been there, experimenting with the faintest tinge of Egyptian blue in the whites of the eyes and the merest touch of green under the flesh tones, all the while worrying that no painted surface could ever rival the subtle beauty of that deep marmoreal gleam. She did not doubt that an unknown hand of two thousand years ago had stood before the Venus of Grenoble and done what she was now doing. Her concerns were to do with the impossibility of knowing with any certainty how the Venus had originally appeared. And deeper still was a still unconfronted question about the political premise of it all. Was displaying the artefacts of the classical world as white marble really an expression – even a promulgation – of an unconscious racism? It was certainly true that the idea of a coloured ancient world had been strenuously resisted long after it had been proven beyond doubt. Faced with the evidence, there were many like Rodin who had resorted to beating his chest and declaring 'I feel it here that they were never coloured'. But did that mean that racism, conscious or otherwise, was behind the persistent myth of a white marble classical world? Might it not be that the simple elegance of monochrome was part of its enduring appeal? The Renaissance had forever identified the white marble of Carrara or Paria with civilisation – abstract rational, refined – consigning coloured statuary to the realms of lesser tribes – primitive, sensual, vulgar. But surely Modernism had played its part, elevating form over colour, openness to interpretation over literal representation, monochrome abstraction above gaudy specifics? Hana had struggled to admire Le Corbusier, and wondered now if he too had added to it all with his rallying cry of 'leave to the clothes-dyers the sensory jubilation of the paint tube'. Art is not what it is, it is what we bring to it, she thought as she ground more pigment on the glass; as the brain does the seeing of what the eye takes in, so a culture creates what the mind thinks of as its own.

All of this passed through her mind as the months passed and the days became shorter in the orangerie. She had expected to be cold as the work stretched into October but realised that under-floor heating and double-glazed windows were keeping winter at bay. It was a perfect place to work, so different from the conservatory at Bzovík, now mostly shards of glass, weeds growing through the flagstones, and long-dead plants stiff and sere in broken pots.

George Palmer also suffered from contrary emotions on his morning visits to the orangerie. He was given no reason to doubt his choice of Hana Kerosi as he observed the Venus of Grenoble re-entering the world of colour. Nor did he question that what he was seeing was as close as art and science could contrive to the original appearance of his statue. Yet he too had his doubts. For all Hana's skill and integrity, there was something doll-like, even kitsch, about what the figure was turning into. Standing before the statue in the light of the orangerie, he had to admit that, to modern eyes, the gaining of colour seemed to be accompanied by a loss of dignity. In his worst moments, he wondered if he was not committing a crass nouveau-riche sacrilege, a crime against taste.

His concerns beat more quickly in his breast on the day the statue was strapped into its harness and lifted back to its niche on the staircase. He tried to fight off the idea that his Venus now appeared as a gaudy Hollywood starlet or something that might be found on a fairground ride or a ship's figurehead. Only when he returned to his study was he able to convince himself that he had made a bold stand against a centuries-old lie and that all the sentiments that rebelled against the colouring were just the surfacing of cultural and racial prejudices that needed to be brought into the open.

On the occasion of the first house party of the new year, Cinzia Fielding had looked up from the foot of the stairs and begun applauding solemnly, her slow hand-claps echoing through the hall. But the companion she had brought to dinner that night, an Italian opera director who had enjoyed George Palmer's champagnes and wines to the full, was heard to say afterwards that it took balls to keep your blow-up sex toy in a neo-classical niche half way up the staircase.

Three years after the Venus of Grenoble was restored, George Palmer died. His heirs, a niece and nephew, placed Flint Park on the market and consigned the contents to Bonham's to be auctioned in situ.

It was only from the chance remark of a colleague that Hana Kerosi learned of the sale. She was now free of debt but running down her savings as she struggled from one unsatisfactory commission to another.

Arriving at Flint Park on the afternoon of the sale, she parked in the staff car park and made her way through familiar corridors to the entrance hall. Even to her, the Venus came as a slight shock. She had never come to a stable view on whether she was proud or ashamed of her work. But whatever the rights and wrongs, she had taken satisfaction in believing that no one could have done a more thoroughly researched or faithfully executed job.

The sale was scheduled for 2 pm, giving her time to revisit the orangerie. Across the lawns, the buyers and spectators were arriving, Mercedes, Audis, BMWs and the occasional Bentley parked up in orderly ranks, almost all of them black, silver or grey. In her time in Munich, one of her professors at Ludvig Maximili had been fond of quoting Goethe: 'People of refinement avoid vivid colours in their dress and the objects that are about them.'

Five minutes to two o'clock. She had thought about

registering in case she might be able to pick up a souvenir of her time at Flint Park – perhaps one of the small water-colours from the guest apartment. She had decided against it. Anything she could afford would certainly be part of a job lot.

The orangerie itself was much as she remembered it except that it was now in use to store the items of furniture and a few of the paintings that the family had decided to keep. There were still traces of pigment here and there between the flagstones, though the stones themselves had been steam cleaned. She left by the side door to the parterre where she had first had tea with George. She had grown fond of the philanthropist over those few months; a generous, patient, unfailingly polite man who had wanted to do the right thing, was how she thought if him now.

First up were the Renaissance engravings and a small collection of seascapes from the Dutch Golden Age, one of which was hammered down for a hundred and fifty thousand pounds. The books came next, followed by the Oriental rugs, the tableware and the contents of the wine cellar. It was five o'clock before the auctioneer announced 'Lot eighty-four in your catalogues' and all eyes turned up towards the softly lit niche on the landing of the great staircase.

Murmured conversation and some laughter were cut through by the auctioneer, anxious to keep things moving. 'Classical antiquity known as the Venus of Grenoble. First-century Roman copy of a Greek original, having been rather heavily restored' – a pause for more echoing laughter – to an approximation of the original polychromy. Shall we say fifty thousand pounds?' Almost without a pause, he went on: 'Start me at thirty thousand.'

Silence, save for some turning of pages.

'Where's twenty-five thousand?'

Silence still.

Hana's heart was pounding, brain racing. She still had untouched the ten thousand that George Palmer had given her as a bonus. She had what was left of her savings. She had her car and just less than three thousand pounds on her credit card.

'Twenty thousand then ....

.... About to be withdrawn.'

And she had Cenek, who could lend her five thousand. At which point impulse took over from calculation and she raised a hand.

The auctioneer swung the gavel in her direction. 'Are you really bidding, Miss?'

Knowing this to be procedure for a bidder without a paddle, Hana stepped firmly up onto the first tread of the staircase, keeping her hand in the air.

'Yes.'

'Very well then, the bid stands at twenty thousand pounds. I'll take twenty-two.'

A pause. The auctioneer raised his gavel. 'If there are no more bids...' – another pause – '... then the lady on the stairs is sold to the lady on the stairs.'

There was general laughter as the gavel came down with a crack that resounded through the hall. Through a blur, Hana became aware of someone in a blazer heading towards her with a clipboard.

The Venus of Grenoble looked still more incongruous when uncrated on the ground floor of the converted glass factory, three floors below her rented apartment. Incongruous, but also astonishing that she now owned the only life-size classical figure restored by twenty-first-century skills to something close to how it had appeared thousands of years ago. What would George Palmer – who had taken her hand courteously and told her she should be more than proud – think of his Venus now if he could see her standing under this grimy north-facing window in Willesden? His obituary in The Guardian had been written by an art critic who had told a story of provoking the philanthropist over an evening at Flint Park by arguing that men being dressed in black and white while the women wore a variety of purples, pinks, blues and reds was just another way in which women were consigned to the frivolous margins of this world while men held the serious centre. The obituary had gone on to describe how George Palmer had responded by inviting all present to return a month later to a dinner at which the women would wear only black and white and the men, rather more reluctantly, had agreed to dress colourfully for the occasion. Good old George, she thought, wishing she could have witnessed the scene but not entirely convinced by the art critic's account of how the sartorial reversal had transformed the conversation over dinner.

The work of the next two weeks was tedious, but not difficult. She had followed restoration's golden rule – record everything and do nothing that can't be undone – so all that was needed was a mild detergent, several value-pack boxes of supermarket sponges, her scalpel, some cheap brushes, and a supply of water from the tap jutting from the breeze-block wall.

The greatest difficulty was in overcoming the feeling of betrayal, not only of George Palmer but of all the care and knowledge and skill – her own and others – that had gone into what had been done. There were times, scrubbing, wiping and brushing —doing the work of centuries of abrasion, damp and oxidisation and logging everything to her file – when she felt as though she were returning the Venus of Grenoble to dignity, even to authenticity. At other times, she wondered if she might be disfiguring the Goddess all over again. Euripides had surely spoken for his times when he had Helen curse her own allure with the words 'if only I could shed my beauty and assume an uglier aspect, as you might wipe the colour off a statue'.

Which direction had been the true sacrilege? It was not a question about which she could be objective, any more than she had been objective about accepting George Palmer's commission. And as first the pigment and then the sealant swirled down the drain beneath the tap in the wall, the only certain satisfaction was in knowing that she and Cenek now had work for many years ahead, starting with the orangerie that would one day make a magnificent studio.

❖

Up on the Downs

In the year 1917, after visiting the battlefields of Gallipoli and the Somme on behalf of the War Department, John Masefield returned to writing poetry in the peace of Lollingdon Farmhouse on the Berkshire Downs. Within view were the Wittenham Clumps, the two small hills to which the artist Paul Nash had returned after painting the battlefields of Flanders in his capacity as an official war artist. Nash was to paint the Clumps twenty-six times before his death in 1946. There is no record of the two men ever having met.

THE OLDER MAN RAISED HIS CANE but the greeting was not seen, so absorbed was the artist in his work. Even on the damp earth, footsteps could have been heard. But the eyes under the soft, rabbit's-hair trilby did not once look up.

At a quarter to twelve, the cane rattled into the pot by the door of the farmhouse.

'Good walk?' Constance, her face flushed, was setting an enamel bowl on the kitchen table.

'Yes. Got a few lines in my head. I think I might have seen that painter.'

'What painter?'

'The one whose brother we met.'

Constance used a cloth to grip the handle of the kettle and began pouring boiling water into the bowl.

'What made you think that's who it was?'

'I remembered that chap telling us his brother was staying over here. Said he was obsessed by those two hills.'

'And is that what he was painting today?'

'Sketching, yes.'

'Why didn't you just ask him?'

The poet was standing in his stockinged feet on the flagstones. 'I don't know. I'd just spotted a kestrel poised not twenty feet above the stubble. So concentrated. So eloquent. Just fine-tuning its tail feathers in the wind. It gave me an idea I wanted to keep in my head.'

Constance scooped Vaporub from a jar with a finger. 'Was the sketch any good?'

'I don't know. I just got a quick look as I passed by. He seemed to be working on the sky and clouds. Turbulent, almost violent.'

'And did it put you off your poem?'

'I think not.'

'So I'll be hearing it after supper?'

On his way back from depositing his boots in the porch, he embraced his wife, kissing her on the lips as the antiseptic vapour rose around them. Constance released herself and began arranging the cloth over the steaming bowl. 'Invite him for lunch if you see him again.'

He closed the door of the study behind him. Constance, smiling to herself, began calling the boy.

The weather was unsettled the next day, acres of sunlight racing over the Downs before prowling cloud shadows and spiteful squalls of rain. Up on Lollingdon Ridge, where hawthorns struggled in a permanent eastward yearning, the poet sensed the beginnings of vertigo, the landscape seeming to heave and roll, raised up by sudden sunlight and plunged down by swift shadows. Like the swells he had seen from the rigging of the Gilcruix, or the heaving mud of Flanders, worlds torn up and tossed to one side, opening dreadful chasms.

Undeterred, the artist was crouched over his sketch-book, the brim of the trilby just visible above the tweed collar of his cloak.

On this occasion, the poet murmured 'good day', causing the other to twist around with a start.

'I didn't intend to interrupt.'

"No, no, not at all. I was just finishing.'

The artist removed his hat to reveal a high pompadour of raven-black hair, parted low to the left side, above a pale, rather pampered face. A long-stemmed cherry-wood pipe, unlit, poked from the corner of his mouth, just clearing the collar of the cloak.

The poet raised his cane towards the two hills on the horizon, topped by their grey silhouettes of beech clumps.

'The Sinoduns?'

'Yes.' The artist turned to the view and began to converse as though the two were intimately acquainted. 'I told my cousins at breakfast – you may be out all day shooting and fishing, but I'm out hunting, too. I watch. I wait. I strike with this.' He raised a delicate twig of charcoal between outstretched fingers. 'What is there to choose, I said to them, between a bird, a fish and a sketch?'

The poet smiled and continued to look to the horizon where two small hills rose from the Oxford plain as though left behind by time. 'I've a mind to find my way over there one day.'

'You really should. Walk on those earthworks. Celtic of course.'

The poet raised his cane to the brim of his hat and was about to set off when he returned the ferrule to the ground.

'As a matter of fact, I was thinking about the Celts myself this morning. It might have been the burning of the gorse up on that bit of heathland'. He gestured to the salient of Lollingdon Hill, now deep in cloud shadow. 'That tinge of smoke in the nostrils. The sharp taste at the back of the throat, you know. Made me wonder about being caged in a wicker man – whether the smoke killed you before the flames.'

Over at Sinodun House, the Wells family supper was followed by the usual musical entertainments and it was after ten when the artist managed to retreat with his wife to the guest sitting room at the back of the house. A fire was already burning in the grate, its light fragmenting on the decanter. Margaret poured Madeira for them both. He pulled the portfolio onto his knees and tugged at the ribbon.

'Might make something of them."

Margaret took the first offered sheet. 'You must have been wet through.'

'There was sun and wind, too. More exhilarating than steadier weather.'

He took out his sketches of the morning one by one, examining each before passing it to his wife. From downstairs, piano music and an occasional interruption of laughter carried through the high rooms of the house, rattling the organ pipes in the stairwell.

'There was another fellow out there today. I think it might have been Masefield.'

Margaret looked up from the sketch. 'What do you mean "might have been"? Didn't you introduce yourselves?'

'No. We just talked about the Celts for a while.'

Margaret gave him her 'look' and took the next sketch.

'What made you think it was Masefield?'

'I recognised him from the newspapers. And you remember John mentioning he'd met him in Chalfont?'

'At the studio, yes.'

The artist took a sip of the Madeira. 'Well, apparently he told him he'd rented a farmhouse on Lollingdon Downs.'

Towards midnight, before following her husband upstairs, Margaret ran a finger across the single row of books on the shelf. Taking down a volume, missing its dust jacket, she crossed to the hearth. The faded red boards caught the last of the firelight, revealing the stamped title and the name – 'John Masefield'. She turned a few pages, tilting the book to the lamp.

> *'Imagine in all that expanse no single tree left intact… imagine that in all that expanse there is no patch of ground ten feet square that has not got its shell hole, gouged and blasted and bedevilled with the pox of war, and at every step you are on the wreck of war, and up at the top of the ridge there is nothing but a waste of big grassless holes ten feet deep and ten feet broad, with defilement and corpses and hands and feet and old burnt uniforms and tattered leather all flung about and dug in and dug out again, like nothing else on God's earth.*[1]

She put the book down on a side table. From behind the mantle clock, she took out the letters she had been re-reading that afternoon. She untied the ribbon and found the page she was looking for, written in her husband's hand.

> *'Imagine a wide landscape… what trees remain blasted and torn, naked and scarred and riddled, the ground for miles around furrowed into trenches, pitted with yawning holes in which water lies still and cold… No pen or drawing can convey this country. No glimmer of God's hand is seen anywhere…*

A dozen or more sketches had arrived with the letter, and she could see many of them in the unfinished painting that now stood in the studio in Chalfont. She turned up the wick to steady the flame and brought the letter closer to the light, its royal blue ink already tinged to bronze.

Sunset and sunrise are blasphemous, they are mockeries to man, only the black rain out of the bruised and swollen clouds all through the bitter black night is fit atmosphere in such a land… the black dying trees ooze and sweat and the shells never cease… tearing away the rotting tree stumps, annihilating, maiming, maddening, they plunge into the grave, and cast up on it the poor dead. It is unspeakable, godless, hopeless.[2]

She extinguished the lamp and remained downstairs for a few minutes, listening to the murmuring of the fire and the faint strains of music from the front of the house.

Dinner at Lollingdon Farmhouse that evening was a homely affair of potatoes and pork chops cooked in cider with a few frostbitten sprouts. When the boy had been read to and the dishes cleared away, the poet carried the cider jar to the open hearth.

'I don't suppose there are any of those peppermint creams left?'

'I let Lewis have the last one. Cider Apple?'

'Not if you want to hear the poem'. He made a face, suggesting that the sweets would glue his teeth together. Pouring cider for them both, he carried notebook and glass to the fireside. 'I've called it "Up on the Downs". For goodness' sake, think of something better.'

Constance sat back, anticipating the edge of a nervousness in his reading voice, even for her, as he strove to avoid any taint of performance. When she lifted her face to the firelight, he began:

Up on the downs the red-eyed kestrels hover,
Eyeing the grass.
The field-mouse flits like a shadow into cover
As their shadows pass.
Men are burning the gorse on the down's shoulder;
A drift of smoke
Glitters with fire and hangs, and the skies smoulder,
And the lungs choke.

He took a drink of cider, gleaming with apple-warmth in the firelight.

Once the tribe did thus on the downs, on these downs burning
Men in the frame,
Crying to the gods of the downs till their brains were turning
And the gods came.
And today on the downs, in the wind, the hawks, the grasses,
In blood and air,
Something passes me and cries as it passes,
On the chalk downland bare.[3]

He looked down at his wife, who was nodding slowly.
'Complaints? False notes? Extravagant praise?'
'Perhaps one too many "downs"?'
He drew a small propelling pencil from the spine of the notebook. In the fireplace, the flames had settled into a quiet heat, save for a torch of gas that burned furiously at one end of a log.
'Especially in this third stanza.'
'And I wasn't sure about "thus".'
He consulted the poem again. 'Bit fustian? Bit Matthew Arnold maybe?'

'And a touch heavy for its line?'

When he had finished making notes, he seated himself in the armchair and reached for her hand across the small space between them.

'They were burning the gorse, you see.'

Constance picked up the poem. After a few minutes, she said: 'Is it about the war?'

He sighed faintly and continued to stare into the fire. She squeezed his hand.

'You said you were going to turn your eyes to beauty again. "Whatsoever things are lovely... think on these things." Remember?'

'It isn't the same, Con. What the eye sees is the same. What the mind sees is changed.'

'Give it time.'

After a period of silence, Constance went over to the revolving bookcase that did not quite hide the patch where plaster had fallen in damp flakes from the wall. He smiled when he saw the book she had chosen. Standing to one side of the fireplace, she read in as normal a voice as she could manage.

So beautiful it is, I never saw
So great a beauty on these English fields,
Touched by the twilight's coming into awe,
Ripe to the soul and rich with summer's yields.

He leaned forward, frowning occasionally, as she read more of the nostalgic quatrains of 'August, 1914'. When she returned to the chair, he reached again for her hand.

'It was a hundred years ago, Con. I can't write like that now.'

'It was three years ago, Jan. You wrote it the week Rupert left. Do you remember? He said you were an old worrier for thinking the Austro-Serbian business might involve us in a war.'

He stroked the back of her hand, and in the quiet of the farmhouse a far-off June day came back in all its innocence, and with it the face of the young man who had thanked God for matching his youth with the hour, and who had died of dysentery on the way to Gallipoli.

In the early hours of the morning, Constance lay in the darkness, kept awake by the rainwater dripping into the bucket, the wait for each malevolent 'zinc' worse than the sound itself. Like the sound of time falling into the void. Like the beat of an inevitable decay. She thought about the plaster flaking from the walls. She thought about Lewis's chest and the winter to come. She thought about whether to keep fires in the bedrooms. She listened to the wind in the beech trees and imagined the galloping horse on the weather vane restlessly changing direction above the barn. She tried not to think of her own spirits, or allow herself to enter the forbidden garden of her loneliness in this place. It would not be forever. But, for now, the peace and isolation were what he needed. In the darkness beyond the brass at the foot of the bed, she saw again the great painting they had stumbled upon that day. They had been walking all morning and had been heading home across the common when they had heard piano notes floating out over the fields. Stopping to look through the open door of a farm building, they had been beckoned inside by a young man standing by an easel. Inside, they had breathed in the smells of an ancient agriculture mingled with fresh linseed and a pungent note of marjoram or thyme. The young man had introduced himself as John Nash, of Iver Heath, and told them that he and his brother, artists and printmakers

both, had rented the old herb drying shed from Tubb's
Farm. As the afternoon had begun to thicken on the fields,
and the piano had continued to play from the shadows,
they had been drawn to a large painting standing on the
floor against a wall. It was a composition of black, blasted
trees and water-filled craters under a dark sky slashed
through with the harsh diagonals of searchlights. The
canvas, charged with a dislocating energy, had seemed to
cry out with anger and despair and, for a moment, she had
seen the battlefield not as it struck the retina but as it must
have struck the heart. Seeing their interest, their host had
informed them that the canvas, unfinished, was the work
of his older brother, Paul, and had been commissioned for
Beaverbrook's planned Hall of Remembrance. Along the
bare edge of the stretcher, written in a loose charcoal
scrawl, the words 'A Flanders Battlefield' had been
smudged out and replaced by 'The Menin Road'.

'Not your own country though?' said the artist.

'No. Herefordshire. Quite different.'

The invitation had been extended merely by the raising
of the Dewar flask and now the two men sat side by side
on the open hillside, sipping tea and looking out on as
perfect an autumn morning as England has to offer.

'And you return there?'

The poet shook his head. 'I've no people there now. And
I prefer to preserve it as it was. Or as it was in the mind of
a child. Cider presses oozing onto dripstones. Bellows
wheezing and charcoal glowing. The coach-and-four
coming over Chance's Pitch with the mail and the London
papers, and the dandies getting out to stretch their legs,
wearing rings on the outside of their gloves. Did you draw
those hills before it all kicked off?

'Yes, I made the first sketches when I came to visit my great-uncle here in '09. It's where we're staying now, just below the Fort Hill.' He lifted a hand to the outline of the Sinoduns. 'They're enchanted places to me. Haunts of old beauty and long-forgotten gods. I knew they were significant straight away, long before I knew anything about them.'

In a heartbeat, some movement caused both men to turn. Not ten yards away, a full-grown fox had stepped out from the damp bracken. It froze on the path now, one paw raised, wary, unafraid. The two men stared in a suspended silence, marvelling at its presence until their visitor, grown bored with admiration, set off unhurriedly down the track.

'There's old beauty for you,' said the poet.

The artist frowned. 'The day we arrived, a neighbour invited us over to Sires Hill to see what old beauty had done when it got under the wire in the night. Only one chicken was taken, but the others! Blood and feathers everywhere, legs and wings torn off, necks bitten through. Utter, unnecessary savagery.'

The poet sipped his tea. 'I suppose it's never far away.'

Neither man felt the need to speak, knowing that the shared experience that can make talk easier can also make silence more eloquent. And in the silence, the poet found his vision straying from the gentle Downs to those tortured, blackened, blasted trees, scarce able to embrace that the man who had painted that scene of heartsick anger and despair was sitting beside him now, sipping tea and making studies for a painting of these two hills and the innocence of their trees.

Almost under his breath, he asked: 'And have you always painted trees?'

The artist paused his sketching. 'I love everything about them. In fact, I worship them, I truly do. I think perhaps I may have got it from Blake. Or Kensington Gardens. When I was a child, there was an ancient beech, its limbs bruised and weather-stained, one branch propped on an iron crutch. Ever since, I've known that trees are really people. And wonderfully beautiful people. Much more so than the majority of people one meets. I paint them as though they were people, because to me they are.'

A distant gunshot from the direction of Kibble Beck brought the artist back to the world and he looked up at his companion with a self-deprecating smile. 'And of course, there's the fact that trees have an obliging tendency to stand still. I've no talent for figure drawing.' After a pause, he said: 'And you can look at a tree all day long without misgivings.'

Constance was applying a rosewater hand salve when he came back from his walk.

'What a strange fellow that painter is,' said the poet, hanging up his jacket.

'He was there again?'

'Yes, we had quite a decent chat. Fellow's more of a poet than I am. Says things like "trees are really people" and "In a wood, everything seems to be listening".'

Constance smiled, delighted with the eccentricity. 'Is he quite all right?'

'I think so – makes sense every now and then.'

'And did you ask if he was the brother?'

'I just assumed. It couldn't be anybody else.'

Constance replaced the lid on the salve and picked up a three-day-old copy of The Times. 'Listen to this. It's just as if nothing's changed.' She blinked twice and read aloud in her best corset-strangled voice: "Wanted: Ladies' maid. Sound character, impeccable references" etcetera, etcetera. Then this: "The successful applicant will have a superior education in the ornamental branches of female acquirements".'

The poet had bent to unlace his boots. 'Sounds like she's supposed to look after her mistress's antlers. I got you some elderberries by the way. They're in my pocket.'

'Better get them out now. Why didn't you invite him to lunch?'

'I don't know, it didn't seem quite appropriate.'

Sitting at the bureau in the music room, Margaret dipped the nib and began again.

> *I am quite ashamed to write this, and would venture it only to you, but I must confess that my conviction sometimes falters when I think of what the men have been through. But then I remember our conversations, dearest Elizabeth, and my faith in our cause is restored by the certainty that if we had a voice and a vote, if we had a say in destiny, then never again would that destiny lead us down the Menin Road.*

Later, before the lamps had been lit, she asked if he had seen anybody out on the Downs.

'Masefield again. I went on a bit about trees. You'd think a poet would understand these things, but I rather think he thought I was demented.'

'And you're still sure it's Masefield?'

'Quite sure – we talked about Herefordshire. And we saw a fox.'

'He's married, isn't he? And I seem to remember reading somewhere she's quite a lot older. Do invite them for luncheon. Uncle would love to meet them and the children have all made paper lanterns.'

Just ahead of where the two men were sitting, a single out-of-season daisy was holding up the advance of winter.

'When I was a child,' said the poet, 'the test of spring was whether you could cover nine daisies with your footprint.'

The artist's eyes lit up with pleasure. 'What a picture that conjures.' He laid the charcoal in its tin box and reached for his knapsack.

'What was it that made you run away to sea?'

It was the poet's turn to smile. 'There's a myth that won't die. I didn't run away. I was packed off to a training ship on the Mersey when I was thirteen. First real voyage was to Chile. Seasick all the way out, sunstroke all the way back. Then a spell on the windjammers.'

'And might I inquire what wind drove you back onshore?'

The poet looked up into another day of intense blue beauty on the Downs. 'A yearning for a foothold, I think. For a place to stand. And in the end, I couldn't wait to get away from the cruelty of ships and the type of men who give a shelf to sleep on and a morsel of daily offal in exchange for a life's work.'

From a sheet of greaseproof paper, the artist proffered a sandwich of homemade white bread, Berkshire ham and thick yellow butter. 'I was sent off to a Navy crammer at that age, twelve or thirteen. Brutal place. Blood and bruises every day without fail. I couldn't ever get through navigation. Hopeless at anything to do with maths. In any case, I'm a land lover. Though I imagine there's beauty at sea, too.'

'Unforgettable beauty. One night in the South Atlantic, when I was alone on watch, a moonbow appeared off the bow. A nocturnal rainbow, I think it's called. Horizon to horizon over nothing but dark sea. So beautiful I thought I'd stopped breathing.'

The artist seemed lost in imagining. At the foot of the Downs, a flock of lapwings lifted off from a flooded field, wings flickering like an old film.

'Even then, the savagery is never far away,' continued the poet, 'and the beauty of the sea can be quite daunting in its vast indifference. I think I needed a more intimate beauty. Something like this.'

In response, the artist lifted a hand to trace a line in the air over the outline of the Sinodun Hills. 'For me, the beauty is a particular thing, an elusive thing. I find it in places where I feel the enchantment, where I sense the presence of a spirit of place. Especially burial barrows, old standing stones, places haunted by long-gone lives that are still here. Especially if there are trees. Sometimes, I find myself quite intoxicated by the clarity of their mystery. I know it will absorb me all my life.'

The older man did not allow himself to smile. 'When will you be leaving?'

'Back to Iver the day after tomorrow. What about you, will you make Lollingdon your home?'

The poet shook his head. 'We'll be leaving soon, too. It might be a haunt of old beauty, but there's no escaping the damp, and it's terribly lonely for Con. It seems we might have the offer of a place on Boars Hill. So I'll be back here from time to time. As you will, I imagine.

'Yes, I'll always be back.'

'And besides,' said the poet, 'I've been known to opine that beauty is to be found anywhere.'

'Even in the most godforsaken of places.'

'Even in the most godforsaken of places.'

There fell another of those silences that might have been occupied with words for the sake of filling a void but with which, up on the Downs that day, both men rested content.

Eventually the artist began collecting up the remains of the picnic. The poet, too, got to his feet.

'So perhaps we may meet again in the spring?'

'Perhaps we may,' said the artist, extending a hand from within the cloak. 'May beauty walk with you, sir.'

'And with you,' said the poet, raising his stick to the brim of his hat.

Notes

[1] *From* The Old Front Line, *John Masefield.*

[2] *From Paul Nash's letters to his wife from the Western Front (published in* Outline, *Nash's unfinished autobiography).*

[3] *The poem* Up on the Downs *was included in* Lollingdon Downs and other Poems, *John Masefield, The Macmillan Company, New York, 1917.*

Sahel

T HE DAY THAT KADRÉ has waited for through the long
months of the dry season had broken without the usual
blinding light. He sits up, and within a second his heart has
begun to pound with the weight of all that the day might
bring.

He rolls his head to loosen a crick in his neck. Just outside
the door a chicken scratches. The sound of pouring water.
And something else. The months of morning dryness have
gone from his throat. He swallows, pleasurably.

'When will you go?'

His mother has placed a bowl of tamarind water by his
mat in silent acknowledgement of anxiety. She is moving
around in the shadows of the hut, setting things straight,
squaring up his schoolbooks, pulling the rush door to one
side, letting in the day. The light is opaque, muted, as if
seen through a block of salt. He tastes the moisture in the
air, pulls the damp into his lungs.

'Straight away.'

When he has washed, he scrapes out the last of the
porridge, pushing in sauce with a shard. She hands him his
shirt, eyes brimming with concern.

Usually, on such a morning, there would be only one topic. For a week the skies above Yatenga had been heavy with promise. And yesterday, towards evening, the first warm drops had spilt over onto the dust of the compound. Soon the whole village had been crouched in doorways, whooping relief from hut to hut in the dusk as the rain, hesitant at first, had begun to insist. 'Yel-ka-ye' they had shouted – 'no problem' – eyes drinking in the dark blots exploding in the dust, darkening the thatch, patterning the jars outside each door. Later, after the meal had been eaten and the youngest children put to bed, a silence had settled on Samitaba as the adults and elders had returned one by one to squat in their doorways, hypnotised by the rhythm of the rain, awed by the completion of the earth's slow stain.

But this morning the talk is not of the night's rains, or of the seeds being sieved from the ashes, or of how many fingers of grain are left on the warm floors of the granaries. This morning the whispers are only of Kadré and his journey to the office of the Préfet.

Assita watches her son go, passing between fresh ochre walls and the still dripping thatch. From today, all of their clothes will need more washing. With a heave she lodges the day's grain on her hip and sets off towards the touré, still watching her son as he makes his way to the road under the eyes of the village. The roofs have been washed, and today the jars will be manoeuvred over the muddy depressions where last night the loose waters splattered heavily onto the earth. All around the familiar sounds of the morning drift across the compound. Firewood being dragged. Water splashing into pots. Utensils being scoured with ash and straw. But all eyes are still on Kadré as he passes the last of the huts and turns towards the road. A few of the women, going about their chores, smile their encouragement. A few of his own age, lacking tact, call out.

Assita crosses the broad circle of chaff and peanut shells, already seeing in her mind her son arriving at the edges of the town, crossing the bridge, passing down the muddy main street to the square, climbing the steps to the veranda of the administration building, standing before the list on the noticeboard, looking to see if his name is one of the ten. She transfers the broad bowl of grain to the other hip. Ten names only. The ten chosen from hundreds, perhaps thousands, from all the schools of Yatenga. The ten who will be leaving their homes and villages. The ten who will be going again to school, only this time many days' journey away. From somewhere nearby a donkey brays, dislodging the crows from their nests. Outside the schoolroom, under the remaining neem tree, an old blackboard long ingrained with chalk has been given new life by the night's rains. Ten who will go to live in the city. Where they have no family. Where they will know and be known by no one. She bows her head in acknowledgement of the elder coming in the opposite direction along the path. Ten who will wear a tie by day and sleep in a bed by night. The elder looks straight ahead but raises a flat palm. A pair of pliers hangs from his neck, in case of thorns.

Ten who will learn about the world, learn to speak in French, maybe even go to Paris. She sets the bowl down by the great mortar, hewn from the trunk of a tree longer ago than anyone can remember. Such things had been known. In the years before the rains failed for the first time, there had been a boy from Koudougu, the village where the well was so deep the water was drawn by men. He had found his name on the list and gone to school in the capital. She steps through the rough carpet of straw, husk, and chaff among which the goats and chickens can always find something else to eat. It was rumoured that he had become a man. That he had gone to Paris. Chickens scatter at her feet as she reaches for the heaviest of the pestles.

He had never returned.

'There is nothing for him here.' Her husband's words, spoken into the darkness as they had lain awake listening to the rains, had disturbed her. That, and the onset of the planting time.

'There is nothing for him here.'

Soon the pestle is flying before her face, thudding into the bowl to the dull rhythm of the woman's drum, jolting the beads of grain from their stalks.

Today the seeds will be risked again in the fields. It would have been his twelfth rains. Lassito's. Her first son. The one who had been born into a parched world, into a colourless land where only the harsh light and dusty shade had defined the shapes of the village. When all across Yatenga – Yense, Kallo, Oufray, Somyaga, Titao – everything had crumbled to the touch. The pestle is sending sprays of white powder into the air as she lowers its rise, easing the muscles of her arms and back. A neighbour passes, heading for the well, and Assita throws the pestle higher, missing a beat and clapping her hands in greeting before catching it again, keeping the rhythm going. When the rains had finally come, they had been the first in two years. And they had come too late. 'Yel ka-ye,' the people had said – 'no problem'. 'Yel ka-be,' they had smiled – 'no complaints'. Until finally, when even the red millet had gone and the roots were being boiled, the time had come for the infants to be given back.

She scoops up the loose grain into the first bowl. From a nearby hut, a child cries and is silenced at the breast. Above the touré, a jay has launched itself from a bare tree. She had taken Lassito to the clinic, stayed with him there, listening to the rain drumming its fingers on the iron roof. But when she had brought him home there had been no food. And she had had no milk. 'Laafi Bala,' the elders had said – 'I have peace and health'. And they were all starving.

She lifts the bowl high and tips the freed grain in a long graceful pour, allowing the faintest of breezes to carry away the straw and chaff to the waiting goats, leaving the hard kernels to rattle accurately into the calabash at her feet, feeling the new touch of the air, the cool and the damp on her skin. It had been just such a morning, fresh and raw, when Hamadé had come to her, carrying the child as a woman does, close to his body. And she had laughed. A man does not carry a child this way. Laughed. Pushing its meaning away. Until it had sunk in that her son was cold against her husband's chest.

Soon the bowl at her feet is full and she begins the second pounding, this time with a grittier thud as the lighter pestle splits the hard backs of the husks to release the tiny white grains; the heart of the matter, the end of the long story that began with the rains and the hoe. 'The water is spilt', the elder women had told her, 'but the jar is not broken'.

And they had been right. Before the next rains, Kadré had been born.

She squats in the shade of the touré, slapping the calabash from hand to hand to the rhythm of another of the dances of her life, working the stubborn husks to the edges of the bowl – slap, tilt, slap – losing them to the waiting earth.

'There is nothing for him here.'

The men have been out in the fields since daybreak, taking advantage of the minutes when the earth is still soft and the air still cool. Across the scarcely perceptible slopes and hollows, groups of figures are bent over the land, blades rising and falling in the sun. Occasionally, a cry of encouragement - 'Wa t'd maaré' – 'let us work' – carries over the land. The rains have come, and the earth is raw and red and greedy.

Hamadé straightens at the end of a row, resting the daba on its blade, surveying the earth he has turned, calculating how much has been done, how much there is still to do. No fence tells him where a field ends and another begins; one man's plot starts where the earth dips... and ends at the broad pool of thin clay that has formed like a skin over the earth; another man's starts at the line of termite hills and finishes at that invisible, meandering line between soil and sand, earth and shale, a dividing line of judgement between fertility and barrenness, a fence of decisions that say 'beyond here labour is in vain'.

For a few moments he watches his son on the road below. On any other day the boy would have been by his side, daba rising and falling in time with his own. His action would not have been as practised, as economical, but he would have refused to straighten his back until his father stopped to rest at the end of a row.

A cart has stopped to offer the boy a lift as far as the crossroads.

Hamadé picks up the daba. Already the tired pallor of the land is returning, the rich colours of the morning drying to a drowsy sameness across the land. All that is different, all that is new, comes from where Kadré is going. From the town. From abroad. The place of diesel engines, dust-stirring motor bikes, steel ploughs and chains, sodium lights and television, Coke and Fanta and yellow beer, razors and zips and baseball bats and brushes for teeth. In all of Hamadé's gaze, the only alien colour is the blue plastic fertiliser bag, split and stretched over poles to make a place of shade in the fields. All else is the colour of the earth, dark with damp or already light with the drying sun. But earth just the same. The earth from which nothing new ever comes; only the meagre grain and the sun-hardened clay, the tamarind seed and the memories of old men. The land of his grandfather's time, and of his own father's memories, has gone. And with it the rich openings of new soil cut or burnt into forest and savannah, the festivals and full granaries. Around him the slopes of Yatenga, cleansed of the tiring dust, glisten threateningly under the sun.

But here at his feet, the land that yesterday would have answered the hoe with nothing more than a cloud of dust can this morning be turned and planted. He bends again to his fields, setting up the rhythm that will carry him to the end of a row. Cut and turn. Cut and turn. Three months, four at the most, in which to replenish the granaries. Cut and turn. He starts another row, breaking a new edge of soil. Cut and turn. Salt and spices you can buy with money. Neer and karite you can buy with money. Cut and turn. Cut and turn. But grain you grow with your own hands. Enough to make the sesuka, the welding between one harvest and the next. Cut and turn. Cut and turn.

He reaches the top of the first field. The boy has gone and the cart is heading in the opposite direction, towards Oufray. The morning is growing old. And soon all living things will walk, crawl or fly from under the weight of the sun; the elders will be finding shade under the eaves, the chickens fussing beneath the granaries, the goats penning themselves up in the strips of shade under the village walls. Even the brilliant beetle, the wife of the rain, seen only when the soil is wet, will have vanished again into the dark cracks of the earth.

He begins a new field, but soon the sound of the blade changes, biting now into shale and sand. It is the sound of half-full granaries, the sound of failure. The sound of why the land glistens. The sound of why the joining of the seasons will not be made. He abandons the furrow and finds a new patch further down the same slope. But the soil here is thinner than the blade's bite and there is nothing to hold the rains. No depth. No root. Instead, the night's downpours send sudden streams scouring the land, earth enriching water, leaving behind only a brittleness so that when the Harmattan begins to blow any soil that is left will fly to the west, as loose as chaff in the winnowing. This is the waré, the quarrel of earth and sky.

He tries again, further up the slope, behind the shin-high stones arranged in broad arrows up the slight incline. Others have left firewood out on the slopes to dry, or the dung of goats and sheep, even the droppings of chickens and scraps of cardboard. Anything to try to hold on to the soil of Yatenga. He looks again down the slopes towards the road to the town. In the wrinkles of his feet and ankles, the mud has dried to a fine clay. It is Ramadan, and he will not eat until sundown.

Kadré arrives at the edge of town, passing between the barracks and the municipal dump. Below the bridge, the river is only a bed of mud in which cattle have left deep, oozy hoof prints.

Lizards scuttle from his path as he walks down the wide street. Everything familiar is made different by the night's rain. As if each low cement building, each water tower, each radio mast, has taken on some new edge of reality. He is nearing the administration building. The walk from Samitaba has been the same, an easy distance that he has covered a thousand times to school, yet on this morning his breathing is tight and his skin feels stretched across his chest.

He passes the grain store, the entrance littered with cycles and iron-handled carts. From the darkness inside comes the sweet, musty smell of sacking and grain. He is about to raise his hand to the foreman who does not see him; the hand goes instead to the pen in his shirt pocket. Outside the depot, a line of new ploughs stands waiting for customers, their naked prows pointing to an invisible future. He stoops to check the label on one of the handles: 'Drome, France, approprié à tous les sols'. He straightens again, and the sun flashes like fear on the bare steel of the blades.

And now his heart is pounding with the insistent coughing of the diesel engine as he approaches the mill, passing between empty carts and oil drums. On the corrugated roof, a makeshift exhaust pipe thuds dirty air into the sky. He hurries past, counting the line of enamel bowls at the feet of the miller. A shout draws his eyes across the street to where a group of men, sitting in the shade, are throwing stones at a goat nibbling at a few vegetables sticking out from the pannier of a motorbike. The men return to smoking and playing cards. A younger man observes them, sitting astride a 250cc Yamaha, a traditional hunting knife bound to the forks with a leather thong.

He enters the broad municipal square. Newly planted trees, fenced against the wandering goats, form an inner quadrangle of acacia, neem, zanga. Behind the trees, on the south side of the square, are the offices of the Préfet. Outside, a battered white Peugeot stands in a strip of shade.

He climbs the five wooden steps to the veranda. On his left, a line of latticed doors give access to the district outposts of various ministries. Through the first of the doors comes the slow clack of a typewriter. Just beyond the flagpole, he can see the doorway and, further along, the noticeboard protected by its wire cage. Inside the cage, he can already see a fresh white sheet pinned on top of yellowing by-laws and curled election notices. Inside the open doorway, the threatening swoop of a ceiling fan.

Assita's lower back is aching as she comes to the end of the last row, finger and thumb rolling seeds over the edge of the calabash, her eyes scanning the road in the direction of town. Hardly pausing, she moves down the furrow, scraping a bare foot over the seeds she has planted, pressing them gently into the earth. If the rains hesitate, even for a week, the new seed will be wasted, the tender shoots tortured and sere, fit only for the goats. Every morning now will see anxious eyes cast to the skies. At the entrance to the compound, the other boys are shouting and laughing, lighting handfuls of straw as they advance on the termite hills that line the road.

At first he is only a speck. But she would know his walk anywhere and hurries to finish the row. There is water to collect, the fire to start, food to prepare. Some of the boys have surrounded the largest of the mounds, waving hands of fire, encouraging the termites that fill the evening air to fly into the flames. Is there a lightness in his step? Later, when enough of the insects have fallen to the earth on frizzled wings, there will be more shouting and laughter as they try their hand at winnowing, pouring the singed insects into bowls at their feet, hoping that imperceptible movements of air will blow away the legs and wings. Or is there a weight in his heart?

A neighbour, smiling, motions to her to take the jar she has just filled. Assita thanks her and lifts the pot onto a bent knee while her hand scrapes the mud from its base.

She slips a coil on top of her head and lifts the jar high, moving swiftly under its weight, straightening her knees and back. She pauses a moment, lets her arms fall to her side, steadies the muscles of her neck, hears the faint snap of a swallow's beak as it takes an insect low over the well.

Mohammed, elder of elders, eyes glinting, hands resting calmly in the lap of his robe, watches as Kadré approaches the first hut of the compound. The boy bows his head as he passes. A boy who shows respect. A boy who knows how to conduct himself.

He follows his progress through the village, observing the glances of neighbours and the way the young man's eyes remain fixed on his own quarter of the compound. Slowly the old man raises a hand to finger the lines carved down his face, cut there earlier than he can remember, in the time when the rains had never failed. Lines of identity. Lines of protection. Lines that once guaranteed hospitality across the lands of the Mossi. He turns his head away as an older youth passes by, carelessly kicking a used battery, scattering earth, ignoring the old man in the shade. Respect that is dying. Dying like the land.

He lifts his head again and runs the fingers of one hand inside the leather thongs that bind the strips of tyre to his feet. It is many hours since any water was set down by his side. He swallows and closes his eyes. Growing old should be an upward as well as a downward journey. For the slackening of muscle and the stiffening of bones, for the loss of teeth and hair, for the sadness of failed hopes, for the realisation of time past grown long and time to come grown short – for all this, compensation is due. In respect. In standing. In the place you have earned in your village. But only in the dying world is it still true. In the world being born, respect is for those who can ride motorbikes and buy what others do not have. He opens his eyes to the late-afternoon sun. To a world built to sharpen the edges of age, where wisdom and usefulness are no more, where all that awaits is pity and tolerance, fading finally to impatience, resentment. Dying like the land.

Very softly, rain is beginning to fall in heavy drops on the thatch. He has heard that floods have collapsed the well at Oufray, and taken away a part of the road.

Assita and Hamadé sit on either side of their son in the doorway of the hut, listening to the hard rhythm of the rain and the undisciplined splatter of the overflow from the gutters. In the compound, the water is running in rivers down mud walls, picking out pieces of gravel, exposing the ends of straws, sluicing through the fence that for months has protected a small shrub. In the distance, the first soft far-off lightning plays around the edges of the sky.

Eventually, Hamadé, who never touches his son, rests a hand on the boy's shoulder.

'The elder of elders came to see me.'

Kadré looks up.

'Here?'

Hamadé's hand grips.

'He came to offer me his congratulations. For my son.'

Kadré swallows and looks down again at the open space in front of the hut. The shallow thirst of the earth is already slaked and reddening pools are swirling under the granaries. Near the wall of the compound, a water bucket made from the inner tube of a tyre is floating slowly across level ground.

'Why did he come?'

Hamadé releases his touch on the boy's shoulder. A touch that will stay with Kadré all of his life.

'He watched you when you came back through the village. He said you carried your disappointment well. He said you bore it like a man.'

Later, when Assita and Kadré are asleep, Hamadé returns to his doorway. This morning, as he had reached his hands into the sweet-smelling belly of the granary for the day's grain, he had felt the bare boards of the floor under his knuckles. This year again, the joining of the seasons will not be made. And he will know the shame of buying grain.

In the fields outside the compound, water from all directions will be swirling down faint inclines, flooding every hollow, pouring into troubled pools and surging in broad, white-flecked streams across the countryside. There is enough money for two sacks, perhaps three. After that, he will have to make the journey to the coast to find work. A thousand miles. And this time he will take Kadré with him.

Under the open night, in the porous rock under the thin soils of Yatenga, the rain is seething through a thousand cracks and fissures, swirling along the centuries of smoothed galleries, pouring down streams and hidden waterfalls to deposit itself into the dark safes of water under the Sahel. But tonight not even the parched earth can drink enough, and the rejected waters turn away, a restless reddening tide, looking for escape. In its path, the leafless shrub finds itself marooned inside its fence. For months it has survived the white sun and been protected from the marauding goats. Hamadé watches its stem rupturing the water's flow, bending before the angry ripple at its base. But the tide, unappeased, is seducing soil from around the slender shoot and slowly, lasciviously, the tender whiteness of the young tree's root is revealed. And in an instant, the shrub is gone, persuaded out of the ground, lifted as painlessly as a child's tooth. A second later, the little binding of earth, freed from the grip of roots, follows after, a small clot in the haemorrhaging blood of the land, swept away to the sudden streams and rivers carrying the soil south to the coast and the cold waters of the sea.

*'Sahel' was awarded the Royal Society of Literature
V S Pritchett Memorial Short Story Prize for 2013*

The Chosen One

HE HAD NOT KNOWN such blackness could exist in the modern world.

The Manor could not be more than two hundred metres from the door of what he was still struggling to call home, but he had not taken into account the lack of street lights. He pressed on cautiously down the lane, darkness and damp fingering his face as if pressing the question – had it been a mistake?

He opened his eyes wide to glean any photon of light that might be available and wished he hadn't worn his white-soled Jimmy Choo sneakers. It had been an unaccustomed problem – pondering what to wear. In the end, he had opted for the unstructured olive linen jacket with the navy T-shirt and pressed charcoal chinos. He must surely be close now, but there were no lights to be seen. He stumbled on. In the city, there was such a thing as twilight, but here night seemed to fall with careless suddenness as if the day had simply given up – all distinctness surrendering to a common oblivion so that only his own self remained separate and alone.

They had known of course that they would be outsiders: anywheres among the somewheres, cosmopolitans removing themselves from the progressive mainstream to a conservative backwater. Privately, he had also worried that they might be made to feel... how could he put it... somehow inauthentic, not 'real people'. All this had been vaguely foreseen; but not the unimaginable darkness. He pushed on towards the Manor, a cold, unfriendly swirl of wind cutting him off even more from the world he had known.

Given time, they would surely adjust. And nothing could alter the fact that the outgoings for the fourteenth-floor apartment in the Surrey Quays – laptops perched on the breakfast bar, printer on a shelf in the airing cupboard – had secured a five-bedroom Victorian rectory with three reception rooms and half an acre of land plus outbuildings. Once it had become clear that they would both be working more or less permanently from home, it had been an obvious move to make, though it had taken the better part of a year to put the apartment on the market.

Might he have missed the entrance? He pressed forward, fortitude beginning to quail. He resisted an impulse to whistle. It was unnerving for one's own footfall to be the only sound in the world.

All he knew about the Manor was that it was the home of the village recluse. This they had learnt from Prentice, who clearly viewed delivering the mail as a primarily social occasion. From the same source, they had gathered that the village was proud of its distinguished if rarely seen resident. And maybe even a little in awe. Voices, it seemed, were to be lowered, shoulders glanced over, when Sir David's name was mentioned.

Some thinning of the cloud that had wept a light rain on the village all day now admitted a thin moonlight by which he made out the gateposts coming up on his left. He turned between them with some relief, sneakers crunching reassuringly on gravel. Peering around, he was surprised to see a flagpole rising up into the night. There was just enough moonlight for him to make out the limp constellation on the flag of the European Union. 'That's the spirit,' he murmured to himself, guessing that the flag was flown in defiance of village opinion. Confidence began to return as he stepped up to the portico, the dark weight of the house barely distinguishable from the night. According to Prentice, no one in the village had ever been invited to the Manor. Yet here he was, barely a month after taking up residence in Compton-upon-Hamble, about to have dinner with Sir David.

A tug on the chain to one side of the door brought a faint tintinnabulation from deep inside the house. He took a step back and surveyed the porch.

He had, of course, looked up Sir David Bridie, KCB, CBE. Somewhat disappointingly, the village recluse had turned out to be a statistician. A long-time director of the Government's Central Statistical Office, his Wikipedia entry also listed him as an Emeritus Professor of Social Statistics at Nuffield College, a Fellow of the American Statistical Society, and a consultant to the Government of India and the United Nations Department of Economic and Social Affairs. The portico itself appeared to be neglected, the lower part of its pillars in the grip of some climbing plant, the stone urns to either side nibbled by weeds.

He was beginning to worry that there might have been some mistake when he heard what sounded like a cistern flushing within, soon followed by the grating sound of a bolt being drawn.

'Ah, yes, you must be... er... Mr Dice?'

'Sir David? Yes, Ingram Dice – very good to meet you.'

The dining room was surprisingly small, oak-panelled, and with a fire burning in the hearth.

'Good of you to invite me, Sir David. I'm so sorry Gaynor can't be here.'

His host, a white-haired man of about seventy, appeared not to have heard but stood looking down at the parquet floor. 'Ah yes, drinks,' he said, jerking himself upright and turning back to the door, as if pleased to have hit upon the idea.

Ingram took up a position with his back to the fire and surveyed the room. The scene was bright enough, though seeming to be lit only by the candles set in sconces around the walls. To each side of the chimney breast, deep alcoves had been shelved to accommodate bound yearbooks of the Journal of the Royal Statistical Society and a powerful-looking laptop. Around the room, the candles glowed splendidly on the oak panelling but seemed to cast everything else into their dark penumbra so that a few moments passed before he noticed that the table was set only for two. He smiled to himself.

There being no sign of his host's return, he began to tour the framed photographs hanging from a dado rail running around three sides of the room. In each, he thought he could identify the young Sir David – here in a flight jacket about to board a light aircraft, there in khaki shorts with one boot on the dimpled footplate of a Land Rover. Moving into the era of colour, an older, besuited Sir David began to appear – garlanded in a garden alongside Indira and Sanjay Gandhi, on a podium with Nelson Mandela and Desmond Tutu, receiving some kind of award from a smiling Jimmy Carter, raising a glass of champagne with Chris Patten in what looked very much like the back quad at Oriel.

He returned to the fireside. Probably it was Prentice who had informed Sir David that his new neighbour at the Rectory was also an Oxford man and that his wife travelled a great deal. With a sudden longing, he wished she were with him.

Gaynor had not worried as much as he about the move. As she saw it, the 'buzz' of the city mainly came down to noise. If she had a concern, it was that they would no longer be able to take it for granted that the people around them shared a similar worldview. So far, they had hardly met any of their neighbours, but it was true that the rack of newspapers in the post office was not overburdened with copies of The Guardian. To their surprise, the village had turned out to have its own Facebook page, though most of the posts seemed to concern potholes or lost pets. As far as they could see, intellectual and social life revolved around the quiz night at the pub and the coffee morning at St Agatha's. In fact, it seemed more than likely that Sir David's reputation as a recluse amounted to little more than having nothing much in common with the good folk of Compton-upon-Hamble.

Warm again now, he crossed to the window. The clouds must have closed in again for there was nothing to be seen but darkness. It was a pity Gaynor had to be away this particular week. She was much better than he at getting things going. Probably at this very moment, as he stood staring out at the nothingness, she would be the centre of attraction at some lunch in one of the private dining rooms at the Met.

He wandered back to the hearth. On the dining table, a few daffodils had been dropped into a tarnished beaker of Indian design. On the screen of the laptop, several windows were open. One appeared to be a spreadsheet. Another showed a web page headed 'Hosting the perfect dinner party'. He scanned the first few bullet points –

For beginners, the 'mise en place' approach is especially helpful, and remember it's best to keep starters and desserts simple so you can concentrate on the main dish. The more expensive supermarket pâtés can be quite extraordinarily good and require only thinly sliced crustless sourdough toast and unsalted butter to make the perfect starter.

Under a colourful border of cartoon raspberries and kiwi fruits, he read:

There is absolutely nothing wrong with fresh fruit for dessert. Serve with a choice of ice cream or crème fraiche.

He glanced briefly towards the door. On the shelf to one side of the laptop was a copy of Wine Folly offering a 'free food and wine pairing chart'. He risked another look at the screen where the third of the open windows displayed a sidebar:

Pay attention to the tablescape but don't over-elaborate – fresh flowers and unscented candles are usually enough. And there is absolutely no need for napkins to be folded like entries in an origami competition...

A loud thump seemed to shake the panelling as Sir David came backwards through the door carrying a heavy wooden butler's tray, which he set down on a trestle against the wall. 'Ah, there you are. Do sit down, Mr Dice.'

'Ingram, please.' On the door being kicked open, he had stepped smartly away from the computer.

'Ingram, you say? Any German connection?'

'Not that I'm aware of, Sir David.'

'Pity. Hope you like duck, young man. Help yourself to wine.'

The notion of pre-dinner drinks, it seemed, had been forgotten. Instead, an opened bottle of Sauternes was lifted to the table, followed by two white plates, each bearing a bare slab of pink pâté.

'Toast,' Sir David announced, producing another plate on which two whole slices of crustless toast were cut so thin as to resemble lace blackened to a brittleness at the edges.

'And your good lady is in New York you say?'

'She'll be there all week I'm afraid.'

Sir David had already begun attacking the pâté as Ingram slid a napkin from its silver ring. embossed with elephants and peacocks. 'You've lived in New York yourself, I believe, Sir David?'

'For a period, I'd say. Quite an interesting city.'

Ingram poured for them both. 'Gaynor and I had a couple of years there. Brooklyn, actually, just off Atlantic Avenue, though I'd rather have been in Manhattan.'

'Couldn't wait to get out of it myself,' said Sir David. 'Sigh of relief every time I swung off on that cable-car contraption to Roosevelt Island. Even deader than Compton-on-Hamble. Ha!'

'Yes, the village is quiet, isn't it? We anticipated that of course. But we'll both be travelling quite a bit. And without all that traffic getting out of London it's nearly as quick to Heathrow as it was from Docklands. I'll be running up there myself next week as a matter of fact. Few days at the Frankfurt Book Fair.'

'Frankfurt you say?'

'Yes, just for the three days before they let the public in.'

His host made no reply, seeming entirely absorbed in the struggle to smear pâté onto the fragments of toast on the plate. Ingram was surprised to discover how well the fruity acidity of the Sauternes complemented the fattiness of the duck. He returned his glass to the table. 'And of course, Oxford's only an hour or so up the A34. Do you still lecture, Sir David?'

'Lecture? Gracious no! Barbarous practice. Medieval hangover from a time when there weren't enough books.'

Ingram smiled his agreement. 'Yes, I must confess to skipping quite a few myself. Most of us did at Oriel. Still, I suppose it's good to hear things from the horse's mouth occasionally.'

'Horse's ass, more likely. Ha! Anyone with anything interesting to say is saving it for their next book.'

Abandoning his battle with the toast, Sir David returned his plate to the tray and sat, fingers locked, observing his guest's progress.

'Excellent,' said Ingram as Sir David reached to take away his plate.

'Shan't be a sec.'

Ingram rose quickly to open the door.

Alone again, Ingram returned to the alcove. Despite the fire that had obviously been burning for some time, there was no mistaking the musty chill in the corners of the room. On the table, the candles hesitated in a draft and steadied again. Getting Sir David into conversation, it seemed, was going to be like turning the key of a car that splutters but refuses to start. Gaynor would have teased and charmed the old man. But Gaynor was in New York. And New York seemed much further away now than it had when they lived in London.

He glanced down again at the open laptop. The window in the bottom right-hand corner displayed the Spotify logo below which a 'Dinner Party Playlist' had been selected – Carole King, Kacey Musgraves, Roberta

Flack, Mavis Staples. A flashing symbol invited the user to subscribe or log in.

When the butler's tray returned with the main course, Ingram found himself confronted by what he believed was known as a 'guard of honour', each of the dozen interlaced cutlets topped with a tiny paper chef's hat. Sir Edward, wearing a pair of floral-quilted oven gloves, lifted an oven tray of roast potatoes to the table, followed by an engraved silver jug.

'Do help yourself, Mr Dice.'

As his host seemed content to eat in silence, Ingram concentrated on the cutlets, wondering whether he might mention the open bottle of Champ des Etoiles Pinot Noir which had been left behind on the butler's tray.

'We did wonder, of course,' Ingram commenced, 'if there might be a degree of resentment toward incomers, but no one seems to have minded so far, though the lady in the post office did seem keen to let us know the old vicar had hosted the annual fruit-and-veg show.'

'Ha!' said Sir Edward, in a tone so disengaged that Ingram doubted he had heard a word, fascinated as he was by the paper hats.

'What would you think, Sir David? Might we encounter some resentment?'

Sir David seemed, at last, to be giving the question his consideration. 'I would think you'd be lucky to encounter anything at all. Ha!' Suddenly remembering the wine, he twisted again in his chair and seized the bottle, filling Ingram's glass and pouring a teaspoonful into his own. Ingram liberated another chop from the rack.

'Of course, from our point of view, it's marvellous. I do quite a bit with the BBC these days and I can get a lot more done working from home. As a matter of fact, I was discussing that the other week on Radio 4. Silver Linings, I think the programme might have been called.'

'Silver linings, you say?'

Ingram raised the glass carefully to his lips. 'Yes, it was sort of an inventory of what might be called positives of the pandemic – reduced air travel, improvements in air quality, more investment in the life sciences and…

'Social distancing. Ha!'

As his host busied himself arranging empty paper hats at the edges of his plate, Ingram took a deep drink and raised appreciative eyebrows. 'Quite superb. Just shows you a Pinot doesn't have to come from Burgundy these days.'

'Burgundy, you say?'

Ingram began to suspect that his host might be a little deaf and raised his voice slightly.

'I was thinking, Sir David, you probably know Fraser Norton-Teller.'

'Teller, you say?'

'Norton-Teller, yes, used to be an MEP? We're having him down for the weekend next month. You must come to dinner and meet him. He'd probably have been one of our Commissioners if we hadn't left the EU.' Here, Ingram shook his head sadly. 'Talk about shooting ourselves in the foot.'

To Ingram's relief, Sir David responded vigorously. 'Both feet and halfway up both legs. Ha!'

'Exactly. You might have seen the little piece I wrote for the London Review of Books laying out the cultural case for staying in. Made not the slightest difference, of course.' Ingram pulled a face suggesting complicity. 'I assume the village was pretty solid for leaving?'

Sir David was pouring a stream of redcurrant gravy onto a roast potato.

Ingram took a rest from the chops and sat back with his wine. 'I think what I found most dismaying was the way facts, statistics, evidence, simply didn't count. I mean it doesn't matter whether we were talking trade, the economy, immigration, the NHS – the statistics simply screamed "Remain! Remain!"'

Sir David frowned and downed his teaspoonful of wine in one swig as if it were medicine. 'I hope you're not one of those people who think statistics are boring, Mr Dice.'

Ingram held up both hands to protest innocence. 'Quite the contrary. Without them one is flying blind.'

'Exactly!' said Sir David, becoming animated. 'Means and measure of progress. Handrail of policy. Dashboard of society … '

From being impossible to start, Sir David's conversational engine had suddenly gone full bore as he went up through the gears of what Ingram suspected was a well-worn monologue on the importance of statistics to policy feedback, resource allocation, political accountability, public transparency… breaking off into a sudden silence as he reached for another of the paper hats.

Anxious to move on from a topic on which he found himself with little to contribute, Ingram attempted to segue his way back to more promising ground. 'I was looking at some interesting stats myself the other day: apparently more than fifty per cent of Londoners are now working from home at least some of the time. That's what prompted our own move down here of course. Bit nervous about it. Not sure what to expect. First thing we checked out was the wi-fi, but we're getting seventy-five gig, which is adequate, don't you find?'

Sir David, who appeared to have no idea what his guest was talking about, finished his chop and carefully added

the paper hat to the line at the edge of his plate. Ingram
tried again. 'Of course, there are some disadvantages, like
not being able to get to the theatre as often, but then again
Stratford can't be more than – what? – an hour and a half?'

Sir David stood abruptly and reached for the tray.
'Dessert next.'

Ingram took advantage of being alone again to pick
strands of cutlet from between his teeth. Who knew how
long Sir David might be gone this time, probably to fetch
what he was prepared to bet would be fresh fruit with a
choice of cream or ice cream. It was comical, really. But also
touching. And, of course, a kind of compliment. Sir David
had gone to a lot of trouble. He was odd, certainly, but
probably not really a recluse: just a widower living alone in
an echoing manor house, eccentricity setting in, social
skills rusting away for the lack of compatible company.
After all, he had wasted no time at all after hearing that the
newcomers at the Rectory were people acquainted with the
world beyond Compton-upon-Hamble.

He rose to stand once more by the fire, taking the liberty
of adding a log from the wicker basket. In the alcove, Spotify
was still winking its invitation as he watched the flames
reach for a fringe of loose bark. The wine was beginning to
dissolve his defences, allowing unwelcome thoughts to
break in. Why this intimate need to be admitted, acknowledged, accepted? He stepped away from the now blazing
fire but the thought followed – questioning the craving for
acknowledgement of his individuality, his status. Surely
someone who so prided himself on scorning elitism could
not be lusting after the thing he despised? The excellent
Pinot Noir seemed to be carrying him on a flood tide of
humiliation and he returned to the table, reaching for the

glass to quell the upswell of self-dislike that pointed toward despair.

When Sir David reappeared, Ingram held his expression in check as a bowl containing a large, unpeeled, greenish banana was set before him.

'Cream or ice cream. Do help yourself.'

Ingram began to peel the banana and adopted what he hoped was a light, teasing tone. 'Well, it's lovely to meet you so soon after moving in, but I really must ask you how come the famous recluse has invited us to dinner?'

'Ah,' said Sir David, again showing signs of animation, 'that was on the advice of my dear friend and colleague Dr Ramalingaswami of the Indian National Institute of Statistics.'

There was a suspended moment of silence. 'I'm not sure I know him?'

'No, no, you don't know him,' said Sir David impatiently.

'But… he recommended inviting us to dinner?'

Sir David looked as if he were beginning to think his guest was eccentric.

'Yes, yes. You see Rama tells me there's now a considerable convergence of evidence to suggest that lacking a social life is correlated with less favourable health outcomes in later life. Quite robust. P-value well below five per cent, though I haven't had sight of the raw data myself. Of course, his research was conducted in Andra Pradesh but he tells me the results have been replicated…

Reeling slightly as Sir David launched into an account of a recent meta-analysis of the relationship between longevity and social interaction, Ingram drank the Pinot and let sink in the idea that he had been invited to dinner for the good of his host's health. Nodding at what he hoped were appropriate points in Sir David's discourse –

which did not appear to require his participation – he poured an unsteady line of cream along the length of the peeled banana and decided that it probably didn't make any difference. After all, wasn't it still the case that Sir David had chosen to invite him rather than any other resident of Compton-on-Hamble?

When his host's enthusiasm for the health benefits of social interaction had run its course, Ingram tried yet again. 'Yes, I can see that it might not be easy to put together any kind of satisfactory social life in a place like this.' Sir David had returned to slicing up his banana with a spoon and did not appear to be contemplating any response. 'Gaynor and I were worried about it ourselves, but we figured we could always invite people down for weekends. As I said, Fraser's coming down next month and Gaynor's already invited some friends from the Hayward.'

As this also failed to provoke any response, he resigned himself to the one topic that seemed to keep Sir David with at least one foot in the evening.

'I'd be interested to see Rama's paper. My own experience of India is rather limited, I'm afraid. Couple of trips to Delhi and Thiruvananthapuram. Can't imagine the difficulties of statistical work in a place like that. I gather you still advise the Government?'

Sir David looked up sharply. 'I hope you're not one of those people who think that India has more important things to do than collect statistics, Mr Dice?'

Ingram shook his head emphatically. 'Not at all, I was just thinking what a daunting task it must be.'

'I can assure you that even the remotest village has its panchayat,' said Sir David, pouring more cream onto a banana that had by now been reduced to a pulp. 'Of course, civil registration statistics are quite straightforward. The difficulty is getting the data on things like nutritional status, literacy levels, contraception rates, seasonal income variability and what-not.' His host was showing all the signs of going off again into a world where he could be speaking to anyone, anywhere. When he paused to pour more cream onto the pulp, Ingram tried to remind Sir David that he was still there.

'Can't begin to imagine how you'd collect that kind of data for – what is it now, more than a billion people?'

'One billion three hundred and eighty million four thousand three hundred and eighty-five at the last census. And not quite as difficult as you might be imagining, young man. Even if we're making estimates for a population in the hundreds of millions, the survey sample doesn't have to be that big. The margin of error, you see, depends inversely on the square root of the sample size, so a sample as small as one thousand gives you a result that's ninety-five-per-cent certain of being accurate within plus or minus three percentage points.'

'I see what you mean...'

'But, of course, it all depends on strictly randomising your sample. Now for true randomness, you'd need to rely on entropy, quantum theory and what-not.' The statistician paused, as if to enjoy observing that his guest was out of his depth. 'Because, you see, it's quite impossible to predict when radioactive decay will occur, so monitor that and you've got your finger on the true randomness of the universe.'

Ingram struggled on gamely. 'I can imagine that might be difficult in, ah, Andra Pradesh.'

'But one improvises, one improvises,' enthused Sir David, pushing aside the remains of the dessert. 'And in fact it's quite simple. Your surveyor locates the centre of the

village, spins a bottle in the dust, and then sets off with his
questionnaire in whatever direction the bottle points. Toss
a coin if the path diverges, count every dwelling as you go,
and derive your random sample from the serial numbers
of the first rupee note you pull out of your pocket. No
quantum theory needed. Ha!'

Ingram had also abandoned his banana and now
reached for his glass.

'Absolutely fascinating.'

'I know. I know. Every bit as good as your high-tech
what-nots.'

'Absolutely remarkable.'

His gratified host poured himself another triumphant
teaspoon of wine. 'Of course, in a statistically advanced
country it's a lot less fun. Anyone can go into their local
library and ask to see the electoral register. Then it's just a
question of opening up a spreadsheet and entering the
formula 'RND' followed by the total number of names on
your list in brackets and voila! You've generated a random
number within your prescribed range. Why, when I
opened the door tonight, I almost said 'Ah yes, you must
be two nine three. Ha!'

❖

Incident in Assisi

LOOKING BACK, there had been warnings of what might be to come. But the true mischief of hindsight is that it would have you believe what happened was foreseeable.

The first small tear in the fabric, as I have come to think of it, came when we invited my brother to join us on holiday. It was two months after Alan had lost his wife to leukaemia, and asking him to come with us seemed the least we could do. If there was any small reluctance on Jane's part, it was only because she and Alan hardly knew each other at the time.

Towards the end of our stay in Italy, we visited the Basilica of St Francis in Assisi, arriving about four o'clock in the afternoon. The day had been blindingly hot and the crypt was blessedly dark and cool. We couldn't have mustered a candle's worth of religious faith between the three of us but were nonetheless stilled into silence by the stale sanctity of the centuries.

We had become separated as we wandered the transept of the lower basilica, the vaults glimmering with the gold of haloes and heavenly hosts. Seeing Jane standing before a large, water-damaged fresco, I crossed the apse to join her. When Alan also appeared by her side, she told us in a half-whisper that we were looking at The Madonna Enthroned with the Child, St Francis and Four Angels, a thirteenth-century masterpiece by Cimabue, one of the founding fathers of Western art. The three of us stared up at the sad-eyed, sallow-faced Francis as Jane told us it was said to be the only actual likeness of the saint. For another minute, we gazed up at the great fresco. And it was into this reverential silence that Alan spoke for the first time since entering the basilica.

'When I was a kid,' he said, 'I had comics with better drawings than that.'

There is usually some tension between brothers whose paths in life diverge. In our case, diverging meant one brother collecting degrees into his mid-twenties and the other leaving school to start work at seventeen. But for Alan and myself it had never been a problem. I have always looked up to him, always known him to be exceptional in ways that I could never be. Socially he was in a different league, with a natural, easy self-confidence and a sideways humour that drew people to him but could also lull them into missing the sharp mind and finely tuned ear for bullshit. He was the elder by only fourteen months, but many were the occasions when he had saved me from my own gauche, teenage gullibilities and I was in no doubt that my passage through adolescence had been eased by the unearned status of being 'Alan's kid brother'.

My strength and passion had been for my studies, his for building a business. And that is what he had done. While still an apprentice mechanic, he had spent evenings and weekends buying, repairing and selling cars and by his early thirties he had a company with four showrooms in the West Riding and a contract hire and fleet leasing service trusted by some of the best-known names in retail. For his part, Alan took nothing but pride in any success that came my way; one year, the only personal news he included in his Christmas message to his employees was that his brother had been awarded a doctorate by the London School of Economics.

Nor could it fairly be said, at that stage, that Jane was the problem. We had met at university and moved in together when she began studying for a Diploma in Art History at the Courtauld and I started a postgraduate course in the sociology of knowledge at the LSE. In this academic environment the differences in our backgrounds – Jane the daughter of a neurologist and a fund manager, myself the son of a chiropodist and a central-heating installer – had not been significant. And knowing how I felt about Alan, she had been more than willing to admire her new brother-in-law.

No, the problem went deeper. And although I resisted bringing it into the light, I had no doubt that its marker was the comment made that day in Assisi. The instant those words had been spoken, the fresco had been transformed as I had seen it through Alan's eyes. Many times since, I have looked at the image online and read about the advance it represented, but I have never again been able to see it as I had before, never again been able to see it through the eyes of my wife.

The following year, Alan came for a long weekend. It was the first anniversary of Carole's death and I wanted us to be there for him. Jane's reluctance had been so fleeting as to be almost undetectable. Yet in my own mind that half-second of hesitation had leapt like an electric arc to the darkness of the transept in Assisi.

We had both forgotten that the Friday was our turn to host the monthly poetry evening. She didn't want to condescend by assuming Alan wouldn't be interested. I knew that, if we asked him, he would say he was happy to sit in. I hadn't read the chosen book and only picked it up on the Friday afternoon while Alan was making calls. To my relief, it described itself as 'a new kind of anthology of relevant, accessible poetry'. Turning to the title page, I came across the heading – 'What is poetry?' – followed by a quotation from Emily Dickinson:

> *If I read a book and it makes my whole body so cold no fire can ever warm me, I know that is poetry. If I feel physically as if the top of my head were taken off, I know that is poetry.*

Jane was out and the only sound was the occasional undertone of Alan's voice from upstairs. Just below the quotation from Emily Dickinson was another from Charles Simic. I hadn't known there was such a thing as the American Poet Laureate:

> *Poetry is a place where all the fundamental questions are asked about the human condition.*

Jane had marked the half-dozen poems to be discussed. I turned to the first of them, a short piece by Paul Muldoon, a former T.S Eliot prizewinner and Oxford Professor of Poetry.

> *Where and when exactly did we first have sex?*
> *Do you remember? Was it Fitzroy Avenue,*
> *Or Cromwell Road, or Notting Hill?*
> *Your place or mine? Marseille or Aix?*
> *Or as long ago as that Thursday evening*
> *When you and I climbed in through the bay window*
> *On the ground floor of Aquinas Hall*

and into the room where MacNeice wrote 'Snow',
or the room where they say he wrote 'Snow'.

'Okay if I use you as an excuse to get me out of this poetry thing tonight?' I said to Alan when he came downstairs.

I only seem to go to gastro-pubs these days but our local, The White Hart, turned out to be a good choice. We carried our drinks to a quiet table and spent a half-hour catching up with each other's news. Finishing our pints, Alan was keen to get into the darts game that was the source of the conviviality in the public bar. We took our glasses through and stood at the back watching. As Alan had thought, the winners were taking on whoever was next on the slate by the bar. I got two more pints in while he chalked our names up and began selecting darts from the collection standing in a cribbage board. By the time we were settled with our drinks, Alan had worked out that the game was 501, double in, double out, with a no-bust rule. The standard was high and the games thudded by until our turn came up.

'Okay,' said Alan, 'let's show them what the Verity brothers are made of.' I hadn't played in years but quickly got the feel of the darts again and was soon scoring nearly as heavily as Alan. When he brought up a cheer by getting out in two darts off eighty-six, we took on the next pair. Ten minutes later, we were knocked off the oche by two of the pub's team players. I chalked our names up again while Alan got another round in and for the next half-hour we watched the play and chatted with the darts crowd. Anyone walking in off the street would have sworn it was Alan's local.

Before our names reached the top of the slate again, the landlord called last orders, which seemed to be the signal for everybody to begin putting pound coins on the bar.

Alan dug out a pound for each of us and told me what was happening: 'Shanghai: first to hit single, double and treble of the same bed wins the pot.' When no one made Shanghai first time around, we all put another pound on the bar and went again, heckled by the landlord who was polishing glasses and insisting we were spinning it out. It was not until nearly the end of the third round, with maybe forty pounds in notes and coins on the bar, that the fencing contractor with the union-jack flights threw Shanghai on sixteens. The landlord, pointing up at the clock amid the din, refused to let him spend his winnings on a round, though the old boy was cheered for trying.

The early summer evening had turned cold as we walked the half-mile home. I wasn't used to drinking beer and, once out in the night air, there was a prickly dryness to my eyeballs and an edgy buzz at my temples. I was also aware that something other than my liver was struggling to cope. Again, I didn't immediately pull it into words or even specific thoughts. But I knew very well what it was. I had enjoyed the evening. Not feeling I ought to be enjoying it. Not telling myself I was enjoying it. As I tried not to look at the sodium street lights, I wondered where that left me.

The curtains were undrawn, trapezoids of light falling on the patch of grass between the front room and the privet hedge. Through the window, a few silhouetted figures could be seen standing around in groups. Alan unlatched the gate and I followed him through, taking a few last, harsh lungs full of cold air and thinking, over the buzz in my brain, that I hadn't saved Alan from the poetry evening; he had saved me.

Half a dozen of Jane's friends were lingering over nibbles and wine as Alan and I carried our coffees in from the

kitchen. One of the lingerers was Gerald Forster, a conceptual artist who had recently had a successful exhibition at
the Whitechapel. My edginess rose a level when I saw him
engage Alan in conversation. Gerald has his good points,
but he would have had no problem with the notion that
reading a poem was like having the top of one's head taken
off or that the precise spot where a poet first had sex was
one of the fundamental questions of the human condition.
He was also, I knew, prone to assuming that anyone with a
northern accent was intellectually challenged. I joined
them, carrying the remains of a cheeseboard.

'And what do you do in the North, Alan?' Gerald was
asking.

'Car dealer, new and second-hand,' said Alan, disingen-
uously failing to allude to the £8-million-a-year turnover
and the string of British Business Awards. Gerald's look
told me he had already subtracted forty points from my
brother's IQ.

'So, how many pubs did you two get to in the end?' said
Jane, joining us and taking the cheeseboard from my
hands.

'Just the one,' said Alan. 'Your husband and I took it
upon ourselves to show the locals how to play darts.'

Gerald turned to me, his frown an exaggerated question
mark.

'Darts, Tom?'

'Pointy things you throw at a board?'

'But surely you need an enormous beer belly tattooed
with the flag of St George?'

'No, just a high level of hand-eye co-ordination,' I said,
attempting to lower the tension by miming the throwing of
a dart at the Agnes Martin print on the living-room wall.
'As you would have had been compelled to agree, Gerald,

if you had seen the Verity brothers in action tonight. I'd forgotten what a great game it is.'

'Played all over now,' said Alan. 'Should be in the Olympics.'

'I'll assume you're not being quite in earnest there,' said Gerald, looking at Alan, as he looked at the world over the top of his spectacles.

'Don't really see why not,' Alan said mildly.

'Well, there may be the suggestion of an issue,' said Gerald, putting his head to one side and blinking with patience, 'in as much as one tends to associate the Olympics with the heights of human athleticism.'

Alan put his own head just slightly to one side. 'And would that be the dressage or the ten-metre air pistol, Gerald?'

Even without my brother's presence my 'Assisi moments', as I had come to think of them, were becoming more and more frequent as the months went by. Almost, one might say, merging into a constant, a different way of seeing.

It didn't affect everything. When Jane got us tickets to the opening of the Velasquez, I could still thrill to the portrait of Juan de Pareja; still wonder at how paint on canvas could reveal its subject with such painful intimacy; still see that it might speak more poignantly of the hurt of racism than the facts and statistics that tended to be at my fingertips. And at Glyndebourne later that summer, I could still hold Jane's hand and feel the togetherness as our spirits rose to Tornami a dir. But the very next minute I would be back in the darkness of the transept in Assisi hearing Alan say that he'd been to pantomimes with more sophisticated plots than Don Pasquale, seen TV soaps with more subtle characterisation and less clichéd dialogue.

Looking back, I can see that it was probably a mistake to have travelled this road alone. But on the few occasions when I had hinted to Jane that I didn't quite see things in the same way, it had not gone well. If I mentioned a newspaper report about a Chamberlain sculpture being carried off with the refuse while being unloaded outside a Manhattan gallery, the silence was steely. When I suggested that the Sarah Lucas exhibition might have been a bit too reliant on sexual gimmickry, she had been tetchy for the rest of the evening.

I knew why. Of course I did. I was nibbling at the edges of her world: the world in which she moved and earned her living, the world where she was known and respected, the world where she had made her place to stand. And so I became more and more silent as the months went by, knowing that I could not hold her hand as I journeyed deeper into the land of honest courtiers and half-naked emperors.

Things deteriorated further when exhibition season came around. For some time now, I had been struggling to see the light of even the brightest stars in Jane's firmament. But silence had seemed the only option. In any case, I had no wish to deny anyone else's enjoyment of Russel Young or dent anyone's belief in the genius of Keith Arnatt. But neither could I participate in the adulation. And whether I remained silent or made half-hearted attempts to enthuse, our journey home was never as it once had been.

I suppose if I search my soul, my responses to her world – to the exhibitions and openings, the critics and the catalogues – did embrace a measure of irritation. In the department where I spent my days, our work involved compiling and analysing data, formulating and testing hypotheses, running regression analyses and controlling for confounding variables, teasing cause from correlation – always in the knowledge that any significant conclusion we might reach would set dozens of other scholars to the task of checking our data, stress-testing our methodologies and checking for replicability. And it was this, I think, that made it harder to accept that Reinhardt's black squares were 'intellectually rigorous' or that Barnett Newman's blue canvasses with the occasional white stripe offered 'a unique insight into the contemporary human condition'.

The catalogues of the auction houses I found particularly hard to take. I don't mind if someone wants to pay a million dollars for one of Yves Klein's plain blue squares but I confess to a mild irritation when Christie's tells us they 'allow the viewers to bathe in the infinite' or that by not having frames 'and therefore no edges… they are windows into the eternal'. If a catalogue says that an empty glass plinth has conceptual clarity or Sotheby's suggests that Jeff Koons' upright vacuum cleaner in a plexiglass case 'addresses social class and gender roles as well as consumerism' then I can't help thinking that the authors of these and a thousand similar statements bouncing around the walls of the art world seemed to me to have awarded themselves a free pass to profundity.

None of this would have mattered in the slightest had it not been for Jane. I could simply have turned my back on it all. But Jane and I shared the same air and, while I was finding that air more and more difficult to breathe, to her it was invigorating oxygen.

I began to make excuses, accompanying her only to exhibitions she had been directly involved in curating. The last of these, in a suite of linked cellars somewhere underneath Clerkenwell, was especially tense. The staircase and cellars were crowded, the air-kissing obligatory. For the first twenty minutes we toured the exhibition together, our senses alerted to art by whitewashed, violently lit rooms. Stopping before each exhibit, drinking our wine too quickly, the tension slowly grew. She knew, and I knew that she knew, as we contemplated a cube of fine Carrera marble wrapped in tangled chicken wire and titled *Sensu stricto*, that this could not go on. Jane appeared to be concentrating, but what she was concentrating on was the silent inner struggle against what she knew I was thinking.

Emerging into the cellar bar, we joined a group of her colleagues and she brightened immediately, swimming out into the mainstream, leaving me on the shores of my apostasy. Always before, I had managed to go with the flow, relying on just the occasional dip of the conversational paddle into the white water of enthusiasm. It was a difficult steer between the Scylla of heresy and the Charybdis of hypocrisy and more and more it seemed to me that my silence was the price of allowing Jane to be happy in her world. And I hated it. Hated that we could not both breathe the same air in that cellar. Hated being the atheist at the Vatican Mass.

There was a small consolation. To my surprise, I found myself taking more pleasure in the aesthetic aspects of the mundane and the mass-produced: in well-proportioned rooms or furniture, in well-designed electronics or kitchen equipment, in the texture and colours and cut of clothes and fabrics, even in the clarity of a web-page. One Saturday afternoon at the British Museum, wandering past the displays of amphora and vases from the time of

Pericles, I even found myself thinking about Alan's appreciation of certain cars.

It was with a sense of relief that I had dropped out of the poetry group and started going to the pub. I had even turned out for the darts team on a couple of Tuesday nights and had become quite friendly with one of the members who managed the local garden centre. Sitting with him one Saturday morning in the conservatory coffee bar next to the plant nursery, I mentioned going to the opening of some new art gallery and he said he often thought of his garden centre as a kind of art gallery where people go to find ways of creating beauty in their surroundings. When I got home that afternoon, Jane caught me staring at her as she came down the stairs.

'What's the matter?' she asked. I said that it was nothing. But it was not nothing. I was thinking about how lovely she looked, and even about her make-up, her hair and her clothes, and about all the time and taste – her own and others' – that had gone into appearing as she did. And about the pleasure that beauty brought into my life.

When Alan called to say he was coming south for a meeting with the fleet-transport manager of a chain of white-goods stores, I pressed him to stay the night. Jane made him welcome, but I could see that wariness had replaced the warmth. I attempted to cook the porchetta that Alan had enthused about in Italy while the two of them sat at the kitchen table offering advice.

I don't think it was premeditated, but after supper Jane launched into a too-detailed account of a performance of Akram Khan's Creature at the English National Ballet. As she talked about its power in a way that seemed almost challenging, I had the sense of a moth fluttering round and round a flame. Alan listened but had nothing to add until she stopped in mid-flow and asked him rather pointedly if he liked the ballet.

'Never been,' he said. 'Like the figure skating, though. Especially the pairs.'

In the silence, I started rattling the little jars of herbs and spices in the rack behind the pantry door.

'That's more of a sport, wouldn't you say?' I heard Jane object. 'More a spectacle than an art form? Isn't it all about competition, about getting eight-point-two for technical merit and, I don't know, nine-point-one for artistic expression?'

I hoped that Alan would back off at this point, but I could see he was engaged, not rushing to reply but thinking about what Jane had said.

'Someone in the English National Ballet must be making judgements on the same things, though – technical merit, artistic expression, musical interpretation and so on. I mean how else do they decide who gets to be the principal and who's in the chorus?'

I tensed as I sensed Jane's exasperation. 'Yes, but the point of it is the aesthetic experience, not the winning,' she said.

Back off, Alan, back off, I was pleading, but he still had the thoughtful look in his eye.

'I'm not sure it isn't much the same thing with the ice-dancing. I think what people really like about watching it is the sheer gracefulness, the flow of movement to music. And giving it a score at the end doesn't really take anything away, does it? Bit of extra interest? Something to talk about? I mean, millions still watch Torvill and Dean on YouTube years after they know they won gold.'

That night, Jane hardly spoke before we went to sleep. I suspect she thought I should have supported her more.

I also suspect that she was putting all the blame on Alan for the change in me. But she was wrong about that. My brother might have helped to jolt me into seeing things differently but my Assisi moments would not, I think, have become a constant if I had not been a sociologist by trade. As it was, any seeds that Alan shook from the tree fell on the fertile ground of Pierre Bourdieu. There were times when I could have wished that one of the greatest sociologists of the twentieth century had been as unintelligible as his contemporaries on the French intellectual scene, but there was nothing opaque about Bourdieu's belief that preferences and taste in the arts are essentially acts of social positioning. Or, as he would have it (I paraphrase) that they 'draw on cultural capital to purchase status and acceptance by demonstrating familiarity with the tastes and standards of the dominant class'. I had always thought he carried things a bit too far; no dragon of genuine preference left unslain, no baby unemptied with the bathwater. But no one had ever accused Bourdieu of lacking intellectual rigour or conceptual clarity, and nowadays I seem to feel his stern, inquisitorial ghost at my shoulder with every expression of taste. So in the end I suppose you would have to say it was the combination of French public intellectual and English car salesman that led me astray.

Things came to a head about a month after that last visit.

Jane and I had settled into avoiding the topics we knew were radioactive. But they were so much a part of Jane's life that they became a kind of black hole in our relationship and as the weeks went by it seemed that more and more of our emotional energy was being devoted to resisting its gravitational pull. But however much we might have wished it, there was no possibility of going back. You cannot will yourself to unsee what has been seen. You cannot kneel at God's altar because it has social advantages. And in our times, all claims to the contrary, it seems to me you cannot serve both art and truth. No, my only option was silence. And as the months went by, we both knew that it was becoming the silence of separation.

It was a mundane matter that precipitated the crisis. Our ageing Peugeot was facing a repair estimate that was more than the car was worth. We talked about it and decided we could go up to £15,000 for a second-hand four-door with built-in satnav, rear-view camera and memory seats. I rang Alan. He said he would call round his floor managers.

He texted the next day. 'Beauty coming nxt wk. Top-rated Ford Mondeo Zetec hybrid / 2 yrs / 1 owner / 8000 mls (!) / Lucida red / auto / LEDs / fully loaded/serviced by us. Lists north of £30k. Going on forecourt at £17,999. Yours for buy-in price £15,500.'

When I got into bed that night, Jane was sitting up with her laptop open on top of the duvet. 'I'd much prefer this,' she said, pushing the screen towards me. The web page showed a metallic grey Renault Megane on the forecourt of a local dealer. I quickly scrolled down to the spec.

'Sweetheart,' I said, as gently as I could, 'it's a year older, it's done four times the mileage, it doesn't have the memory seats and it's more expensive.'

She took the laptop back and snapped it shut. 'You're doing this deliberately aren't you?'

'Doing what?'

'Ganging up on me with your precious brother.'

It's been more than a year now since I've seen Jane and I was more than surprised to be invited to her parents' fortieth wedding anniversary celebration. I suspect it was her father's idea. He and I had always got on well.

As I drove over to Esher, I was thinking, as I often do these days, about what had gone wrong and asking myself if it could have been different. I knew that to Jane it had seemed perverse. As if I had decided to start driving on the wrong side of the road. I also knew that Alan had been upset by our separation. Most people, he said to me on the phone, lived their lives, loved, had children, earned their livings, coped with their problems – all without ever giving art a second's thought. Still grieving for Carole, he found it hard to understand that a marriage could come to an end over something so unimportant.

Most of the guests had already arrived as I turned onto the drive that led between striped lawns to the fine old Queen Anne house that had been Jane's childhood home. The French windows had been thrown open to the fine weather and several generations had spilt out onto the terrace with its parterre and classical stone urns. As I reverse-parked the Mondeo, I saw that other guests were also just arriving.

I watched in my mirror as someone I vaguely recognised from a previous life got out and scooted around to the passenger side of the silver Audi. Even before Jane took his hand, I could see that she was wearing the summer dress that I had always loved. Probably it was silk, but I had always thought of it as gossamer because of the way its pastel colours drifted so gracefully over her body rather than merely being worn.

❖

The Greatest Journey

At the age of twenty-four, wealthy and bored, Apsley Cherry-Garrard volunteered to accompany Captain Scott to the Antarctic. On his return, he was commissioned by the British Antarctic Exploration Committee to write the official account of the expedition. Soon at odds with the Committee, he was on the point of giving up when he was introduced to his Hertfordshire neighbours, George Bernard and Charlotte Shaw. Despite the differences in their ages, temperaments and politics, cooperation with the Shaws helped turn Cherry-Garrard's account of his journey to Cape Crozier in the Antarctic Winter of 1911 into what has been described as the greatest travel book ever written.

Spring, 1920
Shaw's Corner, Ayot St Lawrence, Hertfordshire

'I REALLY AM MOST DESIROUS that you should take a hand, Bernard. Else I'm afraid he might contemplate doing himself a mischief.'

Shaw was already on his feet as if to see his guest to the door but the doctor, having no intention of allowing his friend to evade the question, remained plumply in his chair. 'You might at least leave your card.'

'And that will stop him killing himself?'

The doctor sighed but made no motion to leave. Shaw looked to his wife for help. Charlotte, who had been lying on the sofa, closed her book with a clap. 'And what is it you think one might do for him, Edward?'

The doctor lifted his bag to his knees and forced open the brass jaws. 'I thought you might take a look at these.'

Charlotte took the offered papers. 'Eugh! Where have they been?'

'In his coal scuttle.'

Charlotte held the sheaf of papers away from her gown and gave them a little shake. 'I suppose we might take a look, Bernard?'

It was Shaw's turn to sigh. 'I've no wish to appear immodest' – he ignored the doctor's expression – 'but it does sometimes seem as if every second person in England is writing a book and wanting me to take a look at it.'

The doctor snapped his bag closed and struggled to rise. 'Every second person in England hasn't seen and endured things no man has ever seen and endured before.'

'Unlike you to veer toward hyperbole, Edward,' said Charlotte, smiling as she set the papers down on the piano.

'My dear Charlotte, in all my years I have yet to see the like. The frostbite has the better part of his feet. All his teeth split in the cold. Can't sleep for the colitis. The ague, of course. And heaven knows what internal demons the fellow's struggling with. It's all in there' – he gestured at the speckled papers on the Bechstein - 'and I tell you some of it is heart-breaking.'

Shaw had also risen. 'Fortunately, doctor, I have a heart of stone, else my relations would have broken it long ago.'

'I've heard that line before, Bernard,' said the doctor,

taking the offered hand, 'and I'm asking you as a friend if you would be so good as to take this seriously.'

Shaw lowered his beard to his chest in an attitude of having been rebuked. 'Very few things in life are worth taking seriously, Edward. Plays occasionally. Autobiographies rarely. Diaries never.'

The doctor, accepting his hat, bestowed a look of infinite patience on his host. 'As I have been at some pains to emphasise, Bernard, this isn't your suburban bore opening a tin of salmon of a Sunday and imagining his petty doings to be of universal fascination. He has an astonishing story to tell and no idea how to tell it. And as it's rumoured you are not entirely without merit as a writer, it not unnaturally occurred to me to suggest a little neighbourly assistance.'

Shaw had taken up the papers. 'Neighbour he may be, Edward, but the fellow's also the worst kind of Tory. Day tells me he motors around the blameless lanes of Hertfordshire in a primrose-coloured Rolls with the family monogram on the door.'

The doctor looked uncomfortable. 'Mmm, a trifle vulgar, I'll grant you. However, if you'll read what's in there, I'll venture you won't begrudge the man his quantum of comfort.

'And besides,' continued Shaw, 'didn't I read that he's in the nasty jar? It's said he left Scott in the lurch.'

The doctor shook his head dismissively. 'Armchair explorers! Smoking-room adventurers! Read it, Bernard. The truth of it sings out.'

Shaw smiled at the doctor's passion. 'Yet it's been rejected, you say?'

'Not so much rejected as censored. Some juggins at the Antarctic Exploration Committee has run the blue pencil through just about everything the man really wanted to write about.'

'And what does he really want to write about?' asked Charlotte, releasing the doctor's arm as he turned at the door.

The doctor breathed in deeply through his nose, taking a moment or two to compose his thoughts. 'The pristine beauty of it all. The unthinkable cold. The unprecedented silence. The way the Antarctic touches the human spirit. The way men behave when all hope has vanished. When all the confounded Committee wants is sledging distances and the requisite quantities of pony fodder. And of course, they've absolutely vetoed the merest criticism of Scott.'

Charlotte clapped her hands. 'Oh well played, Edward! There's nothing like the whiff of censorship for getting Bernard to take it up.'

Shaw peered at the title page and read aloud: '"Never Again: Scott, Penguins and the Pole". Dreadful title.' He turned the page and read for a few moments while the doctor waited, hat in hand. Eventually, he looked up.

'In the purdonium, you say?'

'Yes. Dropped it in there when it got the chuck from the Committee. Ever since, he's been… I really do think writing that account was the only thing getting him from his bed of a morning. The man's sunk, quite sunk. Only just past thirty and thinks his life to be over. There's family history as well, by the way. You might have had some acquaintance with Reginald Smith?'

'Fellow who ran that sleepy publishing house? Hanged himself at the end of the war?'

The doctor nodded portentously. 'Our man's first cousin.'

Shaw replaced the papers on the piano. 'I'll take a look, Edward. But I assure you I've no mind to get involved.'

Lamer Park, Hertfordshire

Cherry-Garrard scarcely stirred when the doctor was announced.

'Good day to you, Apsley. May I venture to hope we might have some improvement to report?

'We have not.'

Sunlight charged in through the high window, flashing from glass-fronted bookcases and the polished mahogany bureau as the doctor crossed the room and set his bag down next to his patient's chair. Still without bothering to look at his visitor, the younger man raised both legs to free the footstool, employing one foot to push the slipper from the other.

'I've left your draft with Shaw. He's promised to take a look at it.'

Cherry-Garrard made no response as the maid gathered up his journals, making space for the doctor to unpack his bag onto the side table. When she had withdrawn, the doctor seated himself on the footstool facing his patient and took one foot gently in both hands. 'No doubt he'll apprise us of his opinion in the fullness of time.''

'And what, pray, should I care for his opinion? The man's a subversive, a damned Socialist. And a bun strangler, too, so I hear. I must suppose your society to be limited, Doctor, but I deplore your acquaintanceship with the fellow.'

The doctor paused in his laying out of liniments. 'If it is your pleasure to indulge in incivility, sir, then I suggest you engage the services of a country doctor. The savings in your guineas and my patience would be not inconsiderable.' With that, he returned to the task of unbandaging while his patient continued to look sternly out of the window.

When the layer of gauze had been removed, exposing the blackened feet and swollen, nail-less toes, the doctor experienced a small spread of shame, being well acquainted with the irascibility that is the companion of constant pain. 'Tell me,' he said more gently, 'had you the comfort of a fire or a foot warmer of any kind?'

Cherry-Garrard looked at his physician for the first time. 'My dear Doctor, allow me to inform you that Hut Point bore remarkably little resemblance to your club. Not to mention that a frostbite requires little comforting until it begins to thaw.'

On this occasion, the doctor succeeded in checking his irritation. 'Still no movement in these toes?'

Cherry-Garrard shook his head briefly and continued to frown out at the fine spring day.

With a small 'pop', the doctor withdrew the cork from a bottle of iodine and set to work, so that for the next several minutes there was silence at Lamer Park.

Eventually, he returned the wad of lint to the table. 'Socialist he may be' – he reached for another of the jars – 'but he also happens to be your neighbour and, by the bye, the most celebrated writer in Europe.'

Cherry-Garrard appeared to be giving the remark some consideration. 'I dare say Wells is every bit as good.'

'Yes, I believe you mentioned you were acquainted,' said the doctor as he began smearing salve onto one ankle. 'Though I was rather under the impression that you deplored the society of Socialists.'

After a pause, Cherry-Garrard spoke in a tone of affected boredom. 'Wells is of the better kind.'

'You are of course entitled to think so, but he isn't on your doorstep and would no doubt find it difficult to spare the time from his mistresses.'

When the doctor had left, Cherry-Garrard eased the

slippers back onto his feet and rang for the maid. Hooking his toes under the edge of the footstool, he winced as he hauled it closer. Outside the window, the lawns fell away through dappled sunlight towards a line of birch trees shimmering with the gold and silver of early catkins. Soon, the park would take on the dull weight of summer, but for the moment a thousand tender greens contended, differentiated as subtly as the bluish hues of the pack ice or the infinite gradations of lilac and mauve on the endless snows.

He was about to ring for a second time when the maid appeared with his morning tray. After she had poured coffee from the silver jug, a gesture sent her hurrying to return the journals to the side table. Once she had gone, he pushed a hand inside his smoking jacket and shifted the sachet of warm salts from one side of his groin to the other. The pain in the feet had eased with the fresh dressings and he experienced a brief moment of satisfaction as he sipped the coffee. For some weeks after his return, he had relished hot beverages and hot baths, just as he had enjoyed the colours of the temperate world and the touch of balmy air on his skin. But he had soon grown dissatisfied with ease and irked by the presence of those who now met his every need. He drained the cup and set it down.

The day wore on and the sun streamed in. The room, heavy with Turkish rugs and brocaded upholstery, became stuffy and warm. He brought the first of the journals to his lap and opened it at random.

I have never thought of anything as good as this life, the beauty, the simplicity, the good comradeship of it all. The good times are such as the Gods might envy us. These days are to be with one for all time – they are never to be forgotten.

He let his head fall back on the plush of the chair and

closed his eyes. That had been his time. His time of
knowing who he was. His time of purity at the end of the
world. After a few minutes, he opened his eyes and turned
the page.

> *June 22nd, 1911: A hard night: clear, with a blue sky so deep that
> it looks black: the stars are steel points: the glaciers burnished
> silver. The snow rings and thuds to your footfall... The ice is
> cracking to the falling temperature and the tide crack groans...*

The journal slipped to his lap as he dropped into a half-
sleep, listening for the distant barking of a dog team or the
sound of human voices carrying across the ice, straining
snow-burnt eyes for the sight of valiant men emerging
from the mist.

I never dreamt they were in want.

When he awoke, he was staring directly into the
sunlight. He pushed away the foot stool and wound his
chair to face the shrubbery. Minutes passed, mocked by the
patient back and forth of the grandfather clock. Eventually,
he shifted the sachet of salts and took up the journal. Entry
after entry, page after page, heading towards that
November day when a second Antarctic winter had passed
and the search party had headed south from what was left
of One Ton Depot.

He closed his eyes and rested both palms on the open
pages, living again the discovery of the frozen green
cambric, the never-to-be-forgotten moment when they had
uncovered the marble bodies of Scott, Wilson and Bowers:
Scott with his hands folded across his chest, a tobacco
pouch by his head, his companions on either side. Opening
his eyes to the warm sunlight on the lawn could not stop
him from seeing the snow tomb they had built as the sun

sank low over the Pole, silhouetting the cross of skis against the blazing gold of a midnight sky, a young man's tears turning to ice as Atkinson had read from Corinthians, his breath freezing into the ghost of a blessing.

I never dreamt they were in want.

His own voice had seemed to wake him, unsure if he had spoken aloud. The sun was blinding, the stuffy warmth of his library insufferable, his feet and ankles itching unreachably. When the maid came to collect the tray, he motioned for her to draw the drapes against the great beams of mote-filled sunlight, shutting out the leafy indolence of his park.

Shaw's Corner, Ayot St Lawrence

'I'm afraid he's out, Edward.'

Charlotte was leading the doctor into the drawing-room. 'He was up half the night reading those pages and he'd barely taken breakfast this morning before he was roaring off on that wretched contraption, spitting gravel all over the lawns. He knows he's not one bit skilled at steering but he will keep pestering Day to "ginger it up a bit" and now he's talking of acquiring a motor. Of course you must stay to lunch.'

'Are you telling me he's gone to call at Lamer Park?'

'Indeed he has.'

The doctor lowered himself into his usual chair.

'Well, I suppose that must mean something. Was he taken with it, do you imagine?'

'"Dross veined with gold" was how he described it over his boiled egg. He's asked Blanche to typewriter it all over again so I haven't had the sight of it yet.'

'And you think he might have gone to offer his help?'

'I'm assuming so. And, between us, I think it might be just the thing. You mustn't tell him I said so, but I fear he's at something of a low point himself. Keeps saying Methuselah exhausted his powers.'

The doctor frowned. 'Yes, I've observed he's been a little down of late, though one can't imagine Cherry-G offering much in the way of cheer. I've half a mind to walk over there myself. I fear they may want for a peacemaker.'

'He's really that dreadful?'

'The man has a visceral loathing for Lloyd George, the Land Tax, Socialists, trades unions, suffragettes, the working class, the clergy and Christmas. Not necessarily in that order.'

Charlotte laughed. 'Well, at least they'll have something in common. Bernard would see Christmas abolished, as you know. They'll probably be all chuckaboo by now. Tell me, did he serve?'

'Cherry-G? Went to Flanders as a volunteer, I believe,' said the doctor, leaning to one side in his chair and taking out his cigar-case. 'Some half-baked notion about using his experience with dogs to discover wounded soldiers on the battlefield. The man was in no condition, of course. Invalided home within a couple of weeks. Joined the Home Guard and had to get permission to parade in slippers.'

'You're almost making me sympathise.'

'Well, yes indeed. There's no doubt the fellow has the full quiver of odious opinions, Charlotte, but I can't help feeling a sneaking sympathy. There's the toll on the body, of course, and then being quite unfairly vilified over Scott. But I have the impression that what he really can't get over is the loss of his world – coming back to find the country near-ruined by war, landed estates taxed to the squeak, House of Lords humbled, Socialists and Fabians making all the going, trades unions stirring up the working classes, literary world fawning over the effete and the unintelligible, suffragettes slashing his beloved Velasquez.'

'And, to top it all, Day tells me some woman presented him with a white feather in Ayton High Street.'

'And I doubt a braver man ever drew breath.'

'Perhaps my heart would bleed just a little more were it not for the primrose Rolls. And Lamer Park of course.'

'It's not only Lamer, my dear. He has inherited estates in Berkshire and Oxfordshire and what I believe to be a substantial property in Swansea. Not to mention the house in Watling Street. Rents pouring in from all sides, shouldn't wonder.'

'Oh my Lord! And you know how Bernard gets poked up about unearned incomes. I think perhaps you had better go over there in case they do come to blows.'

'Oh, I hardly think Cherry-G could muster the energy for fisticuffs.'

Charlotte had walked to the window and was looking out for Shaw's return. 'And nowadays he does... what?'

'Very little. Very little. Appears to have piped off life completely. Neglects his estates. Ignores his correspondence. Spot of bird-watching now and then. Bit of desultory book collecting. Spends most of the day staring out of his window. Has his chair mounted on a revolving platform, if you please. Winds a handle to change the view. I believe he still goes up to Glen Prosen for the season. Fine shot, they say.'

'And you wouldn't diagnose a severe case of indolence?'

The doctor stroked his throat and grimaced thoughtfully. 'When you think of all he's done, it has to be something more. Melancholia rather than idleness, I'd say, though it's often difficult to distinguish t'other from which.'

'And he can't sleep, you say?'

The doctor shook his head. 'Says he "knows what dreams await". Wracked by the thought that if he'd pushed on one more day he would have encountered Scott and the polar party and brought them safely in. I've heard him say out loud – when he's dozing in his chair – 'Never dreamt they were in trouble.'

'So why didn't he? Push on, I mean?'

'Apparently Scott's orders were to wait at that particular depot and, at all costs, to preserve the dogs for another winter of exploration. Pushing on any further would have meant killing some of the dogs to feed the rest.'

'How perfectly gruesome! So it's because he failed to rescue Scott that he's in the dirt tub?'

The doctor nodded, pursing his lips. 'Odd thing is – it's not Scott he's obsessed by. It's one of those who died alongside him. Edward Wilson, though for some reason they all called him Bill. A medical man himself, I believe.'

Lamer Park, Hertfordshire

Cherry-Garrard had known on waking that he was in difficulties. Almost before the glue of sleep had begun to soften he had felt the slow seep of depression into every vein and vessel. He managed breakfast, but when it was over he struggled to rise and make his way to his chair with his rug and his footstool. Outside the window, another splendid morning invited him onto the terrace. But though the eyes registered the warm glow of a diffused sunlight, the mind perceived a cold grey fog rolling toward him across the lawns. He sank back, staring at the unseen spring, weighed down by a listlessness thick enough to be carved.

After an hour, he wound himself through a quarter-of-arc and lifted the first of the journals to his lap. A few minutes later, he set it down. The memories now seemed only to deepen his despair. Out on the Great Ice Shelf it had all been different. Being part of others' lives had invigorated his own being and despite the unrelenting demands of survival he had lived in a state that now seemed to him relaxed. A state, also, of perpetual astonishment at the world he awoke to each day, stunned by the antiseptic beauty of an unchanged ice age. And it had not all been blizzards and blisters. There had been days of summer sledging filled with the satisfying whoosh of the runners and the lingering smell of tobacco on the snow at the end of the day. Days, too, of easy passage, daydreaming of dancing at the Ritz with pretty girls and sipping hot chocolate at Claridge's. Cheered a little by such thoughts, he took up the journal from his lap.

We have had a marvellous day. The morning watch was cloudy, but it gradually cleared until the sky was a brilliant blue, fading on the horizon into green and pink. The floes were pink, floating in a deep blue sea, and all the shadows were mauve.

Outside his window, the old Belgian draft horse was drawing the mower over the grass, encumbered by clumsy leather slippers to protect the turf. He replaced the journal on his table with the unopened letters. Would slippers have stopped the hooves of the ponies sinking into the snow? Would dogs like Amundsen's Greenlanders have made the difference? Dimitri's Siberians had been a poor lot. Just as the cumbersome *Terra Nova* had been a poor choice for the pack ice. Most damaging of all, when it came down to it, was the divergence of aims. The pursuit of science or the pursuit of glory? And then that final, fatal decision – the confused orders that had led him to believe he was to wait for Scott at One Ton.

At that moment, the maid knocked and tentatively opened the door.

'A Mr Shaw of Ayot St Lawrence to see you, sir?'

Shaw's Corner, Ayot St Lawrence

'And you found him receptive to the idea?' The doctor had stayed to lunch and had been taking coffee in the drawing-room when the motorbike came to a shattering halt outside the window. A minute later, the man himself had burst into the room, throwing his Jaeger jacket onto the sofa.

'Certainly, I did. Like lighting a fire with damp wood at first, but I soon got him going. To hell with committees, I told him. Publish on your own account and to hell with pests and busybodies!'

The maid had brought Shaw a bowl of soup on a tray.

'Into the purdonium with all that stuff the Committee wants, I told him. Write to please nobody. Write only to share your truth, I said.'

'I can imagine him warming to that,' said the doctor, sharing a smile with Charlotte at Shaw's enthusiasm.

'Unbosom yourself! I said. 'Forget about good taste and discretion. Forget about being the elegant man of letters. Forget about offending people. I may presume you did not climb Mount Beardmore in order to compile a list of equipment? I asked him.'

'I take it you didn't discuss politics, then,' said Charlotte, with a hint of a wink at the doctor.

'What? Politics? No! I observed him steaming up a little when I happened to make some remark about the Vickers strike, but the fellow's a lost cause. Not worth attending to unless he's talking about the breeding grounds of the Emperor Penguin.'

The doctor and Charlotte looked on in undisguised amusement as Shaw's ardency flowed on, interrupted only by impatient sips of soup.

'Do you know what the fellow said when I demanded just one word to express what he felt about the Antarctic? He said it was the "unownedness". Remarkable.'

'Not a word one would have predicted, I'll allow,' said the doctor.

'Exactly! And it shows where the man's heart lies, Edward! All the rest is just fusty old Tory baggage inherited from the pater I shouldn't wonder. Rattles on about how the world is losing its ancient faiths with nothing to put in their place.'

Charlotte poured more coffee for them all. 'So you offered to help?'

'I consider it my duty. The man's experienced unsullied beauty the like of which the rest of us cannot begin to imagine, been confronted with truths that must be brought into the light. Do you know, when I drew him out on what, at the bottom of it, was the point of going to the last unknown place on earth he said: "so that the world may build on what it knows rather than on what it thinks". You may smile, Edward, but I tell you I could make a Socialist out of a man who can say a thing like that.'

'No, it's remarkable! Marvellous, Bernard. Your encouragement will do him more good than anything I could do. No finer cure for the melancholia than being absorbed in some scheme or other that bundles one along, living in the clear flowing stream of enthusiasm rather than the stagnant pond of oneself, if you take my meaning.'

Shaw, who had been bursting to speak himself, instead looked thoughtfully at the doctor.

'I think perhaps it is yourself who ought to be helping him with the book, Edward,' said Charlotte, smiling.

'Nonsense,' said the doctor. 'He has the best advice in the world on his doorstep.'

For once, Shaw seemed not to heed the doctor's compliment. 'He just needs someone to sort it all out. He munges it all so. Nothing's in any kind of order. He just writes things down as they come to him – memories that push their way in, sights that stirred him, reflections purified by starkness and cold. One minute he's describing the purple shadows of Mount Erebus advancing over the snow and the next he's talking about not forgetting the "please and thank you" when things are at the worst. Just starts a fresh page for each new thought and then spends days re-arranging them, endlessly changing his mind and swapping things around. I'm a scissors-and-paste man myself, as you know, but I've nothing on this Cherry fellow.'

'Ah,' said the doctor, 'that may go some way toward explaining the strange abruptness of style.'

'Just so. I also pointed out to him that the waste bin is mightier than the paste brush,' said Shaw, tapping the cane-sided basket by his chair with the edge of his foot.

'And he's going to take it up again under your advisement?'

'I could see the ambition being reborn, Edward. Trust your genius, not your industry, I told him. Write so that readers forget how warm and comfortable they are. Write so that the world may know the truth of the Antarctic. Did you read the part where he says it was the permanent darkness that got to him even more than the cold?'

'I did,' said the doctor. 'And, if I remember rightly, he

ventured the opinion that minus seventy degrees wouldn't be so bad if you could see where you were going. Did you get to the bit where they cut open the dead seal and ate the undigested fish they found inside?'

Shaw pushed the soup plate to one side. 'Remarkable indeed. And, you know, for all his Tory stiffness, the man has a streak of the unconventional. He gave me a copy of his letter to The Times about saving the penguins on some island or other, named after a Scotchman, I fancy. I thought it quite marvellous.' Shaw had taken a folded sheet from his wallet and was scanning down its contents. 'The penguin,' he read, 'has won a little bit of affection from us all because he snaps his flippers at the worst conditions in the world. If we do not help him now we can never look him straight in the eyes again.'

In response to the smiles, Shaw's enthusiasm took off again. 'That's what the fellow's really about, you see – snapping your flippers at the worst the world has to offer and being able to look people straight in the eye at the end of the day.'

Charlotte took the tray from Shaw and placed it on the table. 'And did he say anything about Scott?'

'Only that the committee meant to hush everything up. But Edward is quite right, it's not Scott he wants to write about so much as that other fellow.'

Lamer Park, Hertfordshire

The fingers of both hands batter the Underwood as the coffee cools to one side. He had risen early and hurried from the breakfast room, impatient to commit to paper the thoughts that had surfaced on waking. The maid hesitates in the doorway, alarmed by the frantic clacking of the keys in the usually tomb-like room and wondering how a man who doesn't sharpen his own pencils can be so formidable a typewriter.

Cherry-Garrard ignores her as she approaches to collect the cup, mind and fingers rattling through the morning, time passing unnoticed on the swirling currents of absorption. When the bell rings for luncheon he straightens his back, astonished to see that the morning has vanished, converted into the loose sheaf of quarto on the desk. He orders lunch on a tray and carries on working into the afternoon, pausing now and then to stare from his window at the light of the Antarctic drifting over the ever-changing snows.

... the burnished coppers and rosy pinks of the austral skies reflecting off glittering and translucent bergy whites.

He pauses, unsure about 'bergy', decides to leave it for later, hammers away once more.

When to the beautiful tints in the sky and the delicate shading on the snow are added perhaps the deep colours of the open sea, then indeed a man may realize how beautiful this world can be, and how clean...

The maid has deliberately left the door ajar and summons the cook to witness the extraordinary spectacle. With each pause at the keys, they retreat into the shadows, only to peer in again as a new burst of clattering echoes out into the hall.

By mid-afternoon the bursts are becoming briefer, the pauses longer, as he ponders what to say about Robert Falcon Scott. Should he confess his anger at the pedestalled hero of Empire, the example held up to every schoolboy in the land? Should he tell the truth about the peevish, irritable, moody martyr to British amateurism whose weak planning and confused orders had condemned Evans, Oates, Wilson, Bowers and Scott himself to die in their sleeping bags, their blood turned to ice in their veins? And should he also confess his love for the other Scott, the Scott who had battled so long with his weaker self, struggled daily with his demons and his doubts and faced every danger with a new resurrection of resolve?

He will work on until dinner – perhaps a chop or a roast fowl followed by an hour or two by a well-built fire with a half-bottle of Claret and his beloved Kipling.

'The doctor, sir.'

Cherry-Garrard swivels in his chair.

'Good afternoon, Edward. And before you ask, I think I may tell you that I may not be wasting my guineas on your services after all.'

'I'm delighted to hear it, Apsley. And may I dare to hope that the book is also progressing?'

'I do believe so, Doctor, I do believe so. You'll take tea?'

'Perhaps when I've completed the dressings.'

Cherry Garrard swings round again in his chair and pushes the slippers from his feet.

'And today I really must get you to try a sledging biscuit.'

The doctor looks doubtfully at a plate of ship's tack on the desk.

'Antarctic fare, I assume?'

'Most satisfying biscuit ever confected. Pemmican, y'know. Wilson worked out the formula with the chaps from Huntley & Palmer. Makes a fine hoosh, too, boiled up with a handful of snow. Pity you can't try that, too.'

'A pity indeed.'

Winter, 1922
Cavendish Square, London

The doctor had checked the mantel clock and seen that there was still plenty of time to catch the 12.15 to Welwyn Garden. He poured himself a larger-than-usual peg in readiness for his journey and settled down to peruse the latest notices.

Somewhat oddly, Henry Tomlinson had assured the readers of *The Nation* that 'the man of taste and conscience would willingly forgo a weekend in Brighton [the same cost as the two volumes] in order to buy Mr Cherry-Garrard's story'. Were all of Henry's book purchases, the doctor mused, weighed in the balance against weekends in Brighton? He picked up the Standard, where George Mair had concluded a long and extravagant review by claiming that Cherry-Garrard's book deserved the title 'the most wonderful story in the world'. 'Feathers upon lace,' the doctor mumbled to himself. Mair, he thought he remembered, had been Apsley's contemporary at Christ Church.

He glanced again at the clock and decided he had time to walk to King's Cross.

Shaw's Corner, Ayot St Lawrence

'You realise it occupied Bernard for much of the year?' said Charlotte, resting a hand on the boxed volumes. 'He must have walked many a mile in those spinneys over at Lamer Park, coaxing it all out of him.'

Adjusting his pince-nez, the doctor slid the first of the two volumes from its box, slightly regretting that the pages no longer had to be cut.

'Your good self, too, as I hear, Charlotte. And all without acknowledgement?'

Charlotte shook her head, momentarily closing her eyes. 'He was eager to have GB Shaw as co-author but Bernard wouldn't hear of it. Said it would have rendered the book ridiculous given that his own experience of Antarctic conditions was limited to skating upon the Serpentine in the great frost of '78. I take it he's bucked?'

'Cherry-G? I haven't seen him while I've been away, of course. But when I was there in September he was working away at the proofs and, really Charlotte, I could hardly believe the difference. Appeared ten years younger. Temper marvellously improved. Almost civil at times.'

'The staff at Lamer must be glad of it.'

'I should say so. Attending to his estates again as well, I hear. Goes to show that even the most manifest maladies of the body are in some part maladies of the mind.' The doctor tapped the side of his head with conviction. 'You wouldn't think it of an ulcer, for instance, but the colitis is apparently quiescent and when I last saw him I do believe the feet had eased somewhat. Who knows, even the teeth might show some improvement if he would place himself in the hands of some halfway competent practitioner.'

'Couldn't you find him a dentist in London?'

'I've repeatedly recommended an appointment with the Odontological Society in Leicester Square but he insists on seeing that fellow in Harpenden who, as far as I can see, is to the science of dentistry what Shaw is to the art of steering a motorcycle.'

'Bernard's near as bucked himself, by the way. Just the other day, he told Lady Gregory he thought it one of the great books of the world.'

The doctor chuckled and took out a cigar. 'Seriously, Charlotte, I really do believe the Shaws have saved the fellow's life.'

'And what about Act Two, Edward? Shall the cure be permanent, do you imagine?'

The doctor paused before clipping his cigar. 'One hopes so, but one can never be sure. I confess to a concern now the book is behind him instead of leading him forward, so to speak. The finest physic for the melancholia is undoubtedly the state of absorption. The means rather than the end, I fancy. It's when the business of the mind is entirely directed inward that things go awry. One needs to be caught up in something external, carried along in its flow, so to speak. In such circumstance, one is hardly conscious of the effort required and not always seeking distraction or battling a temptation to desist.'

Charlotte looked thoughtful. 'Yes, I've seen that in Bernard. If he's not absorbed in some great project or other, he has a tendency to sink inside himself. But one can never be sure which might be cause and which effect. A change of scene helps, a sea voyage especially.'

'And is he writing now?'

'No, he is not, Edward. Still saying he's washed up. Says the Metabiological Pentateuch exhausted his creative powers.'

'Remind me, is it still running?

'At the Garrick, yes. And apropos of what you were saying, even when he was working on those plays, I had a worrying sense that he was writing not so much for the end result as to fend off a despair. He's getting drawn into helping Lawrence as well, by the way. Did I tell you?'

The doctor took a few moments to light his cigar, then looked thoughtfully through the wraiths of smoke. 'From the snows to the sands?'

'It would seem so. He was here just the other day asking Bernard's advice. Reminded me quite a lot of Cherry-Gee.

Said "the austerity of the desert was a purification". Bernard scribbled it all down. Really, he can't resist an adventurer. He's got this idea that the true self lies somewhere out there waiting to be discovered by those who would venture. He should really write for the *Boy's Own*. You know he wrote to Kathleen?'

'Scott's widow?'

'Yes. Apparently Cherry-Garrard was poked up about what she might say when the book came out and you know what a church bell she is. Bernard wrote specially to tell her that bringing the greatness of a hero to life means exhibiting his faults as well as his qualities.'

'Just so.'

'And shall you visit Lamer this afternoon?'

'I shall, and I must confess to more than a little apprehension as to what state I may find him in.'

Lamer Park, Hertfordshire, Spring 1923

In the sunlight outside his window, the silhouette of a bird flits back and forth in the ivy. Chiffchaff or willow warbler? The question has barely the energy to break the surface of consciousness. The library, heavy with quiet, glows with innocent sunlight. Spring has returned to Lamer Park, but the field glasses remain in their case even as the shrubberies awake to the chatter of the returning migrants.

Since breakfast, he has scarcely stirred, the morning hours lost to staring from his window. The slightest noise from elsewhere in the house annoys. Yet the silence oppresses. The blood in his veins is viscous, his breathing tense and shallow, his fingers involuntarily gripping the arms of the chair. What in God's universe is the case with him? How can he have permitted himself to be unmanned by so shameful a lassitude? Where within might he find some solid ground from which to push himself free of such quicksands? Was this softening of all fibre peculiar to the man he had become? Were others ever in such a state as this? He makes an effort to sit straight, focus his eyes, breathe deeply, lapsing again as the minutes become hours and the hours see only a soul wandering a maze that leads always back to the scourging post where he flays himself for sloth, for lack of discipline, for his failure of resolve. Though he tries to shut out the sound, he hears his father's staccato demand of him that he consider his blessings, stiffen his spine, knowing even as he hears the admonition that to count his blessings is to add their weight to the forces pushing him into the downward gyre.

As the hour for luncheon nears, he contemplates small determinations – pen a letter to his agent at Wittenham, catalogue the migrant birds returning to his park, unpack the parcel of books ordered from Hatchard's in a happier time – but the meanest of enterprises goes unrealised, having no more weight or momentum than last year's leaves that rise and fall with the breeze across the lawn. He tries to think consecutively, with direction and purpose, but the brain is swaddled into incapability. Obligations eat at the edges of his awareness but he is unable to respond to their call. Humiliated by the passing of time, he nonetheless remains in his chair, devoid of urgency or need, suffocating painlessly, minute by comfortable minute, so that it is only the accumulation of so many such minutes that becomes the unsustainable burden, the ache to be other. From time to time in the maze, he comes to the dead-end of a suspicion that his state is not alterable, not susceptible to any effort of will. That one is who one is and that, as one is, so will one be. And from some vault of memory arise the high schoolboy voices that had once risen into the vaults of Winchester: *Say not the struggle nought availeth, The labour and the wounds are vain. The enemy faints not, nor faileth, And as things have been they remain.*

There have been callers, those he cannot put off, entering his rooms but not his world, their conversation an irritant, their presence an obstacle in the way of returning to himself. Even those whose company he might once have welcomed are now exhibits behind glass, as remote to him as sea creatures in an aquarium. The lives they inhabit, full of ardour and desire, are to be envied but not shared.

At the worst interludes, when even maintaining a façade for the servants seems to demand an impossible effort, thoughts of suicide creep towards him from the shadows. But the notion is insubstantial, fleeting, something that another might contemplate. For his own self there could be no shabbier betrayal of those for whom his esteem burns bright even as the darkness claims all else. He, Bowers and Wilson had not fought against the impossible odds to survive Cape Crozier – singing defiant hymns into the blizzard that had torn away their tent into the Antarctic night – only for him to surrender that life in the warmth and comfort of his library at Lamer. Yet where is the honour in sitting in that library day after day, sifting the sediments of his despair? Looking to the luncheon bell as to a landfall, he repeats the only mantra that has ever stretched out a hand toward him – *This will pass. This will pass* – and by some miracle of unbidden connection he hears the final quatrain of that hymn rising above the portraits of the great and the good: *And not by eastern windows only, When daylight comes, comes in the light, In front, the sun climbs slow, how slowly, But westward, look, the land is bright.*

When he wakes, the tears have dried on his cheeks. The

luncheon bell has sounded. He wipes a hand impatiently across his face.

In the afternoon, he takes a stroll in his grounds; not for the pleasure in being out of doors or in being young and alive and in England on a fine spring day, but merely to afford himself the outer simulacrum of purpose; he walks that he might not be in his chair.

Evening finds him standing before the high double bookcase, key in hand. Behind the glazed doors are his Barries, his Merrimans and Hewletts and the set of gilt-edged Kiplings that had cheered so many Antarctic nights. He unlocks the door and breathes in the emanation of leather and beeswax. Facing him is the copy of In Memoriam, loaned to Wilson for the journey to the Pole. On the shelf below are his journals, in whose pages he has always before been able to find solace. But that prospect, too, palls – mocking his present state with reminders of a better self.

Facing him are the presentation volumes of *The Worst Journey in the World*, bound in a fine roan leather. For weeks over the turn of the year, the sight of the work had stirred a satisfaction, even a pride. But on this spring evening, they evoke only a longing for the time when he still had the writing of them. To contemplate the volumes now is to find the future empty, confronting him not with any sense of achievement or closure but with the companions who, even as he waits for his chop and his claret, are waiting for him forever ten miles south of One Ton Depot. Even the title – upon which Shaw had been so insistent – glitters a rebuke. His co-author has not called. And the luncheon invitation he had thought to extend to Shaw Corner has not been sent. Shaw. Yes. He had seen the signs in him, too, under the bluster. And, of course, in Scott, a braver man than himself. The spines and tooled covers of *The Worst Journey in the*

World stare back at him. Would Wilson ever have countenanced such a description?

It is with thoughts of Wilson that he locks the bookcase and returns to his chair, knowing that if there were a truth to be brought back from the Great Ice Shelf then it would be the truth of the one who had shown them what a man may aspire to. The one whose unselfishness of word and deed had been the star that had guided them all to a better version of themselves as faithfully as Jupiter had guided them through the permanent darkness of that winter. The one whose good cheer had kept all of their fears in harness. The one whose thought was never of himself but of sustaining his companions and whose awareness of the fears and feelings of others had given him the gift of the right word and gesture at the worst of times. He sinks into his chair, struggling to rid his mind of the alabaster effigy that would still be there tonight, preserved under that cairn and the steel-pointed stars. He attempts to conjure up instead the strong forehead and steady gaze of the man as he had been in life – the man who alone among them all had succeeded in leaving himself behind and making the arduous journey to the Pole of other. The one who had made the greatest journey in the world.

After dinner, he falls asleep before his fire. It is not the satisfying slumber of Antarctic nights after arduous days but the sour, fitful unconsciousness of one no longer wishing to be conscious, the sleep of one tired only of being awake. From time to time he opens his eyes and stirs his limbs, awakened by voices calling across the ice while outside his window the blackthorn blossom is beginning to drift like snow.

❖

To Helsinki and back

Kevin

'There's no point talking about it,' Dad said. But I knew it wouldn't be long before he'd find a way back to it. 'Your mother would have known,' he'd say when we were wondering if we could recycle bubble wrap, or 'It's a good job I can cook a bit,' as he made us cheese on toast.

The house was tidy enough, but he'd started smoking again.

Chloe

Mums don't disappear. They just don't. They're always there. And they always answer your messages.

Kevin

It was obvious he wanted to talk about it. In fact, it was the only thing he did want to talk about. But it had to be grudging. It had to be me dragging it out of him.

'Sounds like a romantic idea,' I said.

'I think it was,' he said, failing to suppress the note of self-pity. 'I think it was.'

There was another long silence as he waited for the next prompt. I knew better than to ask anything too direct. That would have been Chloe's way. Girls always go straight at it.

'Of course, I've only heard about it second-hand and you know what Chloe's like. The idea was... what? Sort of recreate your first date?'

He took a sip of beer and stared into the empty fireplace.

'That was basically it.'

'For your twenty-fifth?'

He let the question go unanswered and I left him to it for a bit. We were sitting in the familiar front room but with Mum gone and the tobacco smoke clinging to the curtains it didn't seem like the house I'd grown up in.

'Wish I'd just got her a bunch of flowers,' he said, after a while.

'She didn't much go for the idea then?'

He lit another cigarette, taking his time.

'You know what your mum's like with anything a bit out of the ordinary.'

'But she came round to it?'

'Bit mealy-mouthed to start with. Asked me if I thought the Little Chef at Droitwich would still be there.'

I took a sip of beer. There was a tricky course to be negotiated here. If I was going to get it out of him, I'd need to show a bit of male solidarity. But I was damned if I was going to let Mum down.

'But you went to Helsinki?' I said, as though this were the obvious alternative to Droitwich. When he didn't reply, I reached for the newspaper.

'All I said was,' – he leaned forward – 'all I said was, what about celebrating our silver wedding by imagining we're meeting all over again.'

'Nice one, Dad,' I said.

He gave a little 'look where it got me' shrug and stared at the end of his cigarette. I dropped the newspaper in my lap.

'So where did Helsinki come in?'

He sighed cigarette smoke, the long-drawn-out exhalation of a patient and much-misunderstood man. 'I just thought the idea might work better if we went somewhere different, that's all. Not even somewhere we'd always planned to go, like Venice. Somewhere we'd never even thought of going.'

'And what did Mum say?'

She said: 'I've never thought of going to Helsinki.'

Chloe

When I finally got hold of Mum, she was with Aunty Karen in Hereford.

'Don't worry, sweetheart, I'm perfectly all right,' she said.

I drove straight down.

There was a shepherd's pie and we talked about seasonal immigrants and fruit-picking. I don't know whether it really was Aunty Karen's bridge night, but after supper she put a bit of lipstick on and said she wouldn't be late.

Mum and I washed up and carried our wine to armchairs by the fire.

'It wasn't just Helsinki,' she said. 'We had to go to the kind of restaurant we wouldn't normally go to and choose food we wouldn't normally eat. Then he really got going – new hairdos and new clothes.'

'Oh my God,' I said.

'That's what I thought. No half measures when your dad does mid-life crisis.'

'So what did you say?'

'Well, honestly, I didn't want to be a stick-in-the-mud when he thought he was being all imaginative and romantic.

And anyway I did think it might be quite fun.'

'I wondered about the hair-do.'

'Like it?'

'Mmm. Suits you. Younger.'

'It'll grow back.'

Kevin

Chloe called to let me know she'd seen Mum. When I asked her what had happened, she said Mum had told her about it in confidence and if I wanted to know I should ask her myself. Strong implication that men can't understand these things.

Dad was in the kitchen studying the user manual for the oven. I suggested going out to eat, my treat.

'Save your pennies, I've made us a casserole,' he said in his new 'I don't suppose I'll ever be happy again' voice.

We drank beer and talked football for a while, but before long we were back in Helsinki. Apparently he'd booked a table at an upscale seafood restaurant. 'Ordered kalakukko as a starter,' he said in a voice that suggested a lifetime of frustrated hopes. 'Turned out to be a Cornish pasty with fish.'

But it wasn't how the evening had started that I wanted to know about.

Chloe

Kev is hopeless when it comes to telling you what anyone's said. They'd obviously had a whole evening and I got ten seconds' worth. So he wasn't getting any change from me. Besides, I didn't want him to think I was making fun of Dad, even though we hadn't been able to help ourselves when Mum described how he'd turned up at this sea-food place with a buzz cut and a pair of jeans that were two sizes too tight.

Besides, I wouldn't have been able to tell Kev the important thing. I couldn't quite get my head round it myself. Mum was different. I don't mean the new hairstyle and the tailored skirt when I'd only ever seen her in slacks. It was more than that. Almost as if she were a different person.

I opened the bottle of Bardolino I'd brought from home and poured us each a generous glass.

'He'd said it would be like taking a break from ourselves.' She frowned as she held the glass up to the firelight. 'But I don't think that's what he meant.'

Kevin

If Dad's to be believed, Mum behaved oddly from the off. Okay, the whole thing was a bit contrived, but so what? He'd done his best, chatting up Mum as if it was their first date, asking her about herself and so on. But apparently lots of the things she'd told him didn't fit with the woman he'd been married to for twenty-five years.

'I asked if she liked cricket,' he said, shaking his head in posthumous amazement. 'She said she thought it must have been invented to push back the boundaries of tedium. Well, you know how many cricket matches we've been to over the years.'

Chloe

'And then when I came out of the hairdresser's, I marched myself straight into the cosmetics department at John Lewis and signed up for the "Style and Beauty Experience".'

'You didn't!'

'I know! I never thought I'd do anything like that. Next thing you know I'm with this personal beauty consultant –

about twelve, face like a mask, eyebrows where no eyebrows had ever been before.'

'I know, I always run the other way.'

'Skin-type analysis, tinted moisturisers, and a small suitcase full of brushes for something called contouring. Highlights. Blusher. Caviar eye-sticks. Glass of Prosecco. I had to be firm about eyelashes.'

'Oh God, Mum, I wish I could have seen you.'

'Can't think why I haven't done it before. Only takes a couple of hours.'

'Two hours?'

'Two hours of "Hope I've got a figure like yours when I'm your age" and "Bare Minerals sits well on the mature skin" and "My mother's the same age as you and she's got dry patches". I'm not telling you how much I spent.'

'Mum!'

'Wait for it. Your dad kept saying we should push the boat out so I thought, right Helen, next stop "Wardrobe Refresh – Walk the floor with your Personal Stylist".'

'No!'

'Yes! I tell you, I could get a taste for Prosecco.'

Kevin

Dad was really getting into grievance mode now.

'When I asked what she did at weekends, she said she liked taking long walks in the country. Talk about tedium! Even when I asked about where she'd grown up, she went on about how she'd always wanted to go back and live in Northumberland.'

'It's your mum's recipe,' he said when he served up the casserole.

I'd never have known.

Chloe

We hadn't bothered to turn on the lamps and Aunty Karen's floral wallpaper looked even more old-fashioned in the fading light. By the second glass, Mum was becoming subdued as well.

'The makeover thing was just a bit of fun, but then… it's hard to explain… when I got home it was like something had changed inside as well. I didn't feel ten years younger or anything silly, but when I saw myself I was startled.'

'Because you looked different?'

'No, because it suddenly seemed like I might *be* different, if that doesn't sound completely mad.'

'It doesn't sound like you.'

'No, well, that's what I mean. It made me think about not being me, about who "me" was, about other "mes" that might have been. I'd set off for a fun afternoon and a bit of self-indulgence and I went home feeling upset. Like a chick that's just broken out of its shell and is looking around a bit lost.'

'The way I'm hearing this, Mum, you're twenty-five years out of practice at thinking about yourself.'

The light was very dim now, but I was pretty sure there was a gleam of a tear as Mum sipped the Bardolino. She looked away so I wouldn't notice. The new bob haircut showed off a pair of blue enamel earrings I'd never seen before.

'Anyway, I used half a tub of make-up remover and got back into my jeans but I didn't seem able to get back into myself.'

'Dad didn't see the new you, then?'

'God no! We were going to meet for the first time in Helsinki. We were even travelling separately.'

I think my mouth might literally have dropped open.

'Your parents aren't supposed to do things like this,' I said.

Mum laughed, but the troubled look was soon back.

'When I was packing, all I could think about was who I'd been when we first met all those years ago. And I couldn't remember. I just couldn't remember.'

There were definite tears now and I got up to kneel awkwardly beside her chair to give her a hug.

'Is there any more wine?'

When we were settled again, I tried to reassure her.

'None of us can remember who we were even a few years ago, Mum. And what you can remember is usually embarrassing.'

'I know, but it started me thinking, that's all. And finally I decided the thing to do was to take your dad's little idea seriously.'

'I'm not with you.'

'I know. I'm hardly with myself. But what I thought was – I'd try to enter into it. I couldn't be who I was at our first meeting, any more than I could look like I looked then. But I thought I'd at least try to be *me*.'

Kevin

Dad takes a drink well. Better than me in fact. But we were into the second six-pack now and the problem was he couldn't get past how hard done by he felt. He just kept saying things like 'I've honestly no idea what I did wrong' and 'it was just like she was a different person'. I decided a loss of interest was called for and picked up the *Radio Times*.

Chloe

We'd switched on the lamps now and Mum was calm again.

'I was going to talk to you about it anyway, love, because

it might be something you need to think about as well.'

'You've lost me again.'

She was only occasionally sipping wine now. In the firelight, and with the new bob cut, I noticed how elegant the shape of her face was.

'You see, when you're a wife for all those years, you gradually become someone else. Someone who's not who you were, or who you could have been, and maybe not who you wanted to be.'

'Ye-es.'

Mum put down her glass and held the backs of both hands out towards me. 'So you've got this person who's you, and you've got this other person who's the wife.' She moved the hands together so that they almost but not quite overlapped. 'But of course they don't completely coincide. And the problem is, the partner only sees the partner, not the person, if you see what I mean. They don't see the bit that doesn't overlap.'

Oh my God, I thought to myself, this can't be Mum talking.

Kevin

Dad wasn't getting any nearer to the beef. I put down the magazine and tried giving him a prompt in the backside.

'So maybe you could just tell me what happened, Dad?'

He looked hurt, as if I hadn't been listening to what he'd been saying.

'What happened,' he said, 'is something I'll never understand.'

Chloe

'I didn't plan it. I honestly didn't.'

After all the wine, we'd decided we'd better have something to eat and made ourselves plates of crackers with Wensleydale and some of Aunt Karen's homemade tomato chutney.

'Didn't plan what?'

'What happened,' she said.

I attempted one of Dad's sighs.

'It should have dawned on me from the start,' she said. 'But it suddenly hit me that here I was struggling to make something more meaningful out of the evening when for him the whole thing was just an elaborate sexual fantasy.'

I stared at the plate of crackers. 'How was the food?' I said.

'Not great. Dad ordered something called kaalikääryleet. Turned out to be a cabbage roll.'

Kevin

Dad said: 'We had a lovely evening, wonderful meal, splendid Soave, Koskenkorva chasers – like vodka but better. And I must have told her at least half a dozen times how great she looked.'

'But?'

He shrugged. 'She just carried on telling me things about herself that weren't her at all. How she'd really wanted to go to law school. How she'd like to join a choir. How she liked having lots of friends and giving dinner parties. Even when I asked her where she liked to go for her holidays she said Umbria when we've always gone to the Dordogne.'

'Dad, can I just ask you – where is all this leading?'

'I'm getting to that,' he said.

Chloe

'You really think that's why he suggested the whole thing, the new clothes and hairdos and everything?'

'To be fair, I don't know if that was the idea from the start. I mean even if it was, I mean, okay, harmless. Could even have been fun, if you'll forgive your old mum for saying so, but…'

'Go on, Mum.'

'It's just that I couldn't help thinking that what our romantic anniversary dinner was really saying was that he was a bit bored with me as I am. I'd started to think that maybe what he really wanted was a romantic dinner with someone who wasn't me.'

'Oh, Mum, I'm sure that wasn't it. Don't you think you might be reading a bit too much into it?'

Mum thought for a while.

'Anyway, that's how it felt. Like he was gazing adoringly through the candlelight but he wasn't seeing me. And probably because of the wine, I started thinking that maybe he'd never seen me.'

Kevin

Dad took an awful long time 'getting to it'. First, we had to have the rest of the menu, including the Mustikkapiirakka dessert, which sounded very like blueberry pie.

Chloe

Mum looked at her watch.

'Ethel will be back.'

'And you still haven't told me what happened.'

'What happened was, he suggested we skip coffee and go straight back to the hotel.'

Kevin

Even Dad hadn't been able to bring himself to eat much of the casserole. He went to the kitchen and got us four packets of cheese-and-onion crisps.

'It's Match of the Day in five minutes,' I said.

I thought this might get us over the line, but what it did was give him an excuse to talk about what was going on behind the scenes at White Hart Lane.

I reached for the remote control.

'Anyway,' he said, abandoning the punditry, 'there isn't anything else to tell. We just paid the bill and went back to the hotel.'

I returned the control to the table. 'Dad,' I said, 'just tell me – why isn't Mum here now?'

'I don't know, you tell me,' he said.

And I knew I'd blown it.

Chloe

'So you went back to the hotel,' I prompted.

'Well, first I suggested we have a walk around the harbour. It was really lovely, all the jetties and waterfront buildings lit up in pastel colours, pinks and blues, reflecting in the water. He took one look at it and said "Why don't we just go back?" Well, honestly, before we even got to the hotel, he was kissing me in the street. And I'm not talking peck on the cheek.'

'Doesn't sound all that horrific, Mum.'

'And in the lift.'

Kevin

Dad pretended he had too much on his mind to be inter-ested in Match of the Day and sat there eating cheese-and-onion crisps with a forlorn look that lasted until Spurs got the equaliser.

'Anyway,' he said, when the pundits started drawing triangles on the screen, 'then she wanted to go for a walk round the bloody harbour.'

'And?'

There was a pause, and he must have decided he'd better get it over with.

'Quick canter round the waterfront, back to the hotel, lift to the third floor, get to the room, she produces her key card – then just turns around and slams the door in my face.'

'Mum? I don't believe you.'

He looked somewhere between offended and exasperated. 'Believe it or not, I'm telling you – just said goodnight and shut the door in my face.'

'What did you do?'

'I didn't bloody knock, I'll tell you that. And I wasn't going down to the desk to ask for another bloody room. Next thing, I'm traipsing round bloody Helsinki looking for a hotel.'

'You know she's at Aunty Karen's?'

'I don't bloody care where she is.'

Chloe

'But, Mum, he'd obviously had a few glasses of wine and it's not as if he doesn't love you. I mean love you-you. I mean you're surely not thinking of leaving him over it, are you?'

'Goodness no! It's just that I've come up with my own little romantic idea for our anniversaries from now on. I'm going to wear what I usually wear, do my hair like I've always done it, and leave him for a couple of weeks.'

I felt like I'd got my mum back.

'To help him elp totooto appreciate the real you?'

'To help him appreciate the real me.'

I poured us the last of the wine.

'But you still haven't said what actually happened. You don't have to tell me if it gets too steamy. I'm only twenty-six.'

'Oh, I don't mind telling you. We got to the room and, as he was following me in, I turned around and said "I think we'd better get to know each other a little better first, don't you?" and closed the door.'

The Wine of Forgiveness

For Jon Rohde

KATARZYNA SOKALSKA, known on five continents as Kat, left UNICEF headquarters on New York's 44th Street for the last time on a Friday evening towards the end of a sultry August in 2020. Turning uptown, she easily outpaced the red tail lights crawling up First Avenue.

No hurry now, Kat. No hurry any more.

She had tried to resist any kind of leaving ceremony but friends and colleagues had refused to allow forty years of service to come to an unmarked end. In the event, what she had feared would be an excruciating couple of hours had turned out to be bearable, enjoyable even. The Secretary to the Board had given a glowing tour d'horizon of those four decades and ended by presenting her with a Flightgift voucher for $1,500 and a card signed by almost a hundred present and former colleagues. After that, Marie-Touré had made a tearful speech recollecting the days when they had worked together through the cholera epidemic in the Sahel. Then Faraji, who had given an exaggerated account of how she had cut a swathe through the bureaucracy in the aftermath of the earthquake in Haiti. The Executive Director had arrived late but brought tears to her eyes with the warmth of his tribute.

Halfway up 53rd, she let herself into the four-storey walk-up that had been home since being brought in from the field five years earlier. Closing out the noise of the street, she checked her mailbox and began the climb to the top floor, wondering how much longer she would be able to manage the stairs. Many of those she had worked with over the years had not been able to attend tonight, scattered as they were across the globe. But Venkatesh had happened to be passing through New York and he, too, had embarrassed her by what he had said about her role in the programme to reduce maternal and child death rates in Madhya Pradesh. On the second landing, she paused for a few seconds; the handrail had been repainted so often that the detail of its iron finials had long ago been filled in, but it was a help these days. She began pulling herself up, panting heavily in the intimate silence of the stairwell.

Once inside the apartment, she put the chain on the door and sat on the couch to recover, pushing off her shoes.

There were times when her apartment seemed to her to be a sad little place. For one thing, it had never lost its temporary look despite the wall hangings and gifts from colleagues at her different postings: a batik depicting the Sigiriya frescoes, a genuine Makonde carving, a shiny parol from the Philippines, an antique bronze of Shiva from Thiruvananthapuram.

It had been kind of Chariya, long since retired herself, to come down from Westchester to be there tonight. And appropriate, for Chariya had been there at the beginning. Working with her on that first posting in Nepal, now so very long ago, Kat had at first regretted not going to medical school herself. But by the end of that first year, she had realised how little medical science could achieve without the managerial and logistical skills that had turned out to be her own forte.

Breathing normally again now, she forced up the sash window with the heels of her palms. Not being streetside, the apartment was quiet except for the moan of the air-conditioning units that protruded from the windows of the adjoining block. It was, by a distance, the least prepossessing of all the views she had known over the years. And what a contrast to the ocean-front bungalow in Dar-es-Salaam with the lattice-work walls open to the warm sea breezes on which, she had liked to think, she could detect the spices of Zanzibar. Or the shared apartment outside Nuwara Eliya with the verandah looking out over the endless plantations. Outside her window this Friday evening, all there was to be seen was the zig-zag of converging fire escapes leading the eye to the yard below where litter had accumulated over the years and a pigeon was slowly decomposing.

She showered and changed into her favourite navy dress and open-toed sandals, getting ready for the small ritual by which all the important moments in her life had been marked. Before the mirror on the wardrobe door, she smoothed the dress over her hips. There had been a time when male colleagues had been known to refer to her as 'the Polish princess,' but she was heavier now, her skin stretched by years of other suns, her hair so fine that it could hardly hold the bobbed style she had kept it in all her life. She turned side-on and smoothed the dress some more. Was the lipstick perhaps a shade too bright, the heels of the sandals a tad too high – for a pensioner?

She checked her purse and took her linen jacket from its hanger in case it grew cool later on.

By eight o'clock, she was sitting at a sidewalk table outside an upmarket bistro on Lexington Avenue. She would have preferred her little ritual without the fumes and the car horns and the bellowing of air brakes, 'but hey,' as her younger colleagues would have told her, 'this is New York'.

Without it ever becoming a conscious decision, she had known that this was where she would spend her retirement. There was no one left in Gdansk. Nowhere to call 'home' with any conviction. The only community to which she belonged was the band of friends and former colleagues spread out across the world and this was the place that most of them would be likely to pass through from time to time. More sentimentally, it would also be keeping faith with her father, much on her mind this night. From her earliest years, and from the depths of disillusionment, he had told her many times: 'America is the place to be.'

An order of baked clams with garlic butter came first, the mouth-watering aroma instantly transporting her to Bangkok and the restaurant over the Chao Phraya where she had so often dined with Javid. At the time, both of them had been deeply involved in programmes to rehabilitate Burmese girls being trafficked into Phat Phong's sex industry and, for those first few dinners together, they had talked of nothing but work. But gradually the talk had turned to other things and they had learnt more of each other's lives. And in the silences between, romance had bloomed over the river-shrimp and cracked-crab curries.

Back on the sidewalk, a blaring of car and cab horns was echoing up Lexington Avenue from somewhere downtown, no doubt caused by some obstruction to the Friday evening exodus.

Bangkok had been the first of her regional postings, the hub from which they had supported programmes throughout Southeast Asia. What a posting that had been, and what characters she had worked with! Muralidharan, the Sinhalese who could see off *The Times* crossword in his coffee break. Ayaan, who had protested against the intro-duction of breakfast meetings by declaring that it was like strangling the day at birth; Gaspar in Indonesia, so focused on his work that he had appeared at the office one morning in a suit of blue pants and brown jacket. And Dalisay – 'Daisy' – in Manila, who had defied all the rules by helping to organise a demonstration against companies persuading mothers to abandon breastfeeding in favour of commercial baby-milk formulas. Or Philippe in Saigon, the French former diplomat who was fluent in seven languages and was rumoured never to have said anything sensible in any of them. She smiled to herself as she speared the first of the clams, the tiny, two-pronged fork recalling as always the bifurcated needles that had been the symbol of the decade-long campaign to rid the planet of smallpox.

She had chosen the Carnegie Bistro because it was one of the few restaurants in Manhattan where the wine list included a Miłosz Pinot Noir. She sipped and nodded approval. The waiter poured the first glass as she lifted the first dripping clam from its shell and the car horns downtown reached new decibels of impatience.

She could see now that the obstruction was a protest of some kind and that it was advancing up Lexington. She lifted the napkin to her lips. On the corner of 57th, a kiosk advertised a concert at the Lincoln Centre and an exhibi-tion of photographs from the Kamoinge Workshop. After today, there would be time for all the things people got excited about in this city. But what she looked forward to most was having time to walk the streets, watching the world change with almost every block from the Lower East Side to Chinatown and on through Little Italy, Soho and the Village, stopping for coffee and occasionally coming across reminders of her former lives – a stall offering stewed okra, a sign written in Malayalam, a shop window displaying a figurine of Sitata Mata.

It didn't need to be Polish wine, but Milosz was what her father had always opened at such times – births, marriages, high-school graduations, or the start of a new venture. And of course, it had been the wine he had opened the night she had left from Długi Targ Square. Since the age of twelve, she had participated in the little ritual, her small wine diluted with water. The first glass, this first glass, he had told her then, was for the forgiveness of others, each measured sip to be the dissolving of some residual resentment, the warming of some cold place in the heart.

The disturbance downtown was growing louder as she raised her glass to what she could see of the evening sky. Above street level, above the scaffolding and traffic-viola-tion signs, the fire hydrants and ATMs, the steam vents and awnings, the lights were coming on in the private worlds and unknown lives of Manhattan's apartments and condos. The forgiveness, her father had warned, was not to be glib; it was to be the realisation that other people have things in their past and present that you cannot know about. It was to be an appreciation of life's unknowns, uncertainties, complexities. It was to be the forgiveness proffered by the hand of humility. Had she heard it said that to understand all was to forgive all? Wise as far as it went, he had told her, but to drink fully from the wine of forgiveness was to follow such wisdom to its conclusion – forgiving even if you do not understand.

The protest was now in view, advancing across the whole width of Lexington and provoking a wall of noise from cars and cabs as they fought their way into the side streets in the hope of making more progress. She sipped wine and thought of those she would need to forgive. The lights had changed but the attempt to cross over to Second or Park had produced the predictable gridlock. So few, so few to forgive, she thought, as the Pinot cut through the thin film of garlic butter coating her palate.

Before the aftertaste had quite faded, she was wondering whether her father had been able to forgive the far greater evils that had been perpetrated on so many of his generation. He had been slow to speak of it and, if called upon, was likely to quote just the one spare, terrible sentence from Maria Dobrovska: 'In the morning the Germans were still here, and in the evening we are under Bolshevik occupation.' Humbled by having so little to forgive, she instead took a sip of gratitude for the privileges of her life. And most of all, she imbibed a thankfulness for Javid, gentle Javid, who in his quietly spoken way had turned the world upside down. The chanting of slogans was growing nearer now as the protest reached Starbucks on 55th, though the marchers were still not close enough for her to make out the banners. Her entrée of soft-shell crabs arrived with a basket of different breads.

Javid's paper in the *International Journal of Pediatrics* had not at first attracted attention outside that periodical's specialist readership. But gradually its reputation had spread, first by word of mouth and then through paragraphs quoted and copies circulated by health workers, humanitarian organisations, NGOs and UN agencies until it had assumed an almost biblical status among the international health community. Within a few months, it had been picked up by *The Economist* and the *New York Times* and was being discussed in government circles and international confer- ences. She herself must have mailed out close on a hundred copies to contacts and colleagues around the world.

Over the heads of the crowd, the revolving blue lights of police vehicles could now be seen bringing up the rear of the protest. She broke a piece of bread and sliced into the first of the crabs, pushing aside the tired-looking salad. It has long been an axiom of faith, Javid had written, that only the long haul of sustained economic growth could bring to an end the tragedy of fifteen million children dying every year in the poor world. In the few pages that followed, he had dismantled this 'truth'. More than half of those deaths, he had shown, were caused by four or five common condi- tions that the world already knew how to prevent or cure at a cost of only a few cents per child. Why then, he had asked, was it not being done? His answer had been simply put: those millions of children were dying every year – of measles, diphtheria, whooping cough, tetanus, diarrhoea – because they were the sons and daughters of the poorest and least influential people on earth. And because, to the privileged and the powerful, their lives did not matter.

It felt wrong, tonight of all nights, to think of personal things in the same breath as the challenge that Javid had set before the world, but he had also been one of three colleagues who had proposed marriage to her over the years. Nothing had been settled, and their relationship had not survived postings to duty stations continents apart. Their paths had occasionally crossed afterwards – rather awkwardly – at workshops and conferences. But what mattered was that, in the decade that followed, projects and programmes that could trace their origins to Javid's paper had taken over her life and the lives of thousands of others – immunization managers, government health services, plus UN staff and volunteers working in more than a hundred countries to make happen what Javid had said could be done.

With the first few sips, she had run out of those to be forgiven, but the wine of gratitude had been drained with so much still to be thankful for. She poured the second glass and dipped another piece of bread into the lime tartar sauce. Throughout those years, her skills had been much in demand, especially in the management of mass immuniza-tion programmes that needed the right quantities of vaccines, syringes and sterilising units to be in the right hands at the right times and temperatures. She and Javid had by then been worlds apart, but the sense of working by his side in the great cause had never left her – not even after he had gone forever, cut down by a heart attack while on a field mission to Niger. At their last meeting, at a pledging conference in Guinea-Bissau, all he had talked of was how much more there was to still do – how many were still dying of malaria, TB, pneumonia. And as she contem-plated the second glass on a warm August evening in New York, even the joy at having been a small part of what had been achieved did not stop the tears coming to her eyes: for Javid, for what he had done, for what he had stood for, for how different her own life might have been.

The protest march, whatever it was about, was now only a block away and the waiter was asking those seated outside if they would prefer to move to an inside table. When he approached, she shook her head.

The second glass, her father had told her, with some discomfort deep in his eyes, was the wine of forgiveness for oneself. And this glass, too, was not to be taken hastily, without thought. It was for forgiveness of things done but also of things not done: intentions allowed to languish, principles not adhered to, promises not kept, consequences for others insufficiently considered. Or a self one had not been true to. Had there been perhaps some secret behind that troubled look? Something in his own past that the second glass had not quite enabled him to forgive? Some falling short of honour, some small complicity of the kind that had scarred the consciences of so many of his generation? It had not been easy for her young self to grasp all that he had told her – that just as the forgiveness of others must embrace that which is not understood, so the forgiveness of self must accept failings, flaws, even those that lie too deep to be changed. With some unknown sadness in his voice, he had raised his glass and told her that – from the first spread of the grape on the palate through to the last, lingering aftertaste – the wine of forgiveness should bring an acceptance that you too have your unknown springs of conduct; that you too are mostly a mystery to yourself.

By now, most of those at the sidewalk tables had retreated inside as the photographers and network TV cameras came walking backwards up Lexington. Kat raised her glass to her lips. She had marched, too, in her youth; first in solidarity with the shipyard workers and, later, against abortion laws. In later years, she had only been able to cheer from afar as marches and demonstrations had seen yet another square renamed or another Monument of Gratitude toppled in Legnica or Tallinn.

Reverie ended as the wave of marchers broke over the sidewalk, pressing close, their sweat mingling with the fumes and the aromas of seafood, the evening air taken over by drumming and chanting. 'Black Lives Matter' seemed an odd slogan, a truism if ever there was one. But those were the words printed on the banners and T-shirts crowding past. She raised her glass to the marchers; it was good to see so many coming out to protest racism on a hot summer night in America. But even as she did so, she felt a soul-chill of fear. Not for her safety, not for the closeness of the crowd, but for the phalanx of raised fists, black-gloved or bare-knuckled, marching up Lexington Avenue.

She could see now that almost all the protesters were young, both black and white, a fervency in their faces and voices as they waved their placards above the storm of noise. She gave a wave to one group passing by in lockstep to the beat of an invisible drum and smiled at the nearest of the youths who waved back with his left hand as he punched the night air.

The first ranks had now disappeared from view to be replaced by a more motley crowd bearing other placards – 'No Justice No Peace', 'White Silence Kills'. Kat bit her lip and struggled to see those raised fists for what they were this night in New York. A show of solidarity. A reference, for some, to those Olympians on the podium in Mexico more than fifty years ago. But as her fingers tightened on the stem of her glass, she could not keep at bay images of other fists raised on other streets far from America – or, further back still, of the uncomprehended fear that the gesture had held for a child. Her father had told her the communists had adopted the salute in deliberate contrast to the raised, flat palm of fascism – first in Spain and then in the East. It had been meant to show – he had demonstrated with his own work-worn hand – that feeble individual fingers could come together to make a powerful striking force. But, as he had also told her, the salute that had arrived to proclaim liberation had stayed to become the symbol of a brutal occupation. As a child, she had been spared the details. Only years later had she learned of the mass rapes and murders and the unspeakable events in the Katyn Forest. Later still, in other continents, she had witnessed similar metamorphoses as liberation armies that had courageously raised their fists in the struggle against colonialism had so often become oppressors in their turn.

She brought herself back to the sidewalk and returned her napkin to the table. The marchers in the rear of the parade seemed grimmer, angrier, many wearing the single black glove, their chanting more menacingly insistent. Still, she wished them well while wondering how many of them had set foot outside America or knew how little all those millions of young black lives in the wider world had mattered. Wondering, also, what Javid would have thought had he been able to sit beside her on Lexington tonight. He, too, she imagined, would have wished that the salute of solidarity might have been the open, peaceful, forward-facing palms of the Buddhists. But hey, she reminded herself, this was New York. The march was almost at an end now and she reached to refill her glass as the police cruisers peeled off into the side streets.

The third glass, her father had said, the cheer returning to his eyes – the third glass was just for the wine. She drank to his memory at the same time as becoming aware that twenty or thirty protesters had broken away from the tail of the procession and were heading for the sidewalk tables. Different placards were now being thrust skywards – 'Silence is complicity,' 'White silence is violence' – as the group converged on the bistro with yells of 'Raise your fist! Raise your fist!'

Katarzyna sat straight and still as they crowded her table – 'Raise your fist! Raise your fist!' She was alarmed, but not frightened. This was America. These young people were not Kyungu's Juferi. They were not Mobutu's goons. They were not drugged-out teenagers with chickens strung from their belts and Kalashnikovs strapped over their shoulders. Nor were they renegades from the Soviet Northern Group. She looked from face to face, determined to appear neither frightened nor hostile as the noise rose all around her – 'Raise your fist! Raise your fist!'

In the stalemate on Lexington Avenue, Katarzyna Sokalska had retreated to an inner space where she was quite certain that not only was she not afraid but that she would rather die on this Manhattan sidewalk than raise her fist in obedience. This was her moment. Hers and her father's. And no matter the cause, no matter the sincerity of the frenzied, she would not be intimidated into uniting herself with their demands. For in that moment, in that inner space, it seemed utterly clear to her that the wrong, the dishonour, the eventual evil, would be in the surrendering of herself to the fervent certainties of others; that it was this, in the end, that had led to the very worst that humans had been prevailed upon to do to each other.

In the doorway of the restaurant, a frightened young couple had raised their fists and been cheered, releasing more of the youths to join the crowd at her table where some of the chanting was now less than an arm's length from her face. Yet she remained sitting upright, certain of her inner place, refusing to show fear. However threatening these youths might be, however fiercely the collective zeal burned in their eyes, it was not to be compared to the intimidation her father's generation had faced. Left to her own free will, she might have raised her fist in support of so universal a cause; but not like this. How badly, she thought, how badly it would have been letting him down to give in, here on the streets of America.

❖

Author's note

One part of this story is based on fact. In the early 1980s, the American paediatrician Jon Rohde presented a paper at a medical conference in Birmingham, England, which made the argument that the fictional Javid makes in 'The Wine of Forgiveness'. Dr Rohde's paper began to circulate among health professionals and, in 1980, it came to the attention of the incoming Executive Director of UNICEF, James P Grant. For the next sixteen years, Grant devoted most of UNICEF's efforts and resources to the task of implementing the available low-cost solutions that were the cause of approximately half of the disease, poor growth and early death among the world's children. Galvanising the World Health Organisation, national health services, and non-governmental organisations in over a hundred countries, this effort eventually raised immunisation levels from below 20% to almost 80% worldwide, saving the lives of more than three million children a year. Polio cases also fell from 400,000 to under 100,000 a year (and have continued to fall to fewer than 100 cases a year today). Oral rehydration therapy, almost unheard of in 1980, was by the mid-1990s known to more than half of all the families in poor countries – saving at least a million young lives annually. The full story of the 'Child Survival Revolution' is told in the postscript of my novel The Kennedy Monent (Myriad Editions, 2018). In total, it is estimated to have saved the lives of more than 25 million children, leading Microsoft founder Bill Gates to describe it as 'the greatest miracle of saving children's lives ever'.

Comfort

O N MANY A LONG AFTERNOON in his later years, sitting
out on the balcony overlooking the eel boats moored
along the canal, he had drifted back to the cocktail bar in
the basement of the Cumberland Hotel near Marble Arch.
He had always known that the hour he had spent there, all
those years ago, held some meaning for him. But it was not
a meaning to be grasped at; it had to be allowed to come to
him while he attended at a respectful distance, something
like music. And if his afternoon reverie continued until the
light softened on the ochres and pinks of the little town on
the Adriatic, then the memories and meanings would
gradually acquire the vividness and depth that come only
when slipping the ropes of consciousness and casting off
into the stream of dreams.

He is uncomfortable in the smooth hide armchair, being
unable to either sink back or sit up straight. Fortunately, his
discomfort is not observed. It is dark, designer dark, in the
subterranean cocktail bar. Shadows move to and fro and
even the most innocent pairings have the air of a secret
rendezvous. Ultra-violet leaps violently from the napkin on

the table and the cuffs of his shirt and, for all he knows, the whites of his eyes. Why had he suggested the Nocturne Bar? He does not drink cocktails. He does not pay these prices. On the spur of the moment, it had been the only name that had come to him, and then only because a few months ago he had been invited here by a friend of his parents, visiting from Milan. He glances at the violet face of his watch. Already five minutes past. Obviously, she is not coming.

It is not the leather seat, or the weird light. He can be comfortable in his broken-backed wing chair or in the sagging bed of his rented apartment. He can be comfortable sitting on the folding metal chair with his espresso by the window that opens onto the windy fire escape. He can even be comfortable on a double-decker bus, or in a railway carriage once the possibility of boarding the wrong train is behind him and predictable, uninterruptible time stretches ahead. He shifts his position again. He should have sought out some casual, intimate little wine bar in Soho with check tablecloths and unmatched chairs. Not this desert of culti- vated gloom, this Mecca of meaningless sophistication with its sneering violet light and its never-ending adagios. Of course she would not come. He is also comfortable at his desk in his cupboard-like office on the fifth floor of a dingy post-war building in Holborn, his translations and proofs spread before him. There is even a kind of comfort in having his knee pressed up against the radiator that rumbles and shudders all day long and sometimes registers a tectonic clank that seems to connect him to the bones and bowels of the building.

He has a clear view of the entrance, but as new arrivals descend the stairs they become first silhouettes and then disembodied violet splashes. Even in daylight, he is not sure he would recognise her again. Even if she were to come.

And then why had he chosen this particular alcove, this darker corner of the darkness, the smoked-glass table lit only by unseen spotlights reflected in the bevelled edges of mirrors, bright slivers, mere glimpses and glances of light, gleaming from leather and chrome and glass?

Probably, he supposes, it is his inadequate English that inserts yet one more layer of discomfort between himself and this world, diverting his mind's energies into a cul-de-sac of panic at moments when dealing with the ordinary business of the world needs all his attention. Sometimes, panic even drives his utterances in directions he would not choose, following not what he wants to say but the grooves worn by words and phrases he feels confident of. And for one whose arms are ever circling wildly in the attempt to stay balanced in the company of others, the potential embarrassments of another language are enough to tip him over the edge.

Another silhouette descends the stairs, pauses for a moment to adjust to the unnatural light, and disappears into some recess. A table closer to the bar would have been better. Perhaps the theatre-lit ranks of exotic liquors might have made it easier to see. He drinks the melted ice water in his glass, not knowing whether he is anxious for her to arrive or not to arrive. Either way, he tells himself, as so often in his life, this time will pass. Come what may, in a few hours he will be safe in welcoming sleep. Of all the idioms he has come across in his English lessons, the one that has fastened itself upon him is about sleep knitting up the ravelled sleeve of care. The idea of it had struck him so viscerally that he thinks of it almost every night and often during the day. But any period of comfort, any hour of internal quiet, would do almost as well in the times when he needed knitting up. He had experimented with using 'ravelled' in conversation only to discover that it was no longer a word, or rather it had become 'unravelled', which meant the same thing, like valuable and invaluable, but not like valid and invalid. How could one cope?

A slim, fragmented figure is descending the stairs, pausing on the bottom step, lowering her head as if to look under the darkness; another soul about to cross the Styx into the artificial gloom. But she, too, heads towards a different alcove where her date is waving a lurid hand.

A waiter appears to retrieve his glass, the napkin over his arm a ghastly violet. He orders a second scotch on the rocks. To hell with his budget for the week.

Swallowing the last of his drink too quickly, he recognises the first seepings of internal gloom. It is not only the Nocturne and the language and the being far from home and the girl who is obviously not going to come. Even back in Comacchio, his islands of comfort had seemed to be shrinking, like mudflats in the lagoon as the tide rose. He had thought that being a grown-up would be a stable state and had not expected this lack of fit between himself and his world, the lack of cartilage to stop the bones of his life from grinding. He looks again at his watch.

The problem, he suspects, is the plethora of things that can only ever be understood at the margins: life's vast hinterland of uncertainties, of unknowns and half-knowns, he wilderness of the vaguely guessed-at and the dimly perceived, including the shadows and the mysteries of himself. It is the impossibility of the comprehensive. And, more than this, the lack of any robust framework, any consistent narrative by which to relate things together in a way that offers a degree of comfort, a moment's relief from the blood-tingle of anxiety. All this seemed to become clear to him as he waited in the darkness of the Nocturne Bar that night, a clarity distilled from the gloom of unsettled anticipation. Clear too, it seemed to him, that in his own case the seeds of confusion and uncertainty fell on especially fertile ground, a garden where grew luxurious tensions, thriving weeds, an excess of sensitivity. His second scotch is finished, and she has not come.

He checks the violet wristwatch for a last time. Does he want to see her descending the stairs, peering for him under the gloom? Of course he does. This is why he is here. And he found the courage to ask her because she had a lilt to her, a grace that he could not get out of his mind, and something in her eyes that could tilt his heart. Yet his level of discomfort would surely rise. There was another line from English literature that had struck home: 'To see things steadily and see things whole.' As soon as he had read the words and grasped their import, they had become a private ambition, a kind of Grail-yearning. What was to be implied here of the comfort he sought?

Another female silhouette descending the stairs. Another pause before she moves in his direction, splashing violet. The lights in their eyes meet and he brings both palms to the arms of the chair, preparing to rise. And then she is gone, passing into another darkness, the light in her eyes for someone else.

And it is there in that uneventful hour, waiting and not knowing, not knowing and waiting, that one of his guiding truths comes to him quietly, like the first approach of a gentle stranger who would become a friend. Your Grail is an illusion, his new friend whispers – a chimaera, a sweet siren song to lure you to frustration and disillusionment. To see things steadily and see things whole, his friend says, is not of this age. At best it was a nineteenth-century illusion, implying a single admissible perspective, an absurd notion

of all-seeing, and over-simplified, over-confident narrative
that can lead only to the unsatisfactory comforts of un-
founded certainties and self-satisfactions destined to topple,
with age, into all kinds of bigotry, bitterness and myopia.
Impossible, here in the artificial drama of the Nocturne
Bar, to see even the surfaces of the world either steadily or
whole. But here, or anywhere, it might be possible, even
now, to allow a more modest truth to find him, sit by his
side, take his hand, offer its comfort. Other lines from his
English literature brush against him as he makes his way
out. Though he had not been sure what it was that the poet
had been attempting to touch with such words, he had
known the truth of it; known that whatever it was would
'visit with inconstant glance each human heart and
countenance'.

And inconstant it proved over the years ahead. Grail
illusions had occasionally gleamed again in dark times,
beckoning him to deceitful shores. Because, compared to
seeing things steadily and seeing things whole, his own
seeing has often been uncomfortable, often troubled. But if
he will allow himself a quantum of quiet, allow the ravelled
sleeve to be knitted up, his true friend will wordlessly take
his hand.

All these decades later, out on his wrought-iron balcony
overlooking the canal with the salt air of the lagoon in his
nostrils, he still thinks of that night in London. There had
been no Eureka, only a gradual and partial resolution. The
sharpest discomforts had of course been worn and
softened, like the lettering on much-polished brass. He had
learnt eventually that there are few humiliations from
which it is impossible to recover, few weaknesses of
character and of will that cannot be battled to the point of

self-forgiveness. But those deeper disturbances, those deeper instabilities of self and perception, had taken a little longer. And would take a little longer still.

Below him, the late afternoon light reflects gently from the canal like a second sky. Fifty metres to his right, under the Ponte degli Sbirri, a broad-beamed eel boat is ferrying the day's tourists back from the lagoon. He watches the boatman lean against the rudder, turning the craft in a wide slow arc, rippling the reflection of the bridge that, a moment ago, had been as steady as the bridge itself. A low, unhindered sun falls on the mellow brickwork of the Trepponti, glowing as quietly as sleep. He had, for the most part, moved beyond wholeness as a need. The quest for understanding was undimmed, but with age he had seen that maturity did not demand a fixed view of himself or others, of his past or his future or his world. A re-direction of effort had followed, so that eventually he had learnt something of the art of rewriting his own story into a forgiving, acceptable truth; he had seen that the variants of the story are not competing versions of reality but rather instruments of self-improvement. Knowledge must always be fresh, he has decided, must constantly be perceived anew, even in age. He is tempted to believe that knowledge must always be made up. And, looking back, it was sometimes possible to perceive a certain wholeness. Or at least a satisfaction that had not been evident at the time. A harmony of sorts.

His grandson runs out onto the balcony holding a birthday present, a phone, which he points downwards to take a picture of the painted boats moored below. His father follows, kneeling behind the boy, showing him how to keep the picture steady by resting the phone on the iron rail.

❖

The Institute

THE SPITTLE SIZZLED and was gone. Underneath the church, the cellar was heavy with gloom. At the foot of the steps leading up to the street, one bare bulb gave just enough light to make out a pair of shrouded shapes, like outsize coffins placed end to end.

Tingle stood the smoothing iron on end and turned off the gas ring.

Leaving the kitchen, he approached the first of the shrouds and began folding its edges towards the middle. It was eery to be alone in the cellar, entombed in a crypt of silence when just a few steps away all was daylight and the noise of the street. He began tugging the dust sheet from one end, making a new fold with each tug.

When both sheets had been made into neat packages, he forced a shilling into the meter and gave the key a solid half-turn. A 'clunk' from behind told him the lights had come on and he turned to see, instead of the sepulchral darkness, the brilliant green paradise of the two billiard tables.

Taking the ten-inch brush from the cupboard, he began sweeping the first table, working with the nap and using the tuft of longer bristles to reach fragments of chalk hiding under the cushions. Galaxies of dust rose under the lamps, following his progress, passing through the trapezoid of light and on into the darkness beyond.

Arthur Tingle was pot-bellied and bandy-legged and struggled to reach the centre of the table, his bald head gleaming with the effort. His teeth were stained with tea and tobacco and a slight droop to one side of his mouth gave him an odd permanent grin that wasn't always appropriate. By day, he wore a buttoned white coat to steer his milk float over the cobbles and under the washing lines of the Conways and the Fearnvilles. For billiards nights, he wore a yellow flannel waistcoat with a colourless silk back and half-belt.

Back in the kitchen, he wetted a finger and touched it to the flat of the iron. The slight hiss being just right, he carried it to the first of the tables and began a series of long, slow passes from the baulk end.

Tingle had been married once, but these days he lived alone in a scullery house in the Bayswaters with a coal chute from the street and a fireback boiler. Maureen had known how to use the oven and the damper, just as she had known how to iron shirts. When they had met, at the Saturday dance class above the Astoria, she had been even more shy and awkward than he. They had both known that they were not attractive, and they had not been in love. He had proposed because, after a while, it seemed possible that she might accept him; she had said yes out of embarrassment, and out of thinking, like him, that no one else would be likely to ask.

Standing back to inspect the newly ironed billiard cloth was the best of times – perfect in the evenness of its green lit by the huge Hartley shade that cast light only on the six-foot by twelve-foot field of play, leaving the rest of the world to darkness.

He returned the smoothing iron to the kitchen and unlocked the black metal cue case hanging on the members' rack. Pulling the bottom end away from the wall, he drew out his father's cue.

From his pocket, he took a small square of towelling and ran it up and down the shaft. Maureen had gradually become more confident as the years went by; more likely to put herself forward. The part-time job at Timothy Whites & Taylors hadn't paid much, but she was an organised woman and when she had been made up to manageress her wage packet had been bulkier than his.

Placing the spot ball in the centre of the 'D', he took the cube of chalk from his waistcoat pocket and stood for a moment, holding the block delicately between thumb and first finger, caressing the tip of the cue. He, too, had tried to better himself by enrolling at the night school on Barrack Road, but studying had come just as hard as it had at the Secondary Modern and he had not managed to pass his City and Guilds. One of the men at the depot had told him Maureen was living with a travelling salesman in a semi-detached off Easterly Road.

He splayed his outstretched hand on the cloth, making a firm bridge between thumb and index finger. The wedding ring gleamed under the lights as he struck the white up the board, staring after it along the length of the cue, watching with fascination as the ball travelled obediently to the top cushion and began its journey back. He still polished the shields and cups that his father and he had won over the years. And the chromium biscuit barrel where he kept his shillings for the meter.

He remained down in position, chin resting on the cue. The weight of shot had to be perfect if the white were to come to rest back at its starting point. And it had to be struck dead centre or it would come back from the cushion at an angle. He was within an inch or two after a couple of attempts, getting a feel for the pace of the cloth and the heft of the cue. His father had used this cue, an eighteen-ounce Walter Lindrum Special with the rosewood and ebony butt. Tingle Senior had thought he would never play again after being blinded by the chlorine gas. After the war, he had been a man of even fewer words and, if moved to parental advice, the words had usually come from the Book of Proverbs: 'Ponder the path of thy feet'. Or from Robbie Burns: 'A good name is rather to be preferred than great riches.' Eventually, he had recovered to play top board for the British Legion.

Tingle placed the white back on its spot and played a couple of three-cushion shots to the bottom left pocket, getting comfortable with the angles. The waistcoat was only for billiards nights, and he would not have risked it at all if he had not himself been top board man at the Institute.

By eight o'clock the cellar was full, both tables in action and the names of those waiting to play chalked up on the slate. It was team practice night and Tingle was first up, playing Tommy Bettles. Tommy played off scratch. Tingle owed fifty. It was a lot to make up, but after five minutes he had closed the gap to thirty points. Tommy was at the table now, biting his lip as he contemplated taking on a long pot. Tingle Senior hadn't believed in handicapping – 'Limits the ambitions, lad'. But Tingle liked having to give start to every other player in the Institute. And it wasn't as if the billiards didn't want brain-power: shot selection, planning ahead, estimating odds, weighing what you'd gain if you made the shot against what you'd leave if you didn't. Even the parson, the one evening he had spent in the Institute, had been able to see that it was a mental game as well.

Tommy made the long pot and Tingle took his seat. A couple of new members had chalked their names up tonight. One wore chromium sleeve bands and a tie tucked into his shirt front. The other was a Charles somebody, six-foot-something with deep comb-lines in his hair. Tingle had seen him at the church social, chatting with the parson. There were two children, who might have been twins, and an attractive wife who had worn hot pants to the church outing to Hornsea. Tingle had been silently opposed to opening the club to men who didn't go to the church, but the new parson had argued that instead of the church being a way into the Institute, the Institute might be a way into the church.

Tommy played a thin in-off and looked set for an easy cannon off the top cushion. Tingle took out the square of towelling and wiped between his fingers. He supposed the parson must be right. There were two middle-aged widows at the church. He had tried to talk to one of them at the fish-and-chip supper after the whist drive but the conversation had not gone anywhere.

Tommy broke down at sixteen and Tingle was on his feet, an eagerness in his step that was not to be seen the rest of the week. Low over the cue, mouth slightly open, eyes darting up and down, cue-ball to object-ball, object-ball to cue-ball, he made an easy pot into the middle pocket. Impatient for the red to be re-spotted, he played a half-ball in-off to the top left, bringing the red back down below the middle for another in-off.

Tingle relaxed when he missed a cannon by a whisker. The arrears had been wiped off and he had his nose in front. For himself, he wouldn't have felt right playing at the

Institute without going to the church. He was not religious. Too many unanswered questions. Too many unanswered prayers. But it was somewhere to go, something to belong to. So he mimed his way through the hymns, placed his envelope in the felt-lined plate every week and helped make the scenery for the nativity. He had heard that religious people had happier lives and he supposed that must be right. Why wouldn't you be happier if you thought God was looking out for you?

When Tommy missed an easy pot, Tingle made another eighteen. The game on table two looked to be coming to an end as well. He chalked his cue.

And another thing – why wouldn't you be happier if you believed instead of dying you lived forever in a better place than this? He blew sharply two or three times on the cue tip as he watched Tommy lose position. But for Tingle, it wasn't the bit about everlasting life that appealed. It was the bit about knocking and being admitted; the bit about the meek inheriting the earth and the lowest being made highest and the despised being seated at the right hand of God. Only he didn't think he really believed that either. Any more than he believed 'The honest man, though ne'er so poor, is king o' men for a' that.'

Tommy was having trouble stringing more than three or four shots together tonight and Tingle was soon back at the table. Five minutes later, two or three slow thuds on the floor from the butt of Tommy's cue acknowledged a two-cushion cannon that took his break into the thirties. He had to stretch for his next shot and imagined the other men seeing his head glowing like a Belisha beacon under the lights of the table. He missed the cannon and let Tommy in. Baxter at the Deaf and Dumb kept his cap on, but Tingle didn't think he could risk that.

He took his seat and watched his opponent make a straightforward in-off white to leave himself just behind the red on the top cushion. Tingle understood the billiards, felt at ease with the interplay of angles and weight of shot, the fine degrees of stun and side and follow through. It had subtleties but not mysteries. There was no shifting of perspectives. No wondering what the rules might be today. No questions staring back at him. The crystallite balls and the cushions and the slate bed passed their judgements, but their responses were consistent, and they treated all men as equals. Earlier in the season, he had broken his own club record with a break of seventy-eight; good for the Non-Conformist League, though a long way short of what the best could do. Sometimes, on a Saturday morning, he took the bus into town on the chance that Les Driffield and Willie Smith might be practising at Nelson's. Smith would make a break of three or four hundred and then attempt some impossible shot just to give his opponent board time.

When the A-team had played their matches, Tingle busied himself with the potted-meat and fish-paste sandwiches. It was the beginning of his uneasy time when the lights went up and the chatter began, leaving behind the world where the light fell only on the tables and there was no sound save for the soothing click of the billiard balls.

He finished handing round the sandwiches and looked for something else to do. Tommy was telling the others about his new job at Burton's where one of the machine-shop managers had served in the same unit. Quite a few of the members were ex-servicemen. Kenny Musgrave had been at Monte Cassino and moved himself around the tables with a heavy limp. Harold Hayworth had been torpedoed in the Atlantic. Freddy Hainstock had been bomber crew and had been 'in the drink'.

'How's the day job, Arthur?'

Kenny asked him this same question every week. Tingle had heard all the milkman jokes but couldn't understand why others found his occupation amusing. He had made things worse by letting slip that he took a boy's size twelve in shoes and that the pair he wore on billiards night had a tiny flip-out compass in the heel. 'Which way's north, Arthur?' had been Kenny's club-night greeting ever since. Tingle himself had volunteered for the RAF but had been assigned to a supply division and had spent the war in Aldershot.

There was the tea urn to be tilted and drained and the team sheet to be sent round to check availability for Friday's match against Hunslet Temps. He supposed he should take the teasing in good part, but what he wanted, what he craved, was to be not a figure of fun but a man among men. Tingle Senior had been a life-long union man and shop steward at Braime's. 'Solidarity, lad. Solidarity and pride o' worth.' A few years ago, Tingle had applied for the job supervising the loading bay at the dairy but they'd given it to Bob Little, the polite Jamaican lad who'd been to college and always looked sad.

Tingle went to check the club cupboard again. As well as the Empire brush and the iron, there were half a dozen spare tips and two or three paper-wrapped towers of chalk. Tucked away at the back was a copy of the B&SCC rule book like the one he kept under the biscuit barrel at home. The only other book he owned was 'Every Schoolboy's Pocket Book' for 1936 with the fold-out map of the world showing country after country shaded in red. His father hadn't said it in as many words, but he had made it obvious through the years that being British put you pretty much at the top of the tree – that you were somebody even before you got out of bed in the morning, especially if you were a husband and father as well. 'The man's the 'ead of the 'ousehold, lad, be 'e ne'er so 'umble.' Tingle closed the cupboard. Half a dozen rack cues were leaned up against the wall waiting to be re-tipped.

Second-team practice was finishing now and it was time for the rabbits to have their turn at the tables. Reg Parsons was racking up the reds for a snooker doubles that would probably take a fair while to finish. Reg himself could play a bit. But Billy Hainstock liked to hear the balls smack the back of the pockets and was forever out of position. Freddy, Billy's brother, could never remember what came after the yellow. Johnny Boothroyd was keen, but he was another one who seemed to think the point of the game was to get all the balls on the table moving at the same time. Match night on Friday was the next thing to look forward to. It was an away fixture and the six of them would be steering their cue cases up the stairs to the top deck of the bus so they could get up a fug on the way to the Temperance.

The next two names on the slate were Brian Nevett, the 'C' team skipper, and Charles, one of the new members. Tingle lit a cigarette and took one of the pull-down seats where he could follow the games on both tables. In the dimness around the walls of the cellar were men he sat next to every week, at the Institute, or in church, or on the top deck of the bus. But they dwelt in the shadows of his understanding, their easy way with each other an impenetrable mystery, the centre of a maze he could not find.

'Right, boys,' said Tommy Bettles, producing a coin, 'let's be seein' what you're made of.'

Charles won the toss and broke off. He had apparently
played a bit in the army and looked like he could handle a
cue. For the first couple of weeks, he'd be playing off
scratch until the handicap committee had a look at him. He
was down over the table now, chin on cue, a gold neck
chain looping close to the fine West of England cloth. His
arm was stretched out under the light and scar tissue
glowed red in the gap above the Desert Rat cuff links. His
wife was a regular at church and the two children attended
the Sunday School but Tingle had never seen Charles at a
service, morning or evening. He sometimes wondered
what Maureen was doing; whether she still wore his
mother's brooch, whether she still bought all her clothes in
Schofield's sale, whether she smiled more now. Whether
she ever wondered what he was doing.

On his second visit to the table, Charles made a break of
forty-two, breaking down only when risking a long pot. He
had been counting on the nap of the cloth to keep the red
tight to the side cushion until it dropped into the bottom
pocket, not realising that the cloth on table two had been
turned a couple of years back.

Tingle got up from his seat and went to the kitchen. He
slipped off the waistcoat and hung it on the back of the
door while he rinsed plates in the sink. The clicking of the
balls was less soothing now, and his separation from the
tables felt as cold as exile. He started the drying up,
stacking the half-pint mugs on the rack above the gas ring.
His father would not have approved of the silk waistcoat
anyway: 'Gie fools their silks and knaves their wine, a
man's a man for a' that.' The rubber tube to the gas ring
was perished and wanted replacing.

The drumming of a cue butt on the lino took him back to
look through the serving hatch as a jeer went up to greet a

fluke on table one. Above table two, the brass sliders showed seventy-nine to thirteen. The newcomer must have scored another thirty-some while Tingle was drying pots. Brian missed a regulation pot into the centre, bringing Charles back to the table where he stood for a moment, weighing up options, the cue held confidently between his scarred hands. The way he stood, in fact everything about him, spoke of a man with an enthusiasm for getting up in the morning. He played an in-off with enough check side to leave him a top-board cannon followed, presumably, by another in-off to top left. Tingle leaned his elbows on the shelf below the hatch and watched the new man build his break, moving silently around the table in black leather moccasins with a fringe across the front. When he got into the thirties again, he fluked a red off the angle of the middle pocket and tapped his cue on the edge of the table in apology.

Tingle emptied the sink and turned off the tap but left the waistcoat on the back of the chair. From the club cupboard, he took out the fine-grade sandpapers and the spare cue tips. Baldock tips were the best, with three separate layers so they didn't tend to spread. There had even been talk of an open night when the Women's Institute would be invited in to have a go. Tingle gathered up the half-dozen cues waiting to be re-tipped. He didn't expect to be seated at the right hand of God. But he had liked wearing the yellow waistcoat with the silk back and half-belt.

❖

The Unposted Letter

W HEN I CLIMB INTO THE ATTIC of my mother's house, a few days after the funeral, it feels like climbing into the past. There in the gloom is the standard lamp that had stood in the corner of our front room for all my childhood, its fringed shade still at the tilt. Under the eaves, there is the brass jam pan and the two-bar electric fire, missing its plug, that had been brought down only on the coldest of winter nights. Tugging at a dust sheet reveals our first television, a fourteen-inch Ferguson on whose bulging screen we had watched the Coronation. Moving aside boxes of fabric lengths and rolls of viscose linings, I find the stack of board games – Flounders, Ludo, Monopoly – and the tin with the Woodbine playing cards and the dice still in the chipped egg cup.

My mother had lived to be almost ninety. For most of those years, she had made ends meet on a war widow's pension and what she could earn as a seamstress in our back room. In my memories, she is forever bent over sewing machine or ironing board, pursed lips gripping a row of pins or bared teeth snapping a thread as she sews cocktail dresses and ball gowns for women who pay little and always come back. All of these memories, I realise, have the same sound-track: it is the thrum of the old Singer, stopping and starting, stopping and starting, as her splayed fingers stretch the material tight under the chattering needle.

Against the back wall is a sewing box full of part-used cotton reels, dressmakers' chalks, darning mushrooms, packets of Butterick dress patterns and a pair of pinking shears. Here, too, I find the dimpled velvet pouffe that I always hated and the canteen of 'best' cutlery that, as far as I know, was never used.

From an alcove, I pull out three Florsheim shoeboxes, their cardboard lids split at the corners. I push them to the side of the pouffe, which heaves a sigh of dust as I sit. In the first there are old photographs, sepia relatives in their Sunday best standing stiffly beside potted palms and a few holiday snaps taken by promenade photographers - 'ready to collect by 4pm tomorrow'. The rest of the box is all about me: my first drawings in crayon on sugar paper, my first attempts at writing, all of my school reports in their yellow 'Only to be opened by the parent or guardian' envelopes, some newspaper cuttings of my modest sporting achieve-ments and all the home-made birthday and Christmas cards I had ever given her. The second box holds a dozen Sharp & Thornton rent books, a handwritten list of her customers' telephone numbers, and a set of Yorkshire Penny Bank savings books with the corners snipped off.

At the very bottom of the box is a plain brown envelope. I unwind the wheel-and-string fastening and take out her wedding certificate, my own birth certificate, and the Post Office telegram that I have never seen before and that I read now with tears in my eyes: 'D3/NED/742 □ REGRET REPORT PRIVATE FREDERICK FIRTH KILLED IN ACTION NORTH AFRICA □ CONFIRMATION FOLLOWS □ ARTILLERY RECORDS □ SIDCUP.'

The last of the boxes seems to have been for things she hadn't known what to do with – an order of service from Aunty Ivy's funeral at Ashley Road Methodist, a book of dialect poems that had belonged to my grandmother, a set of pearl buttons sewn onto a card, and the programme for a performance of *The Merry Widow* at the open-air theatre in Scarborough. It is among these odds and ends that I come across a much newer-looking envelope addressed to a 'Mr. S. R. Exley, The Secretary, Garforth, Kippax & District University of the Third Age'. The envelope is sealed and the stamp is of recent issue.

I set it aside with the other papers to be looked at later, along with much else that I decide to keep for no other reason than not wishing to throw away things that so recently had meaning.

The weeks passed and the boxes I had brought home remained at the bottom of my wardrobe. When I eventually made a start, I wondered why I had bothered to keep so much. Among the books was a New English Bible, a boxed set of Readers Digest Condensed Classics, and a dozen Mills and Boon paperbacks with titles like *Leftover Love*, *The Tempestuous Flame* and *Sweet Compulsion*. It was as I was putting these into a box for the charity shop that a folded green card fell from one of the paperbacks. I was about to drop it in the bin with the other oddments Mum had used as bookmarks – old receipts and shopping lists, a postcard from a cousin in Colwyn Bay – when my eye fell on the heading: 'The University of the Third Age'. Noticing that one of the paragraphs had been underlined, I took the card to the window and saw that it was a flyer for a lecture by Terrence R Fielding, MacMillan Professor of Social Statistics at Leeds Metropolitan University. The event had taken place almost two years previously at the Compton Road library and its subject had been 'Are Women Happier for Being Equal?'

It seemed most unlikely that Mum had attended the lecture, or that the underlining was hers. As far as I knew, she had never enrolled in classes of any kind, or ever read a book that wasn't romantic fiction.

I had always known she was clever. In her box of souvenirs, I had come across her final school report from Sweet Street Primary: 'Dora is an exceptionally bright pupil who would have benefited from staying on'. The report, signed by 'Miss E. Hazeldene, headmistress,' was dated 12 July 1929, when Mum would have been coming up to thirteen. After that, she had worked at a haberdasher's, been married, widowed, given birth, and thereafter – when she wasn't sewing all day and late into the night – she was cleaning or cooking or baking, or darning the elbows of my school pullovers, or working the mangle in the cellar, or pegging out sheets on the line across the street, and still finding time to scour the doorstep once a week 'to keep us respectable'. Only in retirement had she come into a little leisure, and by then who could blame her for settling down with the television soaps and *Leftover Love*.

I was about to throw the flyer away when I again caught sight of the heading - 'The University of the Third Age'. And only then did I remember.

In the last box that remained unopened at the bottom of my wardrobe, I found the unposted envelope. Inside was a second envelope and a single-page letter neatly written in the familiar hand:

Dear Mr Exley,
I will be much obliged if you will send the enclosed letter on to Professor Fielding who gave a very interesting talk last

*Thursday week at Compton Road library that I came to with
my friend Mrs Shirley Sutton who is one of your members. I
hope this will cause you no inconvenience. I have put a 10p
stamp on.*
Yours sincerely,
Dora Firth

My phone rang and I had to leave in a hurry to cover for
a colleague who had called in sick, leaving me to wonder
what was in the letter and why my mother, who had never
had the confidence to attend parents' evenings at any of
my schools or to speak to any of my teachers, should at the
age of nearly ninety be writing to a university professor.
And, having gone to the trouble of writing it, why had it
not been posted? These questions couldn't have any significance now. But they nagged at me for the rest of the day,
as even small things do when they can't be reconciled with
the world as you have always known it.

During break, I looked up the University of the Third Age.
As I had thought, it wasn't an official educational institu-
tion but a voluntary organisation of retired people who
arranged lectures for themselves on subjects ranging from
Genealogy for Beginners to The Art of the Japanese
Garden. It still didn't sound like Mum's thing, though I
could just about picture her being cajoled into it by Shirley
Sutton – 'Aunty Shirley' as I had always known her – who
was forever telling Mum she needed to 'get out of the
house' and persuading her to go on coach trips to Temple
Newsam or the Valley Gardens.

I opened the letter as soon as I got home. It was closely
written on both sides in the joined-up 'real writing' she had
learned at Sweet Street Primary and had changed little since.

Dear Professor Fielding,
I hope you will forgive me for wanting to write to you about
your talk at the Compton Road Library a week last Thursday
evening. I came with my friend Mrs Sutton and we both said
afterwards how interesting it was. I am writing this because I
wanted to ask you a question but I have never opened my
mouth in public before and was not able to at the time.

I finished the rest of the letter and read it through again. The only explanation I could think of for it not being posted was that confidence had failed her at the last. I imagined her licking the stamp and her tired face came to me with a sudden, tender clarity.

Another search revealed that Professor Terrence R Fielding had given the same lecture at several other chapters of the University of the Third Age over the past year and was scheduled to give it again the following month in the Garden Room of The Mansion in Roundhay Park, a short bus ride from where I lived.

It was unusual, these days, to find myself one of the youngest in a crowd. I seated myself at the back and took in the audience of perhaps two hundred people. Mum would not, I thought, have been comfortable amid the competing airs of perfume and the confident chatter about foreign holidays. Perhaps it had been different at Compton Road Library.

Fielding himself turned out to be a stout, waistcoated figure who hadn't been able to resist the trope of half-moon spectacles and loosely knotted bow-tie. But he seemed affable enough as he sat smiling modestly through the Secretary's introduction. I imagined Mum in my place, back straight, lips firmly closed, gripping the green flyer in her lap and worrying that she might be the only one wearing a hat.

The professor had his laptop open on a lectern and the portable screen behind was already displaying the title of his lecture. What he had to say this evening, he informed us when he took the podium, was based on longitudinal data stretching back to the 1960s and drawn from randomized sample surveys of women's self-reported life satisfaction in half a dozen OECD countries. Here, he paused to scan his audience with the practised speaker's habit of making eye contact with random individuals. 'The significance of this,' he continued, 'is that it makes it possible for the first time to evaluate forty years of women's liberation in terms of women's overall happiness with life.'

He lingered for a while on methodologies and variables that needed to be controlled for, but this seemed to me not so much scholarly thoroughness as statistical striptease, building audience anticipation for the big reveal. Several slides of graphs and bar charts came and went, their meaning illuminated by the play of the laser pointer, until the professor waved dismissively at the screen and turned to face his audience.

'Cutting to the chase, ladies and gentlemen, what we can see from these data is that over the past forty years there has been a small but statistically significant decline in the proportion of women who report that their lives are "very happy" or "happy" and a corresponding rise in the proportion describing themselves as "unhappy" or "very unhappy". In other words, the available evidence shows that, at the population level, women are not as content with their lives today as they were in the 1960s when the movement for women's liberation first began to achieve real traction.'

It is possible that I was imagining it, but I had noticed on other occasions that the inner responses of an audience can seem to make themselves felt through some kind of social osmosis. And in the audience in the Garden Room that evening, I sensed a great, elderly, male collective sigh of 'I told you so'.

Questions had been queuing up at the back of my mind, but Mum was still front and centre. It would have been the first time in her life that she had been invited to draw conclusions from a bar chart. But it would not have mattered. She was easily intimidated socially and tense to the point of anxiety when she felt she was no longer among those of her own class; yet it was one of the strange things about her that, despite her lack of education, she could not easily be intimidated intellectually. I had first realised this in my sixth-form and university years when, coming home full of myself and my new-found insights, I had often found that her common-sense questions had put those insights to a sterner test than my tutors. And this was how I imagined her now, sitting here beside me in her red wool coat and black beret, torn between social anxiety and intellectual rebellion, twisting the green flyer in her hands.

The professor had switched the projector back on and was about to continue. 'By any and all historical standards' – here he looked down and prodded the laptop – 'one would have to concede that women's progress towards equality in only two generations has been nothing short of spectacular.' Another slide had appeared and the bright red dot of the laser began to dither over a succession of bullet points: 'access to higher education and birth control, career choice and economic independence, reform of divorce and abortion laws, increasing representation at all levels of commerce and governance.'

'But is it not worthy of inquiry,' he asked, returning the pointer to the lectern, 'is it not worthy of inquiry that such unprecedented progress appears to have brought not only no increase but in all probability a modest decline in overall levels of life satisfaction?'

The coy rhetorical question grated, and I prided myself on already having spotted several possible objections to the professor's thesis. I was also pretty sure that Mum would have spotted them too. But it was just such objections that the professor now moved to pre-empt. It was the part of the evening that he clearly enjoyed the most.

'Some of you may be thinking,' he said, 'that the answer to this apparent paradox is what my feminist colleagues like to call "the double shift". In other words, they see declining well-being as a consequence of increasing responsibilities *outside* the home not being accompanied by any corresponding decrease in responsibilities *inside* the home.'

And again it seemed possible to sense that stirring of recognition and assent on behalf of many of the women in the audience. For myself, I was struggling to imagine what the professor's words would have meant to one who had never heard of 'the double shift' but who had worked it most of her life.

Fielding paused to allow his audience to bask for a moment in the warmth of consensus. Then, with a mischievous glance over the top of his spectacles, he very slowly shook his head. 'Unfortunately' – and here he held up both palms as if to stem the tide of agreement flowing his way – 'unfortunately this eminently plausible explanation is not supported by the available evidence.'

The statement seemed to produce a drop in temperature in the room as the audience waited to hear how this could be.

'Because if this explanation were correct,' he went on, as if the conclusion were giving him considerable pain, 'then one might reasonably expect to find self-reported happiness levels declining more sharply among those women with domestic responsibilities who also have employment outside the home.' Here, the pointer went into action again and danced us through the statistics that did indeed show that the decline in life satisfaction held true for all women and not just those presumed to be working 'the double shift'.

He then repeated the trick. 'The other explanation that I'm sure will already have occurred to you all,' he said, 'is that the past forty years have also been years of soaring divorce rates. Is it not likely, therefore, that this accounts for at least some of the observed decline in life satisfaction?'

His audience was not about to be caught out twice and wisely withheld its assent until the next slide appeared. And sure enough, the professor was also able to dismiss this explanation with a wave of his pointer over a chart showing the same decline in life satisfaction whether or not women reported being divorced.

I had now to admit that both of my own immediate objections had been headed off at the pass. And I also had to admire the way the professor had entertained his audience by playing us along, allowing opinion to run free before reeling us into the data.

Taking his time now, he reached to switch off the projector, closed the laptop delicately with the fingertips of both hands, and stepped out from behind the lectern. In this more intimate pose, he brought the lecture to its conclusion.

'Ladies and gentlemen of the Third Age, when such plausible but ultimately incorrect explanations are ruled out, we would appear to be left with an enigma, a conundrum, a mystery. And that mystery might be encapsulated as follows' – he brought the tips of his fingers together – 'why is it that such impressive progress towards equality does not seem to have made women happier or more satisfied with their lives?'

There followed another pause, during which the professor's expression seemed to imply that he shared in the general mystification. 'Unfortunately,' he said, seeming to stir himself and raising both hands with a little shrug, 'the statistics available to us at this time cannot tell us the answer. They can only tell us what the answer is not.' Here, he performed a remarkable little perambulation around the podium before returning to the same spot and again facing his audience.

'It is of course possible,' he said, 'that some of you may feel that the findings I have presented here this evening give rise to the question of whether "equality" was what the majority of women wanted in the first place. Any such conclusion is of course furiously resisted by my feminist colleagues. For myself, I'm afraid I couldn't possibly comment.'

The applause was long and trailed off into a rising murmur of long-suppressed opinion as the Secretary announced that the professor would be taking questions after a short break for the refreshments now available in the foyer.

I made my way through the crowd to the entrance hall. Outside, the cold struck and I pulled a scarf from my bag. A few others had also stepped outside to stand between the blackened pillars of the portico, their cigarettes glowing here and there in the darkness. Somewhere down there in the night was the arena where I had raced track bikes in long-ago summers. Mum had sometimes come up on the tram to watch, sitting out on Hill Sixty with her Bourbon biscuits and a flask of tea. I think now that she came because she imagined that's what a father would have done. The scarf had been her last present to me, a soft blue cashmere, more expensive than she could afford.

The Mansion doors opened, allowing the murmur of many voices to escape from the bar as two more couples came out onto the terrace. Above, the red-and-white lights of a plane, probably from Yeadon, blinked their way across the night sky. I don't know why Mum had not married again, or made any friends, or sought company of any kind. Over the years, I had seen the isolation take its toll. The lubricants of conversation seemed to have dried up so that even a 'how are you?' or a 'thank you' had sometimes not occurred to her. She had rarely initiated an exchange and often failed to respond in the conventional ways or even to smile when that might have been expected. Others had perhaps mistaken this for surliness, but I knew that her silences meant only that she had nothing in particular to say and was out of practice at saying nothing. Shirley Sutton had thought her stubborn because she would not be persuaded to join a book group or an exercise class. But it had seemed to me that this was nothing more than a simple refusal to any longer do things she did not want to do. She had pedalled unremittingly all her life and now what she wanted was to freewheel, to coast to her standstill. She enjoyed her food and her endless cups of tea and her television serials, and I know she looked forward to her visits and holidays with me. But perhaps most of all she enjoyed the simple, unaccustomed pleasure of not having much to do and not having to do much. A few years ago, I had asked my adult-education class to bring along a favourite poem and one woman, recently retired, had chosen the anonymous nineteenth-century poem 'On a Tired Housewife'. To my embarrassment, I had found myself in sudden tears when she read out the final couplet: 'Don't mourn for me now, don't mourn for me never, I am going to do nothing for ever and ever.'

It would not have been everybody's way, but in retirement Mum had seemed far more contented than most people of her age. Or any age. It was unusual, her capacity for contentment, and in many ways I suppose a blessing. But I also thought I understood that it was a contentment bought at a cost. The cost of abandoning dreams. The cost of a lifetime of lowered expectations, of narrowing the gaps between aspiration and reality wherein discontentment breeds.

I took the unposted letter from my inside pocket and brought it to one of the globe lights on the edge of the terrace. Through the window, I could see the professor, glass in hand, surrounded by Third Agers. I had come this evening to see what it was that had caused Mum to step so far out of her own life as to write to him. I brought the letter closer to the light.

Your diagrams showed young women are not as happy as they were in my day and I remember you said that this was taken from what women had said when they were asked. What I wanted to say but couldn't at the time was that I think I might have been one of those women who was asked all those years ago. It was one tea-time when a young woman knocked at the door and said did I have two minutes to answer some questions. She wouldn't have any tea but sat herself down in our front room and I remember she asked if I was contented with my life and I had to say between 1 and 10. I said 'put 8' and I remember after I told her this and she left and I closed the

door to the street I went back to the front room and sat down
and cried and that was something I had never done in all the
years. Why had I said my life was an 8?

When I told my friend who lives two doors down she said she
had given herself a 9. She said if you had your health and a
home and a husband and children you'd be shamed to say you
were a 6 or a 7. Then she said she was sorry because she knew
I hadn't got a husband. So you see in those days it was what
you said. Mamie Singleton in the next street told me she'd said
she was a 9 as well and she was always round our house
crying. So nowadays if a woman says she's a 6 or a 7 I think
it might be because they can tell the truth. Do you think that
is possible? I do. I think if women are only a 6 or a 7 instead
of an 8 or a 9 like they said before then this might mean they
can say what they really feel and I think that is good.

I hope all this does not sound silly. You explained everything
on Thursday but all the time I was thinking it didn't seem
right to put a generation like mine that was brought up not to
complain next to what today's young people have to say for
themselves. I wanted to just mention it because I don't think
staying at school and having all the openings we never had has
made women unhappier.

I hope you will not mind me writing to you like this.

Yours sincerely

Dora Firth

I looked up through my tears into the darkness of the
park. Way out there, I thought I could see moonlight on
Waterloo Lake. Mum told me it had been dug out when
Lord somebody-or-other had hired unemployed men
returning from the wars against Napoleon. She had always
felt for the jobless, always voted for the Labour Party with
no more analysis than 'it's for people like us'. But, like many

of her generation, she had also revered Churchill because he 'saw us through'. Hearing 'Winnie' criticised was one of the few things that could provoke her, not only because of her esteem for him but because it affronted the narrative by which she understood the times she had lived through.

My thoughts were wandering now and I found myself alone on the terrace. Through the window, I could see the professor adjusting his microphone. I returned to my seat as hands were being raised all around the Garden Room.

The next half hour was occupied by members of the audience not so much asking questions as volunteering long-held convictions. The professor accepted each contribution with good grace before answering the question he would like to have been asked. It wasn't hard to understand the appeal of the University of the Third Age, although probably not all of the speakers would be as good as Fielding. Just at the moment, though, he was struggling with an awkward question from a woman who wanted to know why he had given men credit for 'helping more around the house' when no one ever spoke of women 'helping around the house'. He dealt with this handsomely by pleading guilty. I raised my hand.

'Gentleman at the back in the blue scarf.'

Accustomed though I am to public speaking, I experienced something of my mother's anxieties as I came to my feet, letter in hand. But also something of her spirit. Dora Firth, widow not of this parish, was about to speak in public for the first time.

❖

Boiled Egg with Rosie

N O ONE HAD EVER ACCUSED Martin of being a new man. In his forty-eight years, he had never changed a nappy, ironed a shirt, or cleaned a loo. Nor had he boiled an egg until that Friday in April when he had opened up his laptop to look into black holes, a topic much in the news that week.

For the first few minutes, as Rosie cooked dinner, he wrestled with the gravitational effects of invisible forces. But half a dozen promiscuous clicks on ever more tenuous links eventually brought him to a YouTube video on how to boil an egg. Most people, he learned, had no idea how to boil an egg. Or at least not a properly boiled egg. The problem, it appeared, was that the different kinds of protein in an egg were in the habit of congealing at different temperatures, making it tricky to cook the yolk to the point of perfect runni-ness without overcooking the white to the point of imperfect rubberiness. The solution, he gathered, was not to boil the egg at all. Instead, it should be placed in a small pan with enough cold water to cover it by precisely one millimetre. Then, once brought to the boil, the pan should be removed from the heat and left to stand for exactly six minutes.

Twenty minutes later, when Rosie called through from the kitchen to say that dinner was ready, Martin had learnt relatively little about ripples in the fabric of space-time but a great deal about boiling an egg.

On the Saturday morning he came downstairs damp and pink from the shower and announced: 'I'll make breakfast, love. Could you fancy a boiled egg?'

Laptop open on the kitchen surface, smartwatch counting down, he began opening kitchen cupboards in search of egg cups.

'This is perfect, love,' said Rosie, dipping a finger of burnt toast into a yolk of perfect viscosity, having already enthused about the firm but delicately translucent white scooped from the top of the egg.

'Would've been even better if the eggs had been really fresh,' said Martin, turning his empty eggshell upside down. 'Burford Browns would be favourite, but they only lay a hundred and eighty eggs a year as opposed to two hundred and eighty for your average free-range, so you can't always get them.'

Rosie, who shopped once a week on Saturdays, confessed that the eggs in the fridge were a week old and of uncertain pedigree.

Martin opened another cupboard.

'What's for dinner tonight?'

'I just got us a ready meal – moussaka I think.'

That afternoon, seeing her husband stretched out in front of the TV, she assumed he was watching football and that the image of the glistening, golden chicken being lifted from the oven must be a half-time commercial.

When Martin volunteered to make the evening meals, first of all at weekends and then every night of the week, Rosie could not have been more appreciative. With both of them out at work all day, the division of domestic chores had long been a rumbling volcano in their relationship; mostly quiescent, sometimes smouldering, and more than capable of the occasional violent eruption.

Nor was it difficult to enthuse about the results. By meticulously following weights, measures and timings, Martin began producing more-than-acceptable meals almost from the beginning – coq au vin, pork chops with a maple-syrup glaze – even if he could not yet cope with the distraction of vegetables.

It was in this first flush of gratitude that she had offered to take over the washing up, a job which up to that point had been Martin's sole domestic responsibility, albeit one which he had construed as representing fifty per cent of the housework. It was just unfortunate that, as Martin's range and ambition expanded, the kitchen was left looking more and more like a culinary war zone: no pan or bowl unused, no surface spared.

In the same positive spirit, she didn't really mind that he totally ignored her tatty but treasured collection of recipes, a repository not only of favourite meals but of fond memories and the nostalgic comfort that familiar dishes can bring to the table. Instead, it was all 'Nigella does this' or 'Jamie suggests that'. Still, she had to admit that most of the 'top tips' gleaned from hours of clicking away on the internet were often an improvement on the way she had always done things. Her own repertoire had perhaps been a little repetitive, her boiled eggs a bit hit and miss, her pasta not always al dente, and her vegetables might have sometimes mislaid the odd nutrient along the way.

'Do you know what this little lot cost?' she inquired, forcing a smile as she struggled in through the door one Saturday lunchtime. She still shopped once a week, but now her shopping list was generated by Martin's recipe app and sent directly to her phone, though in an order that bore no relationship to the layout of the supermarket.

'Well, if you will shop at Waitrose…'

On the Sunday, he had drawn her attention to an advertisement for the new Aldi that had opened twelve miles down the road.

The same concern for economy, she could not help noticing, did not seem to apply to the Wusthof Classic Icon six-piece knife set on special offer at £357 ('They'll last thirty years, that's less than four pence per knife per week'). Or to the new set of heavy-bottomed, pre-seasoned, cast-iron pans which distributed the heat so much more evenly and would last a lifetime so long as they weren't put in the dishwasher.

She had already moved the ironing board and drying rack out of the pantry to make space for the Kitchen Aid Artisan mixer and a new set of half-shelves for the jars and packets of many new and interesting items from Persian saffron to vermicelli nests. Her phone-charging point and favourite fruit bowl had been moved to make way for the panini press and a rack of colour-coded chopping boards. There was talk of a sous vide cooker.

It was only a matter of time before Martin discovered that most things, even the humble mashed potato, could be made that 'little bit more special' with the addition of a knob of butter or a splash of cream or a glug of olive oil. And as soon as he had mastered the logistics of cooking a vegetable to coincide with the evening meal, he had discovered that leeks, spinach and courgettes also responded positively to a little dairy encouragement. If, to head off calorific catastrophe, Rosie suggested smaller portions, then it was 'hardly worth the time in the kitchen'. If she proposed fewer carbohydrates or using less butter and oil, she was 'taking the fun out of it'. Within a month her blood-sugar levels were all over the place but brown rice and wholemeal pasta were 'the work of the devil' and the words 'glycaemic index' caused his eyes to glaze over. Using leftovers also cramped his style, as did the thought of dovetailing ingredients over two or three evenings in order to avoid the half-used packs of chicken livers or cartons of crème fraiche left to go off in the fridge.

The puritan in Rosie had always thought that eating from a tray in front of the television was a touch slovenly, and she had happily gone along with his suggestion that they should eat at the dining table. But she had not anticipated that 'noticing what we eat' would mean talking of little else. His beef stew (she had been informed that it was no longer thought necessary to brown meat) was indeed out of this world, but might have been more enjoyable without the blow-by-blow account of the subtleties involved in its creation: 'It's the nucleotides in the anchovies that do it: A nucleotide plus a glutamate is basically your savoury explosion.' On occasion, it was after ten o'clock by the time they ate on account of Martin placing too much faith in Jamie's prep times or insisting on hand-making the sheets of lasagne as well as the authentic Bolognese sauce that had to be cooked slowly and required a few drops of full-fat milk to be added at five-minute intervals.

Rosie was not really surprised when Natalie's first words on arriving home for the vacation were 'You've put on weight, Mum. Suits you.' Or when, half an hour later, Ben greeted her with 'You're getting fat, Mum,' as he lifted her in a bear hug. She had smiled and turned away, but not before both of them had seen that she was suddenly close to tears. Later that Saturday afternoon, when Martin had gone out, she found herself forced to stop getting their bedrooms ready and made to sit down with a cup of tea. 'Right, Mum, what's up?'

On that first evening at home – pork belly with black pudding, chorizo and butter beans – it was impossible not to comment on their father's unexpected overlordship of the kitchen, described by Ben as 'Dad's first brush with domestic competence'. But later, when Rosie had said goodnight and left the two of them to catch up on the kind of news that probably wasn't fit for parental ears, she had come back downstairs for a glass of water and, though not exactly listening, had caught the words '…like we always did with Mum'. Lingering just a moment longer by the living-room door she heard the exasperated tones that Natalie frequently used with her younger brother: 'Right, Ben, do you think you can manage anything as simple as that?'

On the second evening – organic chicken thighs in cream and cider – Martin's presentation of the meal failed to cause even a ripple on the surface of the conversation. With the summer holiday still to be decided, Ben was in full flow about the joys of swimming from your own deck at a lakeside cabin in Finland. Natalie had raised her eyebrows and begun checking her messages under the table. At the first pause, Martin asked: 'What about this sauce, then? Are you getting the tarragon?' 'It's fine, Dad,' Ben replied. 'Did you get the link I sent about that place near Raseborg?'

On each succeeding evening – pulled pork with pear gravy, rosemary risotto with crispy sage – the conversation could not be deflected for more than a few seconds from what old school friends were up to or who was worth following on Twitter. 'Marinated overnight. Really amps up the flavour,' said Martin, passing round the pulled pork for seconds. 'Great, Dad. How's the book club going?'

If Ben or Natalie came into the kitchen it was not to marvel at their father's presence there but to eat packets of crisps or even bowls of cereal half an hour before dinner. At least twice a week, one or both would call in at the last moment to say they were running late and would be grabbing something to eat with friends. When they were at home, Ben added salt to everything without tasting and shovelled his food in before rushing out to the pub. Natalie, meanwhile, had persuaded her mother to join her in a diet based on using smaller plates.

As the days went by – duck in marmalade sauce, spiced pork burgers with peach-and-chilli salsa – it was Rosie herself who was the weakest link, occasionally lapsing into a compliment. But even she, as she stood to carry the plates to the kitchen, found herself replying with the same phrase she had heard so many times over the years – 'Very nice, love.'

On a Saturday morning, halfway through the vacation, Martin was checking the shopping list on his phone when Natalie and Ben came downstairs.

'Anything special you kids fancy for dinner tonight?'

Natalie glanced at Ben. 'Don't suppose you could manage that awesome bacon-and-egg pie Mum used to make?' Bowing to Ben's seconding, Martin got up from his computer and went in search of the old recipe book.

'Quiche Rosie,' he announced that evening, lowering the bacon-and-egg flan to the table with some ceremony. 'I saw our old headteacher in town today,' said Ben, 'Scary as ever.' Natalie shuddered. 'I saw Justine Connor. Year above me? I swear to God she was, like, really pregnant?' Rosie ate in silence, amused at the precise arrangement of the tomato slices and trying not to be pleased that the egg mix was a little solid, the flan base a little soggy.

Next day, finding Martin with the family recipe book open on his knee, Ben put in a request for sausage and mash. Wanting to go with the flow, Martin picked up a dozen award-winning sausages from the local farmers' market and, after spending the afternoon consolidating the wisdom of the web, set about producing his own version of 'the perfect sausage and mash', deploying the new potato ricer and gently warming the cream.

'Great mash, Dad,' said Ben, reaching for the salt. 'No wonder you've put on all that weight.' Martin, who still prided himself on his youthful figure, pulled in his stomach as he removed the blue-and-white-striped butcher's apron.

On the Sunday, Ben suggested going out for a McDonald's – 'It's got to be said, no one does fries like McDonald's.' That night over the washing up, Rosie overheard Natalie whispering to Ben 'not to go overdoing it.'

The two of them always felt a little bereft when Natalie and Ben went back to college; the house a little empty, life a little flat.

'Shall we just have a ready meal tonight?' said Rosie as she came down from stripping the beds.

'Fine,' said Martin. 'Maybe watch a film.'

Next evening, he asked if there was anything in the freezer.

'There's some cod fillets that need eating.'

'Fine.'

'I'll do it,' said Rosie. 'We can watch the second half of that movie.'

Afterwards, Martin washed up the two plates, a pan, and the oven tray while Rosie made coffee. On the Tuesday, they had a frozen pizza. Wednesday, a takeaway. Thursday saw them eating leftovers; Friday, a lamb chop with frozen peas.

'I was thinking,' said Rosie on the Saturday morning, 'maybe you could do something special when Mum and Dad come over tomorrow?'

'I suppose,' said Martin, brightening, 'I could do my *arista di maiale al latte*'.

❖

Desiderata

IRIS GEDDES HAD KNOWN from the age of eight that she was not especially attractive. There was nothing ugly about her, but her face was perhaps a little too full and her features a little too crowded. The realisation had dawned in a drip of painful moments, revealed more by comments made about the other girls than anything said about herself. But by the time she entered her teens, shoulders a little hunched, hips tending to heaviness, her opinion of herself had been confirmed.

She had sensed her mother's disappointment and had felt a pressure to excel at schoolwork or sport or to have a bubbly personality. Not being possessed of any of these qualities, Iris had decided she was ordinary and that was that.

When the time had come for leaving school, there had been no special enthusiasm to be pursued. She completed a diploma in management studies without having any ambition to start her own business or climb a corporate ladder. She lived with her parents until it became embarrassing, at which point she moved into a shared flat with two similarly situated young women.

A few months short of her thirtieth birthday, Iris married

a man who worked in the furniture section of a department store. It was not a passionate relationship but they were considerate of each other and tenderness grew as the years wore down the points of abrasion, the jarrings of a less-than-perfect fit, that all relationships encounter. Just occasionally, she wondered what it would be like to have an elfin face and a perfect figure and to be as passionately in love as the couples she saw on TV who could not keep their hands off each other and were forever having sex in lifts. Two children were born, and for a while, Iris entertained the idea that she might be especially good at being a mother.

As her family grew, she read articles about healthy eating and wondered if she fussed too much over the children. She helped with their homework, managed the household budget and saved for rainy days and holidays. She joined a reading group where she worried about having too little to say. She remembered birthdays and anniversaries and shopped once a week for an elderly neighbour. She made time to spend with the children and understood when they did not want to spend time with her. After their first foreign holiday, camping in Brittany, she subscribed for a few months to an online French-language course.

Her employer, a consumer research company, valued her services without seeing any potential. In her cubicle at Marshall & Sons, she entered data from telephone surveys and uploaded tabulated results to the analysts who helped businesses predict customer behaviour. The twenty-or-so cubicles on the second floor were configurable, the cork-board walls personalised with quotations, postcards and photographs of children and pets.

It was in the cubicle next to her own that Iris first noticed the poem. It had been torn from a magazine and pinned up alongside a double-page spread of a deserted Caribbean beach. The first line, with its ornate drop capital – 'Go placidly amid the noise and haste and remember what peace there may be in silence' – struck such a chord with Iris that she assumed she must have seen it before, though the chord it struck seemed deeper than memory. She asked Leah, whose cubicle it was, if she could run off a copy.

In the months that followed, Iris discovered that half a dozen of the other cubicles had the same poem pinned up among the Post-It notes and crayoned drawings. Some were in old-fashioned script on a background made to look like parchment. In others, the title, *Desiderata*, was composed of intertwined wildflowers. Her own copy featured a dark forest with the words of the poem running down a shaft of sunlight.

In time, also, she became aware that the popularity of the poem was a source of some amusement to the analysts on the third floor who occasionally stopped by to request a print-out or a check on a data set. She had heard it called 'The Gospel according to Sharon'. Leah said her husband, an academic, had called it 'Mills & Boon spirituality'.

From her friend Carole, who had the cubicle four down from her own, she learned that the poem had not been found on the wall of a seventeenth-century crypt in Baltimore, as the caption on her own copy suggested, but had been written in the 1920s by a lawyer in Indiana. She was equally unconcerned when Carole told her that it was not really a poem at all but just a piece of writing that someone had chopped up into lines.

It was the first of those lines that eventually drove Iris to a curious habit. She was not religious, seeing herself as too down-to-earth for anything high-flown. But on her way to and from work she passed by the Parish Church of St Peter and St Paul and one day, out of curiosity, she made her way up the path between the daffodils and turned the heavy iron ring. It was a Friday afternoon in spring.

A chill, forbidding sort of place, she thought, smelling of damp stone and musty hassocks. A sign inside the door said the nave was thirteenth century with some later stained glass. She slid into a pew and sat up straight, pulling her coat close. From the first, she was on the verge of leaving, feeling powerfully that she did not belong. What held her in place was the quality of the silence: a protective silence, like the silence of another century, or another life.

On Sundays, there was an eleven-o'clock service but for six days of the week the church stood empty and unlocked. And on Friday afternoons, when Marshall & Sons closed early for the weekend, Iris took to calling in at St Peter and St Paul's on her way home. She told no one of her visits. It was, she told herself, her time of the week to think other thoughts, her reminder to go placidly amid the noise and haste.

Those first few times, stepping down into the church and closing the heavy door behind her, she had not felt at ease. The slightest sound had her on the edge of her seat ready to leave, not wishing to be discovered sitting alone in the middle of an empty church on a Friday afternoon. She hoped the vicar would not appear, lest he approach her with kindly intentions.

In time, her visits came to seem less singular. She sat in the same pew and took time to settle, listening to the silence becoming peace. Sometimes she read slowly the words she knew by heart. Sometimes she let the poem drop to her lap and looked down the columns and arches of the nave. She made resolutions and leaps of hopes. She relived moments of shame, pursing her lips at failures of courage or kindness. She thought about incidents in the past, about her mistakes and attitudes, and attempted to see her worries in perspective. It was sometimes with a sense of relief that she returned to the closing lines of her poem: 'Beyond a wholesome discipline, be gentle with yourself'. She thought about what a wholesome discipline might mean.

If she was troubled by some of the lines, she tried to confront the disturbance but had noticed a tendency in herself to become distracted, her thoughts wandering to the scenes in the stained-glass windows or the spiders' webs of ancient battle flags hanging above a tomb. In the early days, she had been troubled by: 'As far as possible, without surrender, be on good terms with all persons'. As far as she knew, she was on good terms with those she knew. But it was the first part – 'as far as possible, without surrender' – that caused her to seek distraction in the stained glass. Was she on good terms with all because she was all surrender? Because she had no convictions or opinions firm enough to take a stand on? Was her path through life edged by not giving offence on the one hand and hoping to be liked on the other? Finding no answers in the stained glass, she worried that such inward-looking might not be part of a wholesome discipline and resolved to keep it to her Friday afternoons. The truth, she told herself, with some relief and a little regret, was that her knowledge of most things was too shallow to support the kind of firm opinions from which offence is easily given or taken. For someone like herself, she decided, it was only the unschooled opinions of the heart, sympathy and kindness, that should not be surrendered. Afterwards, the lines became easier to read and, in time, seemed to help her to know the few occasions when it was right to resist the suasion of others.

Once or twice she had seen the vicar moving about at the far end of the church where there was a raised area with a red carpet and a table covered in a white cloth. Shuffling just a little way along the pew, she was able to hide behind one of the stone pillars.

Another part of her poem that she had tended to hurry through was the one that said: 'Exercise caution in your business affairs for the world is full of trickery'. On her Friday afternoons, she did not want to be reminded of the suspicious email attachments and the scam phone calls and all the terms and conditions she had accepted but not read. It was her desire to leave life's background hum of anxiety at the church door, like some people left their shoes. And it was with a sense of relief that she came to: 'Let not this blind you to what virtue there is – many people strive for high ideals and everywhere life is full of heroism'. It was these lines that became her cue to take a minute or two to remember, to recognise, the virtue there had been in her week: the kindnesses shown, the times when people had been unselfish and tried to do the right thing.

One Friday, when she had been sitting for twenty minutes in a silence so deep it seemed a sacrilege to even move her feet, she was given a fright by the church organ suddenly starting up. It began with a single note, floating up free as a child's lost balloon through the shafts of sunlight from the high windows. But almost immediately, the grander pipes had joined in, swelling out a sound that seemed too big even for the church; a bullying sound, pushing itself up under the vaults as the pipes themselves were jammed in under one of the arches. For a minute, she had held her place. But the bellowing had built up to something grandiose, triumphant, seeming to insist on a life and aspirations grander than her own and she had gathered up her scarf and her poem and hurried out into the world followed by the exhalations that relented only once she had drawn a curtain of traffic noise between herself and the church of St Peter and St Paul.

The following week, sanctuary had returned. A strange word, she thought, to come to mind whenever she reached to take hold of the iron ring. She was not in danger. She was not pursued or persecuted. Yet her sanctuary it was. Perhaps from the background anxiety; or perhaps from other selves she would not allow to accompany her into the stone-cold honesty of the nave.

The most disturbing of the poem's commandments was only two words. No doubt there were those who could take 'Be yourself' in their stride. And she thought she could recognise them. They were the ones who seemed less hesitant, more spontaneous in everything, more at ease and less worried about giving offence, the ones whose eyes were less troubled. She suspected they might be happier. But she was not one of these persons. To Iris, 'herself' was a vague thing, without substance or edges, a mist forever on the retreat. To others, she supposed, there might be a recognisable 'Iris'. But in her own mind, 'self' was something she struggled to hold on to. And of this, her poem had nothing to say.

As time went by, the vicar seemed to be finding more to do on Friday afternoons, moving about in the raised area, laying down a ribbon in the Bible or putting up the numbers of Sunday's hymns. While he was there, Iris could not settle. She knew that the church had a higher purpose. But seeing him going about his business renewed the feeling that she did not belong, her surroundings rebuking the littleness of her doubts amid the stone-cold certainty of the centuries. If he glanced in her direction, she lowered her poem below the edge of the pew.

'Decaffeinated religion' was also something she had heard said about her poem. And no doubt religion was a grander thing. But the words of the poem seemed more for people like herself. It was, she supposed, a set of command-ments. But commandments so human, so whispered, so gentle and forgiving, that she did not feel judged or admon-ished. Above all, they seemed as if they might be achievable by someone like herself. When she raised her eyes to the stained-glass windows, she sometimes felt that they stood for all that was beyond her. Parables and stories were well and good, she thought, but they didn't always fit what was bothering you. And they didn't always make things clearer. She felt grateful to her poem for not being afraid of naivety. For not dressing things up to seem cleverer than they were. For simply saying: 'Avoid loud and aggressive persons, for they are vexatious to the spirit'. When you read those words every week, it seemed normal to steer yourself away from certain people, if it could be done without giving offence. And, in time, she found herself also avoiding people in the wider world, the world online and on televi-sion, who seemed to her loud and aggressive. And, yes, she thought, her spirit was less vexed as a result.

It was always cold in the church, as if its stones had absorbed the cold of a thousand winters. Yet she looked forward to the drop in temperature when she stepped inside the nave. It, too, had its part to play in her Friday afternoons, signifying some threshold being crossed, a place of otherness entered, a place licensed for the thinking of other thoughts.

In the beginning, the words she had embraced most eagerly were: 'If you compare yourself with others, you may become vain or bitter, for always there will be greater and lesser persons than yourself'. Lord, how right that was.

How obviously right. In youth, she had felt the beginnings of the bitterness. Seen, too, the beginnings of the vanity in those whose beauty or cleverness had filled their sails, taking them to a place where others were not fully acknowledged. Sometimes when she reread the lines in the silence of the church, it struck her how much of the world's noise and confusion was about comparison, making people dissatisfied with their lives, even with who and what they were. How extraordinary, she thought, that all this could be held at bay by keeping those simple words close.

The vicar's comings and goings became unpredictable. Some Fridays he would not appear at all. At other times, he would step out from the vestry just to check briefly around the nave before disappearing again. Once or twice, he had begun to walk down the aisle towards her pew but had always stopped short, finding a prayer cushion to straighten or a dropped hymn book to retrieve. Whenever he threatened, Iris slipped the poem into her bag.

At some point, she had learned that *Desiderata* was Latin for 'things desired' and she thought that fitted. The things the poem spoke of were what she desired. To be on good terms. To see the virtue in the world. To avoid dark imaginings. To have the strength of spirit to stand up to life's difficulties. To be at peace in the noisy confusion of life. But the line that never failed to pierce her, pierce her with a kind of yearning, was the line: 'Remember, you have a right to be here'. Why these words should leave her tearful each Friday afternoon she did not know.

Some Fridays, she found it difficult to concentrate. Her thoughts would stray to the flower arrangements or the church notices. One time she could not take her eyes from a small bird that had found its way in and was panicking all around the nave, fluttering its wings against high windows before settling on a ledge to look down, embarrassed, on an unfamiliar world. And what a world it was, she thought as her eyes came to rest on the windows and she tried to make out the medieval lettering around their borders. 'Blessed are the meek for they shall inherit the earth.' Forgotten Sunday School lessons came flooding back and she was struck by how revolutionary it all was – 'The lowest shall be highest' – and how at odds with everything in the world, even here where the tombs of aristocrats and generals lined the nave. She made out more of the lettering: 'I was a stranger, and you took me in; I was naked and ye clothed me, I was sick and ye visited me'. Yes, she thought, yes.

On one occasion, she suspected the vicar had seen her staring up at the windows. He had kept glancing towards her, perhaps wondering if this would be a good moment to approach. She was ashamed, afterwards, to have pushed her poem under a cushion and bowed her head, as if in private prayer.

Another commandment she had worried about was: 'Enjoy your achievements as well as your plans'. She was not, she thought, a person who had achievements. Middle age was upon her now and what had she done with the years? She thought she had been a good daughter to her parents, though there had been times when she could have done better. She hoped the same could be said about being a partner and a mother. She had tried to put the children first and they seemed to have grown up normal and happy enough. She had tried to be a good neighbour, though she knew her efforts in this direction had been sporadic. She had done her job conscientiously, earned a living, avoided getting into debt. She had paid her taxes and had a standing order to a local organisation that provided work experience for those with learning difficulties. She had, she hoped, behaved with what she believed to be ordinary decency. She had tried not to hurt or offend people, though of course she could not be sure. She had mostly told the truth. Sometimes, as she thought on these things, she felt a dismay that this was more a list of the ordinary, of clichés rather than achievements. But her poem helped her to find some satisfaction in these things – things that had not brought any great improvement in the world but had helped in a small way, she hoped, to keep things going.

Eventually, the time came in Iris's life when she had to consider what it meant to take kindly the counsel of the years, gracefully surrendering the things of youth. And how utterly astonishing, she thought as her eyes travelled over hosts of bearded stained-glass saints, that growing old was the most predictable thing in the world and yet the most surprising when it happens. Sometimes she imagined other things her poem might have said on the topic: 'Beyond a modest care for appearances, do not feign youthfulness' or 'Beyond a wholesome appetite, do not let your BMI drift over 28'. But mostly, she decided, it was a question of appropriateness, a matter of being honest with yourself, undeceived by vanities. How much more difficult must it be, she thought, for those who had set great store by their youth and beauty; how much harder to leave behind the admiring glances, to experience becoming more and more invisible to the young. She saw, then, that the advice to avoid comparing oneself with others was not only for people like herself.

Her father died, and this made Iris feel older. It also precipitated her mother's decline and it fell to Iris to look after her for the years before she was admitted to a hospice. After the funeral, she continued her visits and it was in her Saturday afternoons at the hospice that she began to learn the meaning of: 'Listen to others, even to the dull and the ignorant, for they too have their story'. She had always thought of herself as one of the dull and the ignorant and had sometimes wondered what her story was. But it was as she had been sitting in those high-backed fake-leather chairs at the hospice that she had discovered how difficult it was to listen to those who had not been listened to for years and whose thoughts, in any case, seemed to run only in well-worn grooves. But if you listened with all of yourself, if you really listened instead of passing the time of day, then they did indeed have their stories and their thoughts, things they wanted to say. She had been moved to tears when one of the women she sat with had told her she was tired of being told to live in the present and enjoy each moment by a young therapist who did not seem to understand that one of the pleasures of living in the moment was looking forward to the future.

Only at the last did Iris feel at all let down by her poem. 'Be cheerful. Strive to be happy' was, she thought, an unsatisfactory ending. If you were not cheerful, 'be cheerful' was not a great help. If you were not happy, 'strive to be happy' seemed more like an admission of having nothing to offer, a sigh of defeat. Maybe what the poem was saying, she thought, was that striving to be happy was something you had to work out for yourself. And not just once but every new day.

One Friday in autumn, as an early dusk fell and she sat alone in her pew, she noticed the vicar trimming candles at the altar. She shuffled along the pew as she watched him brushing his hand across the altar cloth. But instead of disappearing into the vestry, he turned to look down the length of the nave, seeming to be enjoying the broad shafts of sunlight that slanted through the mote-filled air. He stepped down from the raised area and headed down the church, not stopping to straighten a prayer cushion or pick up a hymn book.

'Good afternoon.'

'I was just going,' she said, scooping up her poem and scarf from the pew.

'I hope I'm not driving you away? It's not in my job description.'

She smiled and looped her scarf.

'No, really, it's time I was off,' she said.

'I've often seen you here on Fridays, nearly every week in fact.'

It was a simple statement but it took Iris by surprise. She was unused to hearing a human voice in this place.

The vicar made a gesture toward the paper in her hand. 'And would I be right in thinking you always bring the same thing to read?'

'Yes, always the same,' she said, feeling foolish; foolish and worried that, for some reason, the encounter might mean she would no longer be able to visit St Peter and St Paul's on her Friday afternoons.

'I confess to being consumed with curiosity.'

Iris, fearing catastrophe, handed him the poem.

'You're sure you don't mind?'

He lowered himself into the space she had left when she had shuffled along the pew. He began to read.

Iris waited, hands gripped in her lap, regretting she had not left a minute or two earlier. He was sure to bring in religion. That, after all, was in his job description. He was young and nice-looking. If it hadn't been for the collar and the black vest, to which a few petals of trimmed candle had attached themselves, he could have been one of the analysts on the third floor at Marshall's. He had darkish gold hair that seemed too luxurious for a man of the cloth and you could tell from his voice that he was educated and at ease with himself and his world. He said 'offen' instead of 'often', but did not otherwise seem loud or vexatious. She imagined he had a wife with her own career and children at private schools. She imagined he would take 'be yourself' in his stride. She imagined he had barbecues and played tennis. She imagined he was adored by his congregation. She imagined he would be a bishop one day. His knees had to be set sideways in the pew.

He was taking so long that she thought he must be reading the poem more than once. When he eventually looked up, she thought she glimpsed the echo of a tear.

'I'm Stephen,' he said.

'Iris. Iris Geddes.'

He looked down again at the poem. '*Desiderata.*'

She nodded and was about to apologise for something. For being there. For not attending services. For not believing. For being sentimental. For being Iris. She stood up, wanting more than ever to be outside.

The vicar freed his legs and stepped into the aisle. 'I'm sorry to have disturbed you.'

'No, really, I was just going. I shouldn't...'

'May I perhaps say one thing before you go?'

Here it comes, she thought, looking down to the flag-stones.

He handed back the poem and, as she took it, rested his hand ever so lightly on her sleeve. 'I just want to say you are welcome here.'

She blinked as he opened the church door to the glow of an autumn evening. 'Thank you,' she murmured as she stepped out into the porch.

'And Iris.'

Starting down the path, lined now with purple crocuses, she turned. He was framed in the doorway, feet apart, hands clasped before him in a vicarly way.

'Remember, you have a right to be here.'

❖

The Wall

Author's note: To speak of the wall between social classes is usually to speak metaphorically. But occasionally such walls are made of bricks and mortar. One such was the two-metre high, spike-topped wall built in 1934 across a street in Cuttleslowe, Oxford, with the aim of separating the privately owned houses being built at one end of the street from the council-owned houses at the other. There would be no buyers for the new private houses, argued the developer, if 'slum dwellers' were living in the same street.

In 1936, the Communist Party of Great Britain organised a protest against the Cutteslowe Wall. Two thousand people turned out, many with pickaxes, and only a heavy police presence prevented the wall from being demolished. Two years later, Oxford City Council demolished the wall with a steamroller but was forced to rebuild after the housing company took the case to court. During World War Two, the wall was once again reduced to rubble after an army tank on exercises took a wrong turn. The War Office paid for the rebuild.

The wall was finally demolished in 1959 after the City Council purchased the strip of land on which it was built. The park, primary school and shops were now accessible to those who lived in the council houses.

A blue history plaque now marks the site where the Cutteslowe Wall once stood. All that remains of the wall itself are a few fragments on display in Oxford's Town Hall. Memories were briefly rekindled in 2018 when the Highways Department resurfaced the street but stopped where the council houses began. The decision was apparently 'based on need' but this did not prevent the words 'Class War' being spray-painted across the street where once the wall had stood.

When I first arrived in Oxford in the 1960s, the Cuttleslowe 'class wall' had passed into legend and the story gradually faded from my memory. Until, some twenty years later, I came across another 'class wall' in a place very far from Oxford.

The story of the real wall that divided two communities in the city of Colombo, Sri Lanka, provided the opening for my novel Facing Out to Sea *(Hodder & Stoughton, 1996). The following short story is adapted from that novel. It is dedicated to the memory of Stephen Perera and Mohammed Jiffry, who so generously shared their knowledge of life in the slums and shanties of Colombo.*

Maligawatta, Colombo, Sri Lanka, 1985

THE SLUMS HAD BEEN BUILT, long before anyone could remember, in the gardens of what had once been well-to-do homes in the north and east of the Pettah. But with the influx of the poor into every interstice of the city, the wealthy had fled to the suburbs, leaving their grand homes to the landlords and the speculators who had brutally divided them into tenements and built tight rows of slums down the sides of what had once been spacious gardens. Today, throughout the wards of New Bazaar and Maligawatta, the old garden walls compress the lives of the poor as once they preserved the space of the rich and it is for this reason rather than any horticultural attraction that the city's slums are officially known and numbered as 'The Gardens'.

Without any proper entrances of their own, the Gardens find their way out via narrow alleyways so that, from the outside, the only signs of their existence are the stygian clefts in the sun-white façades of the city's streets. Through these restricted throats, the lungs of the slums breathe into the Pettah. But as the alleyways lead only into the Gardens, and as there is usually only an evil-looking drain to be seen flowing from within, there is no reason for anyone to enter save those who live there; and despite housing a hundred thousand souls, the slums are never seen by those who go about their business in the capital.

The entrance to Slum Garden 178 in Maligawatta West, for example, could easily be missed; only an inconspicuous gap, barely wide enough for a hawker's barrow, serves as entrance and exit for its forty or fifty homes and two or three hundred inhabitants. Inside the crack, stone steps, shallow and slimy on either side of the foul drain, lead into a damp-walled passage squirming its way through into the slum.

Here in this private world, the two rows of houses confront each other at a distance of only a few feet, their overhanging roofs leaving only a narrow strip-light of sky down the length of the garden. Permanently shaded under these deep eaves, each of the houses has its own small sitting-out verandah where neighbours, adjacent or opposite, can sit and pass the time of day. From the front edge of these verandahs, painted wooden posts rise to prop up the continuous roof. Nailed between the tops of the posts is a matching wooden trellis, carved and fretted in a poor man's version of the Dutch colonial style. All down the length of the garden, these proud, peeling posts mark off the individual homes, their dark mouths opening into each other across the drain until, at the far end, the alleyway opens out into a bare patch of beaten earth where are to be found the latrine blocks and the washhouses. Here the slum comes to a full stop at the old end wall of the garden.

On the verandah of Number 29, Vijay Jayasinghe is slowly smoking a cigarette. It is a little after seven in the evening. Light swarms of midges are gathering over the drain and the strip of sky between the roofs has turned to indigo, smudged with the smoke of fires. At the top of the garden, a neon light fizzes on the latrine wall. A few of the older children are sitting beneath it, concentrating on their homework under an inspectorate of insects. Somewhere a voice is raised and a dog begins to bark.

As is usual for the hour, the women are embedded in the recesses of their homes, scouring pans with ashes from the dying fires, pouring the cooking oil back into its bottles, lowering the bed-boards, smoothing the worn covers, spacing out the garments that have bunched together in the middle of coir ropes slung diagonally across dark rooms. Outside, the men are relaxing on the verandahs, talking in tones that fall imperceptibly with the light, their glowing cigarette ends tracing their eloquence in the evening air.

Vijay Jayasinghe narrows his eyes against the smoke, frowning slightly at a harsh, incessant barking. A packet of Gold Leaf shows plainly through his shirt pocket. Somewhere he has read that one cigarette, ritually enjoyed at the same time each day, can give more pleasure than ten or twenty smoked carelessly, without postponement or anticipation. The notion had taken lodging within him, meeting his need for economy while permitting the dignity of choice. He slowly releases the smoke, letting it burn in his nostrils. The smell of evening meals lingers comfortably under the deep eaves. This, the first cool of evening, and the first calm hour of the day, is his chosen time.

A sweeter scent briefly brushes aside the pungent

tobacco smoke as Chandra appears from the doorway and steps down into the alley. In a mood to savour, Vijay watches his wife make her way up the garden between the verandahs, wafting aside the midges as she goes, the deep red of her sari seeming to disperse the darkness gathering its strength in the open space around the latrines. Most of the other men in the garden are also following Chandra with their eyes, there being just enough light left. Almost without exception, they draw on their cigarettes after she has passed, all eyes still upon her as she nears the gap in the garden wall and slips gracefully into the gloom.

Vijay's eyes return to his half-smoked cigarette. He hesitates over an old dilemma: whether to make it last by letting it burn away slowly in his fingers or to draw on it, burning the paper and tobacco more fiercely, taking the smoke deep into his lungs, torn between the anticipation and the act. There is no movement in the garden, and his eye is drawn only to a flimsy cockroach scraping across the concrete of the verandah. He flicks the remaining centimetre of cigarette over the low wall and hears it hiss into the drain.

Without the tobacco smoke, the faint smell of the latrines begins to reassert itself. Tilting back in his chair, he sets his feet on the low concrete surround, one bare foot over the other, staring at the break in the wall through which his wife has disappeared. Like the gentle curve of the dagoba or the saffron glow of a priest's robe, the distinctive shape made by the broken brickwork is an icon for Vijay Jayasinghe, an image that summons unbidden a whole universe of meaning as he strains to catch the exact moment at which its silhouetted edges can no longer be made out against the darkness beyond.

The dispute over the breaching of the old end wall in Slum Garden 178 was long past. But while it had lasted it had been an ice age in community relations, scooping deep valleys of division, amassing mountains of solidarity, and sculpting the social landscape for years to come. The cause of the upheaval was, of course, what lay beyond the wall. What had once been just a grassy slope down to the dubious waters of the St Sebastian canal had gradually become a flourishing shantytown of cadjan and cardboard, of thatched palms and bamboo poles, of scavenged planking and rusting corrugated iron. It was a sink of stench and heat, of puddled alleyways and mournful music, of dark, smoking hovels eking out their unvaried food, of wild-eyed dogs with starved rib-cages picking over festering refuse, of energyless children on whose unresisting faces flies played undisturbed. Such settlements were to be found almost everywhere in the city, growing like weeds on land which nobody else wanted – at the edges of canals and railway lines, against the walls of slaughterhouses and public latrines, around the rotting rubbish dumps and waterlogged marshes on the northeast fringe; they were the running sores from which the respectable citizenry averted its eyes and held its breath, and within which it imagined all kinds of fearful vices to be breeding as freely as the families who lived there.

Such was the community that was to be found beyond the wall of Garden 178 in the ward of Maligawatta West.

It would be too simple to say that the battle lines between the wall-breachers and the wall-builders had been drawn between the sexes, although that was how it had begun. By climbing over the end wall of the garden and walking for two hundred metres along the path behind the shanty, it was possible to reach the bridge on the other side of which were the vegetable market, the clinic and both schools. At first, it had been only the children who had scrambled over the wall, pleading that they were late for school; but as they were always late for school, the route had come to be depended on and it had been only a matter of time before some of the younger women had also taken to climbing over with the help of two or three large stepping stones that had one day appeared on the garden side of the wall. There had been some muted grumbling from one or two of the older women, but this would have amounted to little had it not been for the kindly action of Mr P. D. Norman Stanley, the retired cinema projectionist who lived alone at Number 42, the last house in the garden.

P. D. Norman Stanley, being adequately supported by his daughter who was a housemaid in the Gulf, spent most of the day on his verandah, occasionally indulging in a beedi which he took longer to make than to smoke, but mostly just listening to the radio or chatting to his neighbours. To reach the wall, it was necessary to pass P. D. Norman Stanley's verandah and it warmed the old man's declining years to see first the children and, later on in the morning, their pretty young mothers coming by on their way to the shops. Some of the children had even fallen into the habit of stopping by for a few minutes on their way home from school, encouraged by the supply of Fair Ladies and Delta Dots which he kept ready in a screw-top glass jar. In this way, the balance of traffic had shifted so that most of his neighbours were passing by P. D. Norman Stanley's verandah at some time during the day. It was a small thing, perhaps, but P. D. Norman Stanley woke up every morning the more cheerful because of it.

There was only one detail that disturbed him: he did not like to see graceful young women being forced to adopt what he considered to be ungainly positions in struggling over the garden wall. He was sure, also, that they were scraping their delicate skins and what he liked to imagine was the silk of their saris on its rough concrete facing. It offended his sense of chivalry and one morning, having time on his hands, he had solved the problem by knocking out a dozen bricks with the help of a borrowed cold chisel.

It was the dislodging of the bricks that precipitated the crisis. Half of the garden, including many of the older inhabitants, had risen up against the breaching of the wall: it left them exposed; it disturbed social comfort; it punctured the status of the community. The gap was an open invitation, it was said, to all that was undesirable, all that they wished to be separated from. Now every kind of shiftless, work-shy, shanty-dweller would be able to wander freely into the slum and hundreds of foul-mouthed, drug-addicted men with bloodshot eyes and alcoholic breath would use the garden every morning to get through to Kochchikade on their way to look for casual labour at the docks and the fish-processing plant. They would burgle the houses and molest the women while the menfolk were away; they would foul the latrines and break the brass taps on the stand-pipes; they would bring smells and disease and vermin and head lice; most alarming of all, their limitless offspring would mingle freely with the children of the slum.

The horror at the breaching of the wall was by no means unanimous. Most of the younger women and several of the men rallied to the hapless P. D. Norman Stanley's defence: the gap in the wall saved a lot of time and effort; no one in the shanty would ever dare come through into the quiet, private, slum garden; and any who did could be discouraged by the Tamil hod-carriers at Number 4.

The next morning, after an uproarious night of verandah oratory and raised voices in which many a long-suppressed grievance was given an unexpected outing, the garden had woken to find the wall rebuilt, neatly cemented bricks standing out like a red sentinel in the old white-limed wall where the offending gap had been. All that day, smirks and scowls had identified the two parties, but by the following morning the bricks had been knocked out again and those who were yesterday smirking were today seen to be scowling. The bricks themselves had vanished completely, only to be replaced the next night by gritty, grey breeze blocks, crudely cemented in and scratched with a *hooniam*, a curse, on anyone attempting to reopen the wall.

It was on that morning that the battle lines had really been drawn, with the wall-breachers forbidding their wives and children to use the alleyway and the wall-builders forbidding those in their thrall to use any gap that was opened up. Under penalty of the strap, the children of the wall-builders were forbidden to play with the children of the wall-breachers. Elderly dependants, finding themselves in one camp or the other, felt obliged not to speak to those with whom they had gossiped amicably for half a century. Even the tacit agreement about the tuning of radios to the same station had been suspended so that evening time in the slum garden had become a cacophony of classical and popular refrains as transistors were brought out onto the verandahs and tuned to the different stations chosen by the two camps.

At first, guards had been mounted when the wall had been breached or rebuilt, but such vigilance could not be sustained and, within days, built walls were breached and breached walls were built again until, after several exhausting weeks, a wordless process of compromise had begun. First, the wall-building party had left a few bricks out when, in the small hours of one Sunday morning, it had rebuilt a breach in the wall that had remained open for several days. The following Thursday, the wall-breachers went to work again, but this time they left some of the bricks in place, forming a smaller passageway than usual. And so the negotiations continued, a brick offered here and surrendered there, so that the difference between what was considered a wall and what was considered a breach grew narrower until one day, in the hottest part of the year, the gap stabilized to an irregular opening, wider at the top, which bit into the wall to within four bricks of the ground and was just wide enough for all but the stoutest to squeeze through. Within a month, two more bricks had been dislodged by the increasing traffic but by that time no one had cared and within six months all but the most die-hard wall-builders were using the gap to reach the bridge and were exchanging pleasantries with P. D. Norman Stanley as they passed by the verandah of the last house in the garden.

Vijay fought down the temptation to smoke another cigarette. Looking up the garden, he saw his father easing himself sideways through the gap. Under the sodium light on the latrine-block wall, the old man stopped to retie the sarong that had been pulled loose by the edges of the brick-work. This done, he began to wander slowly down the garden to one side of the drain, hands behind his back, looking around in the manner of one who would not at all mind being interrupted for a little evening conversation. A few of the women, their chores done, had come to sit out for a few moments before bed. Radios had been turned low and the garden was settling for the night.

Vijay smiled to himself as his father was persuaded to step up onto the verandah of Number 36, knowing that soon the cigarette smoke would be ghosting out from under the eaves as the card game got underway.

The Second World War had ruined Godfrey Jayasinghe.

On his return from Europe, he had found life robbed of interest by the excitements of the past and the promise of the future. For he had expected to be summoned any day to take up the job in Luton that had been promised him by the Eighth Army captain at whose side he had sworn and sweated from Taranto to Ferrara, and it was this that had prevented him from entertaining any ambition within his own powers of realisation. Instead, he had taken casual work at the docks and brought his bride to a temporary shack in the shanty on the banks of the St Sebastian Canal. A year had passed, then two, and he had ceased going down to the Fort Post Office, just as he had ceased folding his trousers under the bed-board at night. And in the heat of his native land, he eventually found that a sarong fitted him more comfortably than the trousers he had brought back from Europe. Soon afterwards, the shirts with the buttoned epaulettes had given way to sleeveless cotton vests which spread smoothly out over an expanding paunch.

Eventually, he had hit upon the idea of earning a little money from the one trade he had learned in the British Army and had set about teaching the other men to play stud-poker and eventually urging them on to the high-gambling Eighth Army version known in the trenches as 'seven-card roll 'em blind'. Once the game had become established, his own well-honed skills – assisted by his virtual monopoly of the rules – had begun to yield him an unpredictable income from the tea shops and the dimly lit arrack bars in Maligawatta, although it was true that a higher proportion of his earnings than he would have liked came in the form of pawnbrokers' markers, clothing-club coupons, lottery tickets, co-op chitties, broken wrist-watches, teeth which purported to have gold fillings, and paper IOUs which he had introduced and later regretted.

Eventually, the epidemic of poker in the shanties and his own pedigree in the game had opened up another conduit through which a doubtful income had trickled into his makeshift life. Late one evening, long after the oil lamps had been snuffed and darkness had descended on the St Sebastian Canal, two men had appeared outside his hut, hissing his name in low, agitated tones. After a swift and unreassuring survey of his recent conscience, Godfrey had been relieved to find that the men had come to ask him to adjudicate in a dispute over a poker game at Varindra's arrack house. After listening to both sides, he had congratulated both men on the high bluff they had both been playing at the time but pointed out that, technically speaking, both had been in infringement of the admittedly complicated 'when to roll'em' rule and that therefore they should split the pot. When news of this adjudication had spread, other gambling disputes began to be brought to Godfrey's shack or, as his wife Premawathie preferred, to the Bodhiraja Bar where he could usually be found on the two main poker nights of the week. It had not taken him long to institute a small fee of ten per cent of the disputed stake and, as it tended to be the higher games which caused the bitterest disputes, his honorarium, as he began to call it, often came to ten, twenty or even fifty rupees at a time. Soon, he had found himself drawn into adjudicating on sweepstake disputes, chitty draws, election bets, pigeon races and even neighbourhood disputes and matrimonial quarrels.

The card game at Number 36 seemed to have ended and Godfrey, seeing his son sitting out, joined him to smoke another beedi, glancing nervously to check that Premawathie was not hovering in the doorway.

'Dog house?' asked Vijay, smiling.

'Dog house,' sighed the old man, lowering himself into a string-backed plastic chair.

The previous evening, Godfrey and two or three other men had been celebrating a mild win on the horses and had returned well after midnight, waking up half the garden with their farewells. His wife had lain furiously silent on the bed-board as he had entered, none too steadily, and begun to undress. Then, in case anybody should still be asleep, an elbow had sent Vijay's framed diploma flying from the top of the display cabinet, shattering the glass on the concrete floor. Gunatilleke from next door had banged angrily on the planking, disturbing Susil who had begun to cry, and waking Chandra. Premawathie had lain awake for two hours more. Godfrey had gone straight off to sleep.

Now, as he was rolling his beedi, Premawathie came out onto the verandah and seated herself, tight-lipped, on the narrow bench with her back to the wall. Godfrey decided to delay lighting the beedi and instead looked away up the garden.

Premawathie, straight-backed, arms folded, hands gripping each elbow, pulled the cloak of her anger ever more tightly around her shoulders. A few feet away, her husband shifted in his seat in a little exploratory move to test the prospects of leaving without attracting any undue attention. Catching the small movement, Premawathie turned to look at him with all the accumulated resentment of her married life. Godfrey slowly sank back in his seat.

Premawathie continued to stare, her bitterness only increased by the fact that would surely not have troubled her husband's memory – that tomorrow would be the forty-second anniversary of her marriage to the slim, ambitious young man who had returned from Europe promising her the world. For months she had believed him when he had told her that it was only a matter of waiting until things settled down after the War, that they were going 'home' to England, that he was going to be a man. More embarrassed than depressed, she had helped erect their makeshift shack of bamboo poles and plaited palms on the banks of the St Sebastian Canal, a temporary shelter until word came from Luton.

She looked at him now as he sat in his off-white vest, picking at a loose strand of plastic in the seat of the chair. There had been no particular moment when it had become apparent that casual employment and a home in the shanties were to be the permanent reality of their lives. But gradually, as his bus journeys to the post office had become less frequent, her hopes had faded with the colours of her two good saris. After a few more years, the subject of England had become as painful to them as a dead child, never to be mentioned again.

Chandra had returned from her errand beyond the wall and was bringing the tea tray out onto the verandah, balancing the chromium cake stand on which she had set small slices of Victoria sponge in the hope of softening her mother-in-law's mood. Godfrey blew on his tea and rested his feet on the verandah rail, taking an interest in the dogs that had found something worth fighting over in the drain. After a while, he started to reach for a piece of cake but made the mistake of looking up and, at one searing glance, he withdrew his hand and scratched his knee. Premawathie shooed away the dogs. Godfrey lit the beedi, blowing smoke towards the cloud of midges over the drain.

Eventually, Premawathie untightened her lips in order to drink. In compensation, she glared over the teacup at Godfrey, who was wisely still staring at his feet on the rail.

She blinked in disgust and turned instead to her son, who was also waving away the cloud of midges. For a decade or more, she had refused to have a child at all, hoping that the shame of it would force her husband into getting a proper job. Now she looked down at the cake stand but could not bring herself to eat, teeth clenched, thinking of the thousands of such cakes that she had made over the years when her cupcakes and butterfly buns, maids-of-honour and Victoria sponges, had been their only dependable income. For if her husband's losses at the card table had been taken into account as well as his winnings, a method of calculation which he had never completely grasped, the truth was that she had also been the family's main breadwinner.

After twenty minutes of being silently roasted on the spit of his wife's disapproval, Godfrey was wondering whether he might still slip out to Varindra's bar for an hour or so before bed. Reluctantly, he decided that he had probably not yet served his time and began to fiddle miserably with the dial of the radio. Premawathie looked at him with no slackening of her hostility, daring him to start trying to find the BBC. 'Going home', she thought bitterly. 'Going to be a man.' It had never mattered to her. It was not against some imagined life in another country that she had set her life in the shanty; it was against the modest hope of a proper, legally occupied home with solid walls, a latrine instead of the river, and somewhere to wash in private with clean water. Even as the months had stretched into years, she had never ceased to regard with horror the crude hut on the bank of the fetid canal. Nor had she ever ceased to loathe the filth and the stench and the heat, the interminable flies all day, the millions of insects scratching in the cadjan at night, the festering heaps of rotting refuse, the beaten earth floors which turned to mud in the rains, the corrugated iron roofs held down by tyres that were constantly having to be replaced, the motley of woven palm and rough planks which formed her four walls, the lean-to kitchen with room only to crouch over the battered oil-drum stove and the blackened stones of her fire. Beyond anything, she had hated having to choose between the public latrines across the bridge, with their maze of slimy, excrement-smeared walls and almost unenterable smell, and the undignified bottomless hut built out over the river on bamboo poles with its screens of flapping plastic torn from old cement sacks and filthy fertilizer bags. Twice a week she had arisen at two o'clock in the morning to walk the half-mile to the public facilities on the Mihindu Mawa where she could wash in piped water without crowds or queues. At other times, she had been forced to join the women of the shanty who gathered on the stone steps to bathe and wash their families' clothes in the St Sebastian Canal, upstream from their own latrine but downstream from the hundreds of other shanties and latrines that nowadays stretched back through the crowded suburbs of the city. Sitting on the verandah of the slum garden, oblivious now to Godfrey, Premawathie's face had grown dark and fierce with her memories. Accommodation had never been her way; she had never bowed her head to such a life, never compromised her contempt. For more than four decades, she had regarded her home as temporary, keeping locked in an old tin trunk the framed photographs of her parents and grandparents, the china tea service, and the other refined household items which had been part of her dowry. For to put such things on display would have been to subject herself to the daily mockery of her circumstance. Nor would she allow herself to sip from the cup that was the one great solace of the shanties – the solidarity with the other women, the shared hardships, the scraps of gossip, the ritual complaints and mild conspiracies, the helping hands and small midweek loans, the little mutual insurance of sisterhood. This, too, she held herself from; for to accept it would have been to accept that she had become a part of it all; and while other women had turned plump-armed and unkempt from starchy food and social surrender, Premawathie, tight-strung to every slight touch on her respectability, had remained wiry and thin from the fires of resentment consuming her from within.

Only when her eyes fell instead on her son was the knot of her resentment loosened. She had always known that it would be through her son that the day of her recognition would come, that it would be Vijay who would lift her out of the shameful life that she had been brought to. She had always been sure that this boy, with his height and his looks, was destined for greater things. She motioned to Chandra to take the radio that was in danger of falling from her husband's sleeping hands and in that moment the truth appeared like a blister on the perfect surface of her resentment: Godfrey, for all his fecklessness, had made the one essential contribution. She had been able to speak some English before her marriage, but her husband had returned from the war speaking like a sahib. And by speaking English to their son at every opportunity, he had taught Vijay to speak the language as well as any boy from St Thomas's College. There had never been any doubt that he would take the school English prize and with it had come the place at the City Catering College. Three years later, when Vijay had collected his Diploma in Catering and Allied Studies, Premawathie had expected him to be offered a position in one of the grand international hotels along the coast. But after six months had passed, and then a year, she had been forced to acknowledge that Godfrey had been right: her son lacked the one qualification more essential than any diploma. He had no one with any influence, no one who owed his parents favours, no uncles or aunts who could breathe the right words in the right ears, no money for the *kappang* to oil the hinges of employment's gates. But in time the tide had turned. All along the coast, the cry had gone up for hotel staff who not only had diplomas in English but who could also speak something of the language. One day, despite his helpless shrug of the shoulders when asked about the two-thousand-rupee sweetener, Vijay had been hired as an under-waiter at the Galle Face, unquestionably the oldest and most prestigious hotel in the city.

Now the flame of his mother's ambitions had risen from the embers which she had kept glowing over the years in the iron grate of her will. She had gloried even in the deductions from his pay packet: the union dues, the medical insurance, the sick-pay contributions, the provident fund. Even net of all these symbols of a salaried job, his Friday-night envelope had contained more than eight hundred rupees. And no one knew better than she that its real worth was many times more. Her son was now a catch. He would be able to command a dowry in sovereigns, in gemstones and jewellery, in china and cutlery, in bed linen and Manipuri for saris, and perhaps even a sewing machine or a TV set. The problem now was that after so many years in the shanty, her acquaintance was not such as to furnish acceptable brides. And in any case, the shack on the canal was not the sort of place to which one invited respectable families to take tea strained from the china pot with dainty cakes served from paper doilies. For months she had worried about finding a suitable wife for her son, finding satisfaction only in dismissing the shanty women who had daughters and who had suddenly begun to treat her with a little respect.

Then had come that dreadful, sickening day when her son had returned home and announced out of a clear blue sky that he had made a proposal of marriage to an eighteen-year-old girl who lived in a shack on the opposite bank of the St Sebastian Canal. Premawathie had felt a chill on her skin rapidly contracting to a cold cage around her heart. 'Vijay, she has no family. There will be no dowry.' But she had known, even as she had spoken the words, that she would not prevail. Her son was now the head of the household, possessed of all her own stubbornness and unrestrained by any pressure from kinsfolk, any overwhelming obligation to the family name, any parental wealth to be disowned by, any real understanding, despite all she had done, of the importance of station. For the rest of that day she had pleaded with both words and silence. But at night, lying on her bed-board listening to the scratching of the insects in the darkness, Premawathie had come as close as she had ever been to admitting defeat. And after a week of concentrated acidity to which Vijay had proved impervious, she had wordlessly begun preparing for the wedding.

As the day had neared, the atmosphere inside the little hut had been thick with fumes from the engine of disapproval revving furiously within her. And then, exactly a week before the wedding day, Vijay had come home unexpectedly in the middle of the afternoon. Finding his mother alone, he had told her he had something to show her. Tight-lipped, she had covered a batch of cakes with a clean cloth and followed her son up the embankment to the high edge of the shanty. There they had walked alongside the old wall to a point where a dozen or so bricks had been removed. Without the slightest circumspection, Vijay had stepped through the gap and was reaching back to help her through.

It had been a quiet time of day in the garden. The latrine blocks and washrooms were unoccupied, and there was no one at the standpipe with its dripping brass tap. In the one open space, the ashes of a rubbish pile were smouldering. Under the shade of the wall, a dog slept peacefully. Chickens strutted about, pecking at the earth. Passing the latrines, they had proceeded down between the houses with their dividing posts and fretted wooden verandahs. Only P. D. Norman Stanley, sitting out listening to the radio, had seen them enter but he had shown no surprise and merely smiled a toothless smile at Vijay who was leading his mother by the hand.

When he had persuaded her to step up onto the verandah of Number 29, he had told her that his salary had secured the loan for the year's rent in advance, with enough left over to pay the outgoings, and that the house she was now standing in was to be their new home. Premawathie had listened, numb, as he had asked if he and Chandra could move in first and be alone for their wedding night. Then she had let herself be taken by the hand again and led back into the depths of the house. With the silhouette of her son framed in the doorway behind her, she had walked through two rooms to the kitchen with its stone basin and kerosene stove. Slowly, she had examined the concrete floor with its incised diamond pattern and then raised her eyes to the tiled roof. Reaching out a hand to spread her fingers on the concrete wall, she had wept for the first time in forty years.

❖

Acknowledgements

As always, I would like to thank Lesley Adamson for commenting on each story as it was written and giving unfailingly honest and much-valued criticism.

Many thanks also to Chris Brazier for his sensitive copy editing and always perceptive commentary, and to Candida Lacey and John and Mary Marzillier for their support and encouragement.

My thanks also to:

Rod Craig, for again providing a brilliant image and design for the front cover. More of Rod Craig's paintings can be viewed at https://rodcraig.com

Charlie Webster of Production Line for top-of-the-line typesetting and production advice.

The late Marjorie Bellhouse – a much-loved mother-in-law who bears more than a passing resemblance to the character of Dora in *The Unposted Letter*.

Philip Bellhouse – whose comment inspired the story *Incident in Assisi*.

Jon Rohde – who wrote the actual paper attributed to the fictional character of Javid in *The Wine of Forgiveness*.

Bernardette Kabré and Marie Touré Ngom – who are responsible for whatever insight there may be in *Sahel*.

Stephen Perera and Mohammed Jiffry – who helped me to understand something of life in the slums and shanties of Sri Lanka as featured in *The Wall*.

Arthur Adamson and the members of the Men's Institute at Harehills Congregational Church, Leeds, in the 1960s – for the memories behind *The Institute*.

A note on the stories

I need you to be Harold was included in the 2022 Bridport Prize Anthology and shortlisted for the H. G. Wells Memorial Prize.

Sahel was the winner of the Royal Society of Literature V. S. Pritchett Short Story Award 2013.

Boiled Egg with Rosie was shortlisted for the 2020 Mogford Prize

Up on the Downs was first published in 2022 by the *Journal of the John Masefield Society*.

Comfort was first published by Montrasio Arte of Milan as one of three short stories accompanying a retrospective exhibition of the artist Bepi Romagnoni (1930–1964).

The Wall is an adaptation of the opening chapter of my novel *Facing out to Sea* (Hodder & Stoughton, 1996)

Other work by the same author is available at
www.peteradamsonwriting.com